**This Large Print Book carries the
Seal of Approval of N.A.V.H.**

GUARDIANS
OF THE TRAIL

**Center Point
Large Print**

GUARDIANS
OF THE TRAIL

JACKSON GREGORY

CENTER POINT PUBLISHING
THORNDIKE, MAINE

LP
Gre

This Center Point Large Print edition
is published in the year 2009 by arrangement with
Golden West Literary Agency.

Copyright © 1941 by Jackson Gregory. Copyright ©
renewed 1969 by the Estate of Jackson Gregory.

The text of this Large Print edition is unabridged.
In other aspects, this book may vary
from the original edition.
Printed in the United States of America.
Set in 16-point Times New Roman type.

ISBN: 978-1-60285-443-7

Library of Congress Cataloging-in-Publication Data

Gregory, Jackson, 1882–1943.
   Guardians of the trail / Jackson Gregory.
      p. cm.
   ISBN 978-1-60285-443-7 (library binding : alk. paper)
   1. Large type books. I. Title
PS3513.R562G83 2009
813'.52—dc22
2008053283

GUARDIANS
OF THE TRAIL

CONTENTS

CHAPTER I
THEY HAD KILLED HIS FRIEND

THEY had killed his friend. That was in a day when friends were as close as lovers. They lived together, together they fought the wilderness, they shared thoughts and the last bite of food; they saw no one else, just themselves and the mountains and plains. Men like them could swap thoughts without speaking. Silent men, given to grimness because life was grim, with rare flashes of humor—and very, very young. Not so young, either, because though their combined ages would have summed up to about forty, they had been men full grown since they were seventeen.

They had killed his friend. And he knew who they were. Bud Briscoe and his gang, a murderous crew who romped through the Southwest into the Far West, stopping nowhere very long, engaging in brawls, laughing their big laughter, singing their wild raucous songs, raising what they liked to term Merry Hell. They, too, were old young men, Bud Briscoe himself with a silky golden beard like corn silk, not over twenty-two or twenty-three. Like an angel to look at, Bud was, a handsome devil.

They had killed his friend, partly for Bob's forty dollars, mostly in fun.

And so he dug a grave in a pretty spot under a big tree and blew his nose—and followed their tracks.

CHAPTER II
FOLLOWING DIM TRACKS WESTWARD

HE was Jefferson Davis Morgan, the youngest of the Civil War Morgans. A great clan, those Morgans. Their women were as beautiful as moonlight on rippling waters. Their men were blue-black bearded and fierce eyed—until they laughed. They didn't laugh at everything, but when they did, the rafters shook.

They lived among hominy, moss roses and gun powder.

Young Jefferson Davis Morgan, the War over, refugeed as did so many others. There was nothing left at home, not even father, mother, brother, sister. He had ridden with Morgan's men. He was seventeen when one night over a camp fire Morgan beckoned him aside.

"I've had my eye on you," said Morgan, the Raider.

"Yes, sir," said young Jeff.

"You're a lieutenant now," said Morgan. "Take a dozen men and go raid the town. See how many horses you can bring me back."

Young Jeff saluted and turned red with pride. Then Morgan shook him by the hand.

Young Jeff was seventeen that night. Before morning he was a man full grown; a grim and determined man.

He had come to grips with stark tragedy, and it had seared into him, so that for a time his soul was like a scrap of saddle leather that had been thrown into the fire.

Then the War broke down. It was all over, only bitterness left within him. But he found a friend and the two, on spent horses, fared westward. They had their times; they were full fed and they starved; they laughed and they scraped danger.

And now he shoved the dirt over the dead face of his friend.

And he started following dim tracks.

Still westward.

CHAPTER III
THE GIRL AND THE SPY GLASS

HE was a tall young man; he made you think of a whiplash ready to snap. He walked like an Indian, silently, sure-footedly, keeping himself to himself. Girls looked at him and turned their heads to watch him out of sight. Men looked into his eyes, and their own eyes narrowed.

He didn't talk much, hardly more than a cool "Howdy" to a stranger. He didn't ask questions; that is, his tongue didn't though his eyes and ears did. He was very polite, always ready to lift his old black hat, ready to step aside for a lady, young or old, or for an old man or a child. No, he didn't talk much, but word got about that he was

11

looking for something, for some one perhaps.

Roads didn't amount to much. There were trails; you could take your pick. Mostly you traveled horseback, though there were stages rocking along on leather straps for springs. Young Jefferson Davis Morgan rode his own red bay Morgan horse, and led a rangy sorrel which not only carried his canvas roll but also provided a fresh mount at a pinch, and there were pinches.

He stopped on a high place where the narrow trail, about to dive straight down, made a kink among the pines and boulders, and looked down into the likeliest green valley, threaded by a lusty small river, that he had ever seen. He drew a deep breath; he tightened the belt about his lean, flat stomach. He shoved his hat far back and a gleam came into his eyes.

"I like it here," he said aloud.

He broke short off, realizing he had done a lot of talking. But he did like the place. That valley far down yonder, sort of crescent shaped and as lovely as a young moon, as gay as a young maiden, caught his fancy. More than that. He made up his mind, when he had done with the Bud Briscoe gang, to come back here and make this place his place. Down in the heart of the valley was a gentle knoll darkly green with a growth of timber: he'd build him his cabin right there. He'd go in for stock. He would hang up his saddle, turn his horses out to pasture, lie on his back and look up at the sky. Home, that's what he had found. And he knew it.

Yes, down in the heart of the valley was a gentle knoll darkly green with a growth of timber. He couldn't see the long log cabin that was already there, and he couldn't possibly see the girl.

But she saw him.

He was two or three miles away, but she saw him quite clearly, and gasped. Her uncle Dick had just come out to California from Boston, by way of the long traipse across Panama. He had brought her a present, a spy glass, which he had won from the ship's captain in a card game.

To her it was a magic thing. You could look through it across the miles, and a rock that had seemed no bigger than a crab apple grew into a boulder of tremendous size. She watched a hawk perch on a dead limb, and felt that she could scrape him off with a ten foot pole. She looked at the high pass where the trail snaked through, and saw young Jeff Morgan.

He was riding westward and it was late afternoon, so the sun flooded him. It picked out silvery glints all about him; a belt buckle, a gun at his thigh, a silvered bridle shaken by his horse's tossing head. He was all brightness to her; he was like one of the young princes in her fairy tale book. She turned scarlet.

And there were those two or three miles between them, and he did not so much as dream that any

13

human being beside himself was within miles.

He pulled his hat forward, jerked on his lead rope and rode on down into the valley, lost in the shadows of a steep walled gorge.

CHAPTER IV
THE AFFAIR IN BLACK GULCH

ALICE BRISCOE was seventeen, almost eighteen. She was as sweet as the little wild flowers hiding in the valley grass. When she came slowly back to the long log cabin, the faded calico was tight over her breasts and there was a tremulous glow, warm and tender, down in the depths of her eyes.

Uncle Dick looked at her shrewdly; he had known her for only a couple of weeks, but he was a wise old owl and saw signs that some others failed to see. He was a slim, small man of sixty with hard, bright blue eyes and needle-pointed salt-and-pepper mustaches and a bit of an Empire beard which his agile fingers strove to make into a corkscrew.

"Hello, Allie," he said. "You look like the sun was still settin', with all that red in your face. See anything through them spy glasses?"

Alice felt her cheeks growing hotter as it seemed to her that those shrewd eyes of Uncle Dick's were drilling down into her secret heart. For a second she just looked at him; then her words came tumbling out:

"Oh, it's the most wonderful spy glass, Uncle Dick! It's like magic! You can see—why, you can look right up into Heaven with it!"

She ran off to her room laughing, the spy glass hugged tight to her breast.

"He is going to come back," she whispered. "I seem to know he is. Real soon, too!" And she fixed her wild hair with her fingers as though she expected to turn and see him standing there in the doorway the very next minute.

But he rode on, across the lower end of Green Water Valley, up to the high country on its western rim, and so just as it was growing dark came to the little remote town of Black Gulch. He had heard of Black Gulch in his travels; it was rumored that Bud Briscoe and his merry men at times favored the mountain settlement with their rollicking presence.

He stabled his horses, stuck his thumbs into his belt and strolled along the high plank sidewalk of the one street, a street in name only through courtesy and imagination; a country road, it was, deep in dust and gouged with ruts. It was the hour when first lamps and candles were being lighted.

In the stillness which at the moment lay over Black Gulch the air did not stir, the powdery dust in the road lay like dust in a picture, there were no voices. Even Jefferson Davis Morgan on the plank sidewalk came to an involuntary stop, listening to hear something, waiting for something to happen.

From a door here and a window there, from many doors and windows, pale light gushed out from the candles and lamps. The first stir came when the blundering, fuzzy-winged moths came from nowhere and hurled themselves bumblingly toward the lights they saw. Sudden sounds awoke: A door slammed somewhere. A man on horseback came racing into town; from not far off could be heard the measured creaking of an oncoming wagon. Voices spoke up in more than one place. The hush had lasted perhaps half a minute. It was just a natural phenomenon. Jeff Morgan moved along again, the warped boards complaining dryly under his boots like asthmatic old men.

He looked to right and left as he went; for one thing he was glancing in at all open doors, noting the few men already gathered in the barrooms, and then too he had his mind on a lunch counter. A cup of coffee and a bite to go with it was what he required right now, for he hadn't eaten to speak of during a long day and he was conscious of a queer sort of sensation, an oddly prickly feeling, that he was going to need a steady hand real soon. There were times, his mother had told him in the southern pastoral long-ago before the war, when Morgan men could hear the whisperings of coming events. He thought, Bud Briscoe's town; and he made sure that his gun was free in its holster, and was very watchful. He sniffed the air as though the little night breeze, just now awaking, brought him some sign, some hint. There was stealth in him then as he moved along slowly, as he watched through saloon doors and looked also for his lunch counter, his two appetites primitive. The hunger to live and to kill.

The wagon with two plodding horses, a darkly moving shadow-shape, came creaking into town all but blotted out by the dust the horseman had raised, creating further clouds of dust of its own. Jeff Morgan passed along, still glancing in through open doors, or over the tops of the half swing doors that gave broken views into the emporiums of alcohol and games. There were not many men to be seen, in one place two or three, in another half a dozen, and nowhere any sight of woman or girl or any young child.

The thing that he succeeded in sniffing first, after his nostrils were cleared of the dry dust, was the warm and fragrant smell of coffee. At a corner, where a dark and narrow alley cut across the street, was a coffee room not much bigger than a piano box, and a greasy, bullet-headed, close-cropped negro had just made an oversized pot of coffee. The door was open and Jeff Morgan, stooping his elongated frame so as not to knock his hat off, entered. There was a lunch counter made of a couple of foot-wide boards flanked by a bench made of one board. Morgan got a leg over the bench and sat down. Across the counter he faced a small grimy window which peered like a bleary eye upon the blackness of the alley.

"Coffee," he said, and asked, "Got any pie?"

"Yazzuh," said the black man.

He poured the boiling black beverage into a tin cup; he cut a thick and generous wedge of a pallid pie and dumped it down on a tin plate. Then he proffered a tin spoon and some lumpy, not over-white sugar in a second tin cup.

The coffee was so hot that Jeff couldn't drink it; the cup so hot that he couldn't set his lips to it. He asked for a second cup and some cold water.

It was dried apple pie. He tasted the crust, spooned it away, dug into the succulent interior; not bad as the insides of most pies went. He had a sip of his coffee. Bad, yes; but warming. He gulped down half a cup—

Just then it was, all of a sudden and all without warning, that a furor broke out that seemed to shake the town of Black Gulch to its flimsy foundations and which had the effect of exploding in Jeff Morgan's ear, so close to him was the crash of the uproar. At one moment the silence was so deep that the hissing of the cook's fire was emphatic; a second later the silence was torn to shreds by shouts and gunshots. And the fracas, whatever its exact nature, was taking place in the alley, just the distance of half a dozen feet beyond the thin wall which Jeff Morgan faced as he straddled his bench.

"Lawdy-lawd!" yelped the negro, dropped to the floor as though shot, lay there quivering, hiding his black face in his trembling hands. Then he began whining, "It's dem dam' debbil Briscoes—"

Jeff Morgan was off his bench and out through the door like a shot. As he swung into the dark mouth of the alley he heard a fresh fusillade of shots; he saw red and orange streaks and blobs of flame and smelled the black powder burning. And as he turned the corner he came upon two dark forms, standing their ground and blazing away, and made out some forty or fifty feet farther down the narrow way—it was impossible to judge distance with any accuracy—the spitting flames of several guns.

For an instant but for an instant only he stood uncertain. Then one of the two men not a yard from him, the two with their backs to him, all unknowingly cut him in on the game. For the man, sounding throaty with rage, shouted,

"Damn you, Bud Briscoe!"

That was all except that he kept on emptying his gun. And to himself Jeff Morgan said, That's all I need to know!

And he, stepping closer to the two in the mouth of the alley, joined the battle, slinging his lead the way theirs went, seeking a shadowy target there in the dark where all the hot flashes of flame were blossoming.

Naturally the two strangers to whom he lent

such prompt and willing aid did not stop to ask questions or speak up a Thank you, stranger. The three proceeded to empty their guns in methodical and businesslike style. Jeff estimated that they were outnumbered perhaps two to one; he thought, it's the whole Briscoe gang that we're up against.

He heard a thud nearby and knew it for a bullet striking flesh, and heard the grunt jolted out of one of his companions. He had squeezed in between the two; he didn't take time to look to one side or the other to note which man was hurt or how badly; he narrowed his eyes to a moving form that was as dark as a drop of black ink on a purple surface, and squeezed the trigger again. And in reward he heard a sharp howl that sounded like pain and rage commingled.

Then the next thing he knew was that he was alone in the mouth of the alley; his two companions had slipped away, one helping the other, turning the corner, quitting the dark alley for the lighted street. He heard their boots clumping on the wooden sidewalk at a half run, an awkward sounding, scrambling, limping sort of run. And then there were shouts, from other men drawn out from barrooms, and then hoofbeats in a thunder of sound dying swiftly into the distance.

Jeff Morgan in turn backed out of the narrow street and turned the corner around the lunch counter, and began refilling his gun. He saw that a

20

score or more of men had gathered, and that all of them now were looking at him. He moved back a step to get his back to the wall while he finished reloading. He didn't note the negro cook; he had forgotten all about him. But the black boy, with the shooting stilled, was on his feet again, and his eyes were wild and he had in his hand a stick of stove wood as thick as a base ball bat. With a grunt he brought it down on Jeff Morgan's head.

As Morgan slumped down the negro, his black eyes rolling in seas of glistening white, muttered angrily,

"He's a bad man, he shore is. He done et my pie an' he drunk my cawfee an' he run out an' neveh guv me nawthin'. He's a damn Briscoe, 'at's what he is."

CHAPTER V
GUARDIANS OF THE TRAIL

SHERIFF AL JAMESON, at times called Long Jim for short, was a wise old bird or it might have gone unduly hard with young Jefferson Davis Morgan that night. When in due coarse young Jeff gasped and shook his head and blinked his eyes and began to mop the streaming water off his face, he looked into a pair of hard, shrewd, incalculable blue eyes which drilled away at him as steely as a shoemaker's awls.

He saw a small, lean, wiry man holding a drip-

21

ping water bucket in his leathery hands; he took stock of the man's vest, black and white cowhide with the hair still on it and glossy with use, ornamented with a sheriff's badge, looking old, battered and soiled. Jeff, sitting up on the floor, his hands at his sides propping him upright, blinked again and looked at his surroundings; they were in a small bleak room unfurnished save for a pine table, a stove, a shelf and two chairs and a sawdust box nearest the chair with arms. There was one door; it was closed.

Young Morgan got up then; standing near the other man he towered over him a good twelve inches. He dragged out a bandana and did a more thorough job of mopping his head and face; he looked around for his hat, saw it crumpled and soiled in a corner; stepped to it, stooped—and groaned as a searing pain zigzagged through his head—straightened slowly and put it on. Next he fingered his holster and found it empty. Again he looked the room over, looked the man over too. His gun was not in sight; the sheriff, a two-gun man, wore both of his hanging loose and low on his spare hips.

Even then Jeff didn't ask any questions. He simply looked at Sheriff Al Jameson, called Long Jim through courtesy, with a question in his eye.

The sheriff set his bucket down, went over to his arm chair at his rickety table and sat down.

"You was out good and cold, young feller," he remarked mildly. "For a spell I took you for dead on me. That was the second bucket of water."

Jeff, his long legs uncertain under him, groped for the chair across the room and sat down in it. Again he ran his hand over his head, his fingers exploring this time.

Long Jim shook his head.

"Nope," he said. "You didn't stop any lead. Alabam slugged you with a stick of stove wood. Alabam," he explained, since Jeff was so obviously a stranger here, "is the black boy at the Alabama Lunch Counter. He says you stole pie and coffee from him, claimin' you gobbled and run off and refused to pay."

Jeff Morgan, hearing him out and giving the situation due thought, came close to smiling. But he didn't feel like smiles just now.

"You've got my gun, I suppose?" he said.

"Reckon," said the sheriff. "You wouldn't be wantin' it back, would you?"

"Want me running around naked?" said Jeff, short of temper. He had never known a man's head could ache the way his ached now. It seemed to dilate and throb and shudder with the blows of a hot hammer pounding.

"You're brand new here," observed Jameson thoughtfully.

Jeff nodded, then winced. Next time he'd say Yes or No, and keep his head still.

23

"It's kinda funny, ain't it, that you got into a gun fight so almighty quick after hittin' Black Gulch?"

"Maybe."

"Want to spend a while in the calaboosa while I figger things out?" asked Jameson, and seemed both hospitable and very polite in his invitation.

Jeff Morgan stared at him and a bright hard glint came into his eyes.

"Don't be a damn fool, Sheriff," he said, very crisp. He added, "What's your name anyhow? You are the sheriff, of course? Me, I'm Jefferson Davis Morgan and I don't give a damn who knows it."

"Me, I'm Al Jameson. Yep, I'm sheriff and I've been sheriff since about the time you was pupped. And if I like to be a damn fool, that's my business."

"I heard a feller tell a story once," said Jeff reminiscently. "One feller says, like you, If I'm a fool, that's my business. And the other feller ups and says, Got any other business?"

"You won't have to walk far to the jailhouse, Morgan," said Long Jim. "Come ahead; let's get goin'."

"Fire ahead, Sheriff. I'll answer your questions. What's on your mind?"

"Known Bud Briscoe long?"

Jeff Morgan hesitated. Come right down to it, he didn't know Bud Briscoe at all; he was just looking for him. So in answer he started to shake his head, caught himself in time and said, "No."

"What are you throwin' in with him for? You one of his crowd?"

"Me? Throwing in with Bud Briscoe? Didn't I tell you once not to be a damn fool?"

Sheriff Al Jameson shoved his hat far back and scratched a high and shiny forehead with a grimy forefinger. Meantime his eyes, slitted and agate-hard, probed deep into Jeff Morgan's which certainly just then looked frank enough.

"Better do some talkin', kid," said the sheriff, and jerked his hat forward again. "Tell me just how come you got into this fracas and why and all about it."

"That's fair enough." Having thought it over, Jeff deemed it eminently fair. So he drew out the makings and began the slow rolling of a cigarette; his head wasn't as clear as he'd like it and he wanted to go slow until he got the drift of things. "It's like this," he said, and licked his cigarette and swept a match along his thigh for a light. "I was in Alabam's place, the way he said—"

"Come out of the brush, kid, and get goin'!" The old sheriff was growing impatient now; there was a lot of uncertainty within him but a lot of surmise and suspicion too. How could it be otherwise! He commanded curtly, "Leave out the trimmin's and tell."

"All right." Jeff straightened in his chair, expelled a lungful of blue-gray smoke, crushed out his cigarette after the one drag. "I heard two men in the alley. Just before the shooting started. They were right by Alabam's window. One of them yelled, 'Damn you, Bud Briscoe!' So, me, I hopped along and took a hand." He paused a moment, studied his man, eyeing him levelly, then said simply, "You see, Sheriff, I'm out to get Bud Briscoe if I have to trail him the next fifty years. He murdered a pardner of mine; he did the job in cold blood; he did it for forty dollars and the fun of it!"

The sheriff's heavy, crooked brows came down in a scowl which put deep puckered creases into his brow. He seemed briefly lost for words. Then he queried in a queerly quiet and gentle sort of voice,

"Who in hell was you shootin' at?"

"Why the Briscoes, of course!"

"And who was the two gents you was standin' alongside of, helpin' them fight their fight?"

Jeff Morgan made an impatient gesture.

"How should I know? Why should I care? Just so they were fighting it out with Bud Briscoe—"

Long Jim stared at him more solemnly than ever. Then he got up and moved about restlessly a moment; with a sudden gesture he jerked off his hat and sent it spinning into Jeff Morgan's hands.

"Look it over!" snorted Long Jim.

Wondering, Jeff did so. Looking up he said,

"There's a fresh bullet hole through the damn thing!"

"And I've been wonderin' who put it there! Might have been you, Mr. Jefferson Davis Morgan! Now hold your horses and don't go callin' me names any more. Whether you're lyin', I don't know; anyhow I'll tell you a story. A few minutes ago, Bud Briscoe and his cutthroat cousin Nate Briscoe, half drunk, come roarin' into town. I knew they was comin' this way because I got tipped off by a man who didn't stop to drink along the road like they did. They pulled off a robbery, just the two of 'em, yestiddy it was, over to Yellow Jacket. And, maybe it was accident and maybe Bud Briscoe didn't give a damn, they killed a woman. She was Big Belle; ever'body knows Big Belle, used to run a boardin' house for dance house girls over to Nevada City. Big Belle, when drunk, wore jewels on her what-you-call ample boozum like they was colored glass you bought a handful for a dollar. Well, these two gents grabbed the jewelry and headed this way. And I had six men with me when we seen one another in the alley. And now the Briscoes are gone, and one of my men is shot up bad—and look at that hat!"

"Look here!" It was Jeff Morgan's turn to frown. "I don't get what this is all about. You mean—"

They talked it out for an hour. By that time the whole thing was clear to both men; by that time they had come to accept each other. And Jefferson Davis Morgan, thunder-struck, red with rage, with a tremendous yearning to kick himself all over town, came to understand that in the fight in the alley he had chipped in on the wrong side! The two men with whom he had joined forces were Bud Briscoe and his cousin, Nate Briscoe! True, Jeff had heard Nate Briscoe call out angrily, "Damn you, Bud Briscoe!" But that, as Sheriff Jameson was in a position to explain was because the two were always damning each other, because though they worked together they distrusted each other; that tonight, as the fight began, Nate was railing at Bud Briscoe for getting them into this jam.

And now, with Jefferson Morgan's timely help, the two Briscoes were well on their way on horses they had kept handy; and one of the sheriff's deputies was being probed by old Doc Shandy for a bullet; and Long Jim Jameson's fairly modern Stetson was clean ruinated.

"I could slam you in the jailhouse, and it would serve you good and right for comin' into another man's town and runnin' hawg wild before you knowed your way around," observed the sheriff and pulled open a table drawer, giving Morgan his gun. He stood back and watched the way young Morgan hefted the weapon, touching it like the hand of an old friend; sliding it back where it belonged, giving it a gentle pat like a mother putting her baby to bed. The older man's lips twitched. He said morosely,

"Well, the damn Briscoes are clean away again, and their pockets full. They tell me Big Belle was wearin' a ruby wrist-thing that was worth ten thousand and maybe twenty thousand dollars, and had two rings to match. Think of that! In Bud Briscoe's pocket now, tomorrow to be stuffed away with a lot of the rest of his ill-got gains in some hole in a mountainside. And you, you leather-headed young jackass, you're anyhow part to blame."

"Think it makes me happy?" Young Jeff glared at him. Then he shrugged. "Well, it's a long trail that don't get somewhere sooner or later. Which way do you reckon Bud Briscoe went?"

"Anybody knows that: Straight back down into Briscoe Valley. Green Water Valley folks used to call it and some do now. That's the way he went, all right. I watched him and Nate high-tailin' over the rim, headed down the old Rim Trail."

"That might be the pretty valley, long and deep and green with a little river winding through, that I crossed coming here tonight?"

"That's her," said the sheriff. "Some of the Briscoes moved in down there a few years back. There's a whole tribe of 'em. Mos'ly damn thieves and cutthroats."

"You're not going down?" Jeff looked at him curiously; he sensed something steely-hard in Long Jim Jameson, nothing soft or yellow.

"Nope," said the sheriff. "Them two boys got

too much the head start on me. Hell's bells, they'll have vanished off the face of the earth long before I could get down onto the valley floor. There's seven million hideouts in the mountains lockin' Green Water Valley in, and Bud Briscoe knows every one of 'em. Nope. I'll wait."

Jefferson Davis Morgan turned to the door.

"See you later then," he said.

"Better be like a fox and keep anyhow one eye open, kid," said the sheriff. "If you don't, well, I'll see you get a bang-up funeral."

"I'll go see Alabam first," said Jeff.

"Hell, Morgan, you can't blame him! He took you for one of the Briscoe boys."

"I'm just going to pay him for my supper. And I didn't finish my coffee, either; I've got half a cup coming. So long, Sheriff."

He moved along the deserted sidewalk. Those men who had been a party to his fracas with the sheriff's party and with the Briscoes, had been given their dismissal by Long Jim when once they had conveyed the unconscious man to his office; they had promptly wended their various ways to the bars of their several choices, to comment briefly upon the event of the evening, to speculate idly as to any future happenings which might hinge upon it, thereafter to drop back into their habitual Black Gulch ruts. So Jeff Morgan had no parley with anyone until he returned to the Alabama.

Alabam himself showed the whites of his eyes and looked as ready to run as any frightened rabbit. But Jeff merely got a leg over the bench again, demanded the half cup of coffee which, with great sternness, he accused the colored boy of having stolen from him, drank a fresh cup instead, paid his bill and went back along the street to the stable. He estimated that it would be folly to try to follow Bud Briscoe tonight, else Sheriff Jameson would already be in the saddle; yet folly came easy and natural to him, and he meant to ride anyhow.

He selected his fresher horse, the rangy sorrel built alike for speed and endurance and sure-footedness, made a tight snug bed roll behind the saddle, left his Morgan horse with the stable boy, and rode. As he passed down the slope at the edge of town the full moon, looking as big as a balloon and as yellow as butter rolled up above the black timber on the far rim of the valley. As yet the valley itself, far below him, was as dark as some deep, vast pit.

He remembered the down trail, the trail he had followed so short a time ago coming up; it was so steep in places and so narrow, winding down steep-walled gorges that he loosened his reins and gave all responsibility to his horse. It would be nearly an hour, he knew, before he reached the gentler lower lands.

He thought what a tricky jade a man's Fate

could be. Here for so long a while he had sought Bud Briscoe, here tonight he and Bud Briscoe had stood so close together that their elbows touched at one time—and there was Jefferson Davis Morgan, with a damned Briscoe on each side of him, fighting their fight!

The night was one of an ineffable, lonely beauty, but he missed its beauty because there was just then no loveliness within his heart, nothing but bitterness that rankled, hatred that burned like acid. He was a man who did not forget; he would never forget his last day with Bob, never forget how Bob died in his arms, Bob young and so over-flowingly full of life with its joy and zest and eager ambitions, Bob trying to tell him good-bye, trying to tell him good-bye with a laugh, as though they would be meeting up again in no time at all.—Well, perhaps they would!

He rode mostly in darkness because of the timber and brushy growth through which his trail snaked, because of the gouges, shadow-filled, in the cliffs and the overhang of rocky ledges. But presently the moon, riding higher, flooded the nearer rim of the valley with a light which seemed green, so richly green were the meadows and the foliage of the willows and alders along a tributary brook, and the tender young leaves which dawning summertime was strewing through the oak branches. Even the star-shaped tip-tops of the young pines were of the same lovely, tender hue.

And at last, though but fleetingly, though not deeply yet troublingly, he did begin to sense some small part of the glory of the lonely night here in this hushed solitude. For there was never a sound not made by the scuffling of his horse's hoofs or the jingle of bridle and creak of saddle leather, or the faint whisper and rustle of the softly blowing night wind through the trees.

And then all of a sudden, startling him, there was a clamor. How abruptly silence can be broken, shattered to bits, and how it flees like a frightened thing and how slow and timid and shy it is in its coming back!

He had reached the valley floor, coming down a final gradual descent, and was just looking up-valley where the moon now revealed the swell and ripple of the meadow lands dotted with ink-black groves of big live oaks, when the clamor broke out and his horse came close to jumping out from under him. Right at hand, close under a bank where the slope broke down, was a clump of mountain laurels; with a savage growling that broke into a wolfish howl, two lean grayish bodies hurled themselves toward him, and only in time did his horse dance out of the way and only in time did Jeff Morgan, sitting so loosely in the saddle, save himself from falling.

At first he could think of nothing but that he was being attacked by a starving wolf pack, though why wolves should be starving here in this valley at this season was beyond him. But as he whipped out his gun he was stopped from firing by the timely realization that he had heard a rattle of dog-chains; that the two animals, whether wolves or not, were chained there among the laurels at the base of the trail, that they had sprung to the end of their chains and the episode was concluded. Even yet, whether the big brutes were wolves or dogs he could not for the life of him make out. Ugly, mean and vicious brutes they were in any case.

The two snapped with fangs which he could see gleaming in the moonlight, glistening sharp fangs which worried the chains holding them, which would have worried a man's throat. Then they sat back on their haunches, the two like one, like trained animals, and put back their heads and howled to the high heavens. There was a fierce cruel savagery in those reverberating howls which put a shiver in a man's blood, a purely primal sort of uncontrollable dread. Though Jeff Morgan slowly holstered his gun his hand remained lingeringly on its grip.

Then the howling ceased abruptly; for ten seconds the night again was still save for the restless pawing of his horse's nervous hoofs. And then, like a belated echo to this devilish din of wolf-howls, there came from afar, from somewhere up-valley sounding a mile or more away, the long sustained baying of another dog or wolf, of one or perhaps two. And while Jeff sat there stone still and listened, and while this second rape of the moonlit silence was ebbing away, he thought that he heard, still farther away, faint with distance, something like a still receding, still belated echo. He sat there a moment pondering the thing. Here, to begin with, were these two great gaunt, flashing-fanged beasts, slavering to be at a man's throat, chained—and he knew, though having ridden this way during the late afternoon when the light was still good and he had his eyes and all senses about him, that there wasn't a house within miles. He knew these trail-guardians had not been here in the late afternoon. What he didn't know, though later he came to guess at it, was something that Long Jim Jameson, had he bethought himself, could have told him: Bud Briscoe was at home in the valley, and already, though half a dozen miles to the north, he would be knowing that tonight the valley had a visitor!

CHAPTER VI
THROUGH THE CABIN WINDOW

"GOOD night, pups," said Jeff Morgan, and gave his eager horse its head at last, striking northward, on up into the spreading valley. His departure and his voice together started up another series of blood-troubling howls; he shrugged distastefully and touched his horse with the spur. "No reason we shouldn't lope out on 'em, Dandy," he said.

"We've got not much more use for Briscoe dogs than we've got for two-legged Briscoes. Let's breeze, boy!"

They swept along in the open, a black centaur shadow running at their side, and for a time all they heard above the soft thud of the horse's hoofs was the wolfish duet they were leaving behind. But as the first half mile fell away, and the howling behind grew fainter and then died away altogether, Jeff Morgan was a second time treated to the eerie effect of a postponed echo drifting down-valley from the north. Louder and clearer and closer it was this time, sustained and vicious and menacing, growing all the while still louder as he pressed on.

A queer admixture of sensations, of emotions, flowed through him with his bloodstream. The beauty of the night was almost too perfect for a mere night on earth, partaking of something unearthly and heavenly, and here he rode on an errand of death. The soft summer moonlight, the glint at times of winding Green River, the breath of an incense laden breeze from the hill slopes was all about him—and in his ears was the hideous din of wolf-howling. He had loved this hidden valley from the first glimpse of it and loved it now, and he loved the night and swift riding through it—and he was planning to kill Bud Briscoe. He thought of the deed as an execution; that was rightfully the name of it. He meant to be impersonal about the whole thing. Bud Briscoe was to be executed and Jefferson Davis Morgan was appointed by his destiny to play the part of executioner. And the night was divine!

He even wondered whether he hated Bud Briscoe? Here was the funny part of it: He hated with all the fierce might within him the man who had killed his friend, young Bob Lane, and that man was Bud Briscoe. True enough. But he had never seen Bud Briscoe's face, not once, not even tonight when they had fought elbow to elbow in the Black Gulch alley. And how the devil can a man rightly hate another man when he can't for the life of him summon up a mental image of the fellow to focus his hatred upon?

And so this was Briscoe Valley? This valley with which he had fallen in love at sight as a man may with a woman, this valley which he had vowed instantly he would some day make his own? He was glad that things fell the way they did; before he was through he hoped to take, along with Bud Briscoe's life, everything that belonged to him.

"Except his damned dogs!" he muttered, and twitched his high shoulders as the barking in the north, having ceased for a moment while no doubt the dogs cocked their ears listening, broke out more furiously than ever.

His horse had struck into a broad, hard packed trail; there were even wheel tracks, very faint in the grass, for a wagon seldom traveled this way; the trail led straight on toward the second outpost of guardian dogs, and Jeff Morgan was quite content to follow it. By now he understood well enough what purpose these sentinels served; he could only wonder how many of the surly brutes there were and how widespaced, and hence how far it was to the hideout where he must seek Bud Briscoe.

With the sky clear and the moon well above the timbered eastern ridge, he knew that he and his horse could be seen, were any on the lookout, from afar; and dwelling upon the thought that where there are watch-dogs there is a master keeping an ear open for their report, he bethought him of making his approach somewhat less conspicuous. Therefore he turned aside from the trail and rode down a gentle slope to the dark line of the river with its bordering of willows and poplars. Here the trees dropped long black shadows and he kept pretty much in this semi-dark as again he headed up-valley.

Thus he did not come as close to the second pair of chained dogs as he had to the first, yet he saw them clearly enough, lunging at the ends of their long chains where they howled at his passing from a grove of live oaks. Again their ferocity put a twitch into the involuntary uplift of his shoulders.

He rode on another mile; he heard still other dogs, barking in the distance ahead of him. And then at last he saw a light, the shine of a lamp through an open door or window, he judged, and made out the vague, dim outline of the long, low rakish log cabin on the knoll. He halted in a pool of shadow on the river bank and asked himself,

"Now what, Mr. Jefferson Davis Morgan? Here you are; right yonder, you can bet your bottom dollar, is the man you're looking for. And by now he is no doubt looking for you to show up, too. He's been told enough times! And, like enough, he's got his whole gang with him! Now what, Mr. Morgan? You've got what you asked for—a man generally does—"

He sat where he was, thoughtful and watchful. He even builded himself a cigarette, hiding the flare of his match, cupping the cigarette's glow in the palm of his hand. The length of the cabin was mostly in the shadows, but the full moon flooded the slope on the nearer side and made golden-green patterns under the oaks. And presently his narrowed eyes made out a figure moving swiftly across an open, moonlit space. It was the figure of a man, seen only fleetingly, lost again in the dark, just emerged from the cabin, passing deeper into the oak grove. And while Jeff Morgan sat still where he was and watched, he saw another figure and still another and yet one more, until in the confusion of them he could not be sure how many; say half a dozen in all. And there were two or three of the big dogs running with them.

Jeff Morgan's natural thought was, There are more of them than there are of me, and they're just as ready for things to happen as I am. And yet he was of no mind to draw off and let his chance go by to have it out with Bud Briscoe; he had come too far, he had waited too long for tonight. And the night was still young, and it was a part of his experience that if a man hung on to what he wanted and bided his time, he'd find his chance.

And now, all of a sudden, and all unexpectedly from a most unexpected quarter, at least some modicum of that chance was gratuitously proffered him. He heard a challenging shout go up, a man's voice rich and deep and vibrant, and he knew it must be Bud Briscoe's, because it was the voice of one of the two men at whose side he had stood in Black Gulch, and it was not the voice of the man who had cried out, "Damn you, Bud Briscoe." And in swift answer to Briscoe's shout there came back an answer from somewhere on the farther rim of the oak grove, and then there rose a rollicking storm of laughter.

All this was at some distance from where Jeff Morgan sat his horse, but the night was so intensely still that sounds carried clearly, and further the little night breeze drifted down his way, and he made out a word here and there and understood how his good luck had stood at his elbow.

". . . and those damn dogs of yours, Bud! I like to have shot 'em. . . ."

". . . but I never thought it might be you! Wondered if that fool sheriff. . . ."

". . . Oh, dry up you boys. Come in, come in."

Here evidently, almost on Jeff Morgan's heels, had come some friend of Bud Briscoe's, and both he and Bud himself took it for granted that all the uproar made by the sentinel wolf-dogs was because of him. Out in Green Water Valley visitors were not likely to arrive two in a single night; two in a month would be more like it!

Morgan watched the several men return to the cabin, followed by the two or three dogs. Then he rode deeper into the jungle-like tangle of trees and brush making a dense high thicket along the river bank, and hid his horse in a spot which the moon would not enter for another hour. There was a rifle in its boot on the saddle; he left it where it was, content with his belt gun in case of trouble. Then on foot, as curious as any cat to find out anything he could about Bud Briscoe and his outfit, he began making his cautious way toward the cabin in the grove.

First, still on the river's rim, he went several hundred yards farther upstream. Then, hurrying across the open spaces, he hurried from one spreading oak to another, keeping when he could one of the big trees between himself and the cabin in the grove. And so in a little while, unseen he was confident, certainly awaking no fresh din from the watch-dogs, he came to the rear end of the Briscoe cabin. He stood very still; from here he could see no light, but he heard voices; jolly voices they were, it struck him, carefree voices, the voices of men glad to be at home after a jaunt into the outside world.

And still never a dog barked. He moved along the cabin wall; it was a crazy sort of building, long and narrow, but none too straight, angling out at one spot, jutting out at another; you could visualize it in the making, with a single room to begin with, then other rooms added in a hit-or-miss style somewhat as a careless child might line up a series of odd blocks. In an angle of the wall he saw a small window; a dim light shone through.

And still there was no barking of dogs. It was then as he had hoped it might be; the men trooping back into the cabin had had no thoughts of the dogs underfoot, and the two or three running loose had slipped inside along with their masters. Again it seemed to Jefferson Davis Morgan that this was his lucky night; well, in his time he had known occasions when everything went right, other times when it all went wrong. You took it as it came.

He felt sure that the men were gathered in a room at the front end of the crooked string of rooms; nevertheless, meaning to fill his hand tonight with any knowledge which might come his way, he peered in at that first small, high, lighted window.

At first he judged the room unoccupied; all that

he could see was part of a bear skin on the floor, the corner of a table, a shelf with some odds and ends on it of which he made nothing in a sweeping glance, the back of an obviously and crudely homemade chair. Then he heard a faint sound, next someone moved from the hidden portion of the room into full view—and Mr. Jefferson Davis Morgan received one of the major shocks of his life.

It was a girl! A girl here in this Briscoe den of thieves and killers! And such a girl!

He had known girls and women in his time, not very many, to be sure, but more than just a few; pioneer women, of course, since he himself and all those with whom he came in contact were of that breed; fine women, loyal and true, and sweet, too, and womanly. Beautiful, some of them, with a sort of nobility, Junos, deep-breasted, robust, made to be the mothers of still further pioneers. But in his innocence it had never quite dawned upon him that anywhere created on earth was a girl like this one. She was the loveliest thing, he swore, that ever was on land or sea, in heaven or on earth. And so for the second time that day it may be said that Jefferson Davis Morgan fell in love; with a valley, to begin with, one that belonged to the Briscoes. With a girl now, Bud Briscoe's seventeen-year-old sister, the darling of Bud Briscoe's otherwise warped and evil life.

And never had little Alice Briscoe looked lovelier than tonight. Had she known who was outside the window looking in at her and marveling as Jeff Morgan marveled, had it been given to her to suspect even that the young man whom she had watched so eagerly through her new spy glass was within half a dozen steps of her, drinking her in with his eyes, even then she could scarcely have sparkled more or opened her shining eyes wider or turned pinker or in any way have painted the lily of her own beauty. For all alone, she had just finished dressing in her finest, a frilly little dress of forget-me-not-blue organdy, with big ribbon bows; and she wore her one nice, tight-until-they-hurt pair of blue slippers—and as Jeff Morgan entranced watched, she was just beginning to bejewel herself!

At first young Morgan, obsessed with the girl, paid not the least attention to her fingers busying themselves with her adornments; there was a scrap of a looking glass on the wall which he could not see, since it was beneath his window, and she was looking into it, which was almost the same thing as looking straight at him, and so for his part he looked deep into her eyes. They were big with happiness, bright with the moment's excitement, warm and liquid eyes always. He could even see the shadows of her long lashes making a lacy fringe on her cheeks. The redness of her mouth, smiling and so close to his, was a provocation and a temptation. What did it matter whether she decked herself out with a ribbon, a flower or a glass bead?

She preened as he had seen birds preen in the springtime, a-thrill with their own new raiment. But just as she whisked about, with a last fingered touch to the warm glory of her abundant curly hair, he did see the glowing ruby necklace kissing the round whiteness of her throat, and he saw the great ruby ring burning on her finger. Then her skirts billowed as she was whirling and he saw her blue stockings, and she ran out of the room and so he lost her.

So now each in turn had in a way spied upon the other without the other knowing. She had said to herself, He will come back! As he watched her pass through a door leading toward the front rooms he knew that, for good or for evil, he was going to see her again. And something rankled within him and tortured him already: It was that she was wearing Big Belle's jewels, that even now she was hastening to show Bud Briscoe how pretty she looked in his gift.

The way she led, Jeff Morgan followed, she within the long cabin, he stepping along softly, close to the wall outside. There came another lighted window; he got just a wisp of a glimpse of her, of her billowing blue dress, rather, as she hurried on her way. He, too, hurried. Another lighted window, and no attempt made to protect those within from being spied upon by anyone outside, and that struck Jeff Morgan as queer even then, when he was still bemused, when his mind was all but filled by such a girl as a man may dream about but may go a weary long lifetime without ever seeing in the living, breathing flesh—yes, it struck him as downright odd that men like Bud Briscoe and his crowd, especially on a night like tonight, when they came so fresh from murder and robbery, when they had so recently fought it out with the sheriff's men, should sit in a lighted room with never a shade drawn over a window! Brave men, were they, recklessly bold and foolhardy—or just fools? Headlong devils he had known them by reputation a long time, but it was hard to judge them tonight. Most elaborately they had arranged to be warned of anyone coming into their valley— and then had let the house dogs go into the house with them! A man standing where Jeff Morgan stood could shoot through the window and pick off any of them he chose. Yes, and could run to his horse and be away with none ever to know who had fired the shot!

This was the largest room of all that he stood looking into now, and there was a big fireplace at one end, a long sturdy table down the middle, benches along the walls, chairs even, bearskins on the floor. And there were several men in the room. Jefferson Davis Morgan did not immediately know how many and he did not take particular notice of any of them at first; and when he did single out one man it was only after the girl in the blue dress entered the room.

She stopped when just across the threshold; with finger and thumb she lifted her skirt ever so gracefully, ever so slightly, just enough for the gleaming buckles on her little blue slippers to catch the lamplight. She was laughing and her eyes were very bright, and in a gay voice which she pretended to make quite serious, she demanded,

"How do you like me now?"

And then, without waiting for any answer, as swift as a swallow, she darted across the room and threw herself, her feet clear off the floor, into the arms of the big young man standing at the fireplace. And so it was this man who drew and held Jeff Morgan's scowling interest.

CHAPTER VII
INTO THE THICKER DARK

THIS big young man set Jeff Morgan frowning disapprovingly. In the first place, the fellow was too infernally handsome for any man to be. Every bit as tall as young Morgan himself, he was of heavier build, yet there was no excess weight, no fat on him. He made Morgan think of a picture in a picture book at home in the drowsy old Ante Bellum summer days: A Young King of the Saxons. He had yellow hair and it was long and

47

curled at the ends, and there was a tendency toward curls at his temples; his eyes were as blue as ever were California's skies, and as clear; he wore a small beard that was like fine silk, the color of ripening corn silk. And despite his overdose of good looks, he was deep chested and stalwart and manly to look at. And his arms, huge and powerful like a blacksmith's, swept the girl high and held her locked tight, and his deep, hearty laughter came rumbling out. Jeff Morgan could see them, could hear them, as though he were in the room with them, from where he stood at the side of the window. There was even a chance that they might see him, were they looking his way. But within the cabin all eyes were on the girl—save when presently they drifted from her to the man who held her in his arms until she began squirming for freedom.

Jeff Morgan had no fancy for the scene. First of all, he had no clue to their relationship, and had he known it he still would not have liked it. He had no way of knowing that she was Alice Briscoe, that he was Bud Briscoe. No stranger, seeing the two together, would ever have guessed them brother and sister. They were as unlike as the summer sun at high noon and a little wisp of a new moon.

She had leaped a willing captive into Bud Briscoe's embrace, but now began beating at his vast chest with her small clenched fists, panting,

"Let me down, let me down, let me down! You—you great big grizzly bear!"

He tossed her upward toward the high, bare, black rafters and laughed at her bit of a half frightened, half laughing squeal, and caught and set her down as lightly as thistledown and went on laughing. And she gave his bearded face a bit of a slap, just a love-tap it was, and it did young Jeff Morgan no good at all. And even yet he could not be sure that this, rather than any one of the others, was Bud Briscoe. He did find time to wonder whether the two were engaged to be married; not married yet, he was sure, for she wore no ring save that blazing, bloody ring of Big Belle's.

Nor, as it happened, when the girl spoke again, free now, tossing her hair back, smoothing her dress, then displaying her new adornments, did she give him any clue even then. For whereas most men, and women too, called her brother "Bud" to her he was and ever had been Charlie. Charles Briscoe he was christened, Charles he had been to his mother until her death, which was speeded by the grief he caused her and which she until the last hid from her one little daughter. Charlie always to Alice, just as she was Allie to him.

Laughing, she pretended to pout.

"Charlie, you bad boy," she said, adoring him with her eyes, "I dressed just for you, to show you how pretty your ring and necklace looks on me, and you haven't said a thing! I asked you, don't you like me?"

Bud Briscoe leaned back against the chimney and put his big hands into his pockets and grinned at her.

"Allie," he began, and you could see that he was trying to think of just how to say something a girl would like to hear, "I'll tell you—"

But she cut him short, making a face at him, turning to the others in the room. And then Jeff Morgan ticked them off one by one and carefully. After all one of them was without doubt Bud Briscoe.

Beside the big handsome young man with the corn-silk beard and the corn-flower blue eyes, there were, as he discovered now, four other men in the room. There was a slim, wiry little old man, with blue eyes as hard as steel and as sharp as needles and a small pointed beard which he never ceased twisting; that was Alice's newly arrived uncle Dick, the donor of the precious spy glass through which Alice Briscoe's lovely eyes had already looked upon Mr. Jefferson Davis Morgan who would have leaped out of his boots had he been aware of the fact and of her own reaction. There was a thick shouldered, heavy set, dull looking man of middle age, spade-bearded, heavy-handed, George Briscoe, father of the young Briscoe generation. Then there were two others, young men both.

One, whom even a stranger might know for one of the clan, was Nate Briscoe, a cousin. He was like a pallid copy, a colorless imitation of Bud Briscoe, smaller, of less boldness though perhaps of more craft, good looking but only in a commonplace sort of fashion, his eyes not unlike Bud's but furtive and narrow; altogether the sort of replica which a master craftsman should smash with his hammer and toss into the scrap heap. He kept watching the girl all the time; he seemed fascinated by her . . . or was it the blood-red stones she wore which fascinated him? They were of tremendous value, a value much greater than Bud Briscoe guessed. Certain it is that Nate Briscoe kept slanting his eyes and that now and then, under his small blond mustache, the tip of his tongue touched his lips.

Now when Alice Briscoe turned her back on Bud and faced the others there was a gleam in her eye that had a dash of sheer deviltry in it, and it was not to her father nor yet to Uncle Dick, not to her cousin Nate that she turned, but to the one other man in the room, the newcomer over whose arrival the dogs had raised a din so fortunate for Jeff Morgan. She said,

"And you, Mr. Cass Burdock? You've hardly said good evening to me, have you? And you haven't told me how you like me in my new things that Charlie brought me!"

So Jefferson Davis Morgan's eyes started drilling at Cass Burdock. He discovered a tall

51

young man whom he did not like, whether through prejudice or through an alert instinct. Cass Burdock was another tall young man, much of young Morgan's build and dark, too, like Morgan. He was dressed, one noticed first of all, with a certain elaborateness: His boots were new and expensive, the fancy cowboy boots of the Southwest, and the hat twirling in both lean, long fingered hands was a fit companion piece for the boots, a fine piece of goods in a dove-gray Stetson with a broad band about it with a silver buckle. There was a dash of the dandy in him with his scarlet silk scarf and his fresh shirt checked in big squares and his carved leather holsters and belt, and the tight fitting breeches stuffed down into his boot tops. But, despite the dandyism, the man looked as hard as any cactus thorn, and his eyes were steady and somehow commanding and had a way of pouncing upon the object they looked upon that was predatory.

For a moment he looked down into the girl's face without smiling; his jaw was lean and prominent then and his mouth small. Then he did smile and the expression upon his somewhat saturnine face changed entirely, so that his eyes almost grew warm.

"Miss Alice," he said in a quiet voice, very low, "I sure do like you in your new things. You sure do look powerful nice in them, Miss Alice." His smile broadened, making his expression soften still more, making him look really friendly. "But you always do look mighty nice anyhow. You sure always do to me."

Little Miss Alice had got more than she asked for, and turned red in confusion. A scowl dragged down Bud Briscoe's brows, but he didn't move, didn't say anything, just looked for a while at Cass Burdock, then looked curiously at Alice.

Nate Briscoe shifted his feet. Then he cleared his throat.

"You're quite a talker, ain't you, Cass?" he said. "Kind of a spell-binder, huh? I hear tell over 'round Yellow Jacket as how all the girls go crazy over you and your elegant speeches."

Cass Burdock turned and looked at him, then looked elsewhere quite as though he had not seen him. It was Bud Briscoe who said curtly, "Shut up, Nate. You must of et something today that didn't agree with you."

The little old man with the twisty scrap of beard—that was Uncle Dick—spoke up in his quiet way.

"You come here, Alice, an' let me look at you," he said. And when she came at his bidding and stood in front of him he put out his weathered claw of a hand for hers, and she put her warm fingers into his. He turned her hand this way and that, studying her new ring.

"I kind of noticed," he said when he gave her hand, ring and all, back into her keeping, "how the gold shined in the light but how there was a place on it that didn't shine. Looks like blood on it. How'd you do that, Allie? That ain't lucky with a new present, you know. Kind of like blood on the moon!"

She whipped back from him, startled.

"Uncle Dick!" she cried. "Don't you say such things!"

But she held her ring up in the full light and studied it, and some of the glee and sparkle went out of her eyes. It wasn't altogether just Uncle Dick's words; it was the queer, grave way in which he spoke them.

Bud Briscoe began to laugh. He stepped with his long swinging strides to where Alice stood bending over the table lamp, and took her hand and slipped the ring off her finger. He looked at it and laughed again, his laughter a series of rumbling chuckles.

"Pshaw!" he said, and wiped the ring vigorously on his shirt sleeve. "Don't you listen to his foolishness, Allie. Some folks are always seeing blood on the moon if only it's the end of a red nose they're looking at, and maybe their own nose at that!" He examined the ring, blew his breath on it, rubbed it on his sleeve again. "I'll tell you, I had that ring in my pocket; I showed it to a feller over to Black Gulch while we was having supper, and it fell into my soup. Guess I didn't wipe all the stuff off. Here she is, all cleaned up."

Alice extended her finger for it and over her shoulder darted a small gleam of triumph at Uncle Dick. He didn't say anything, didn't even seem to notice; those shrewd old eyes of his were intent on Bud Briscoe's face.

Cass Burdock was looking at him too, and now, when Bud had finished speaking and the ring was back on Alice's finger, he said, businesslike,

"You sticking around here for a spell, or just passing through? I dropped out for a little talk with you, you know."

"Let's talk now then, Cass," said Bud. "We just dropped in to say hello, and are changing horses and riding again right away. What's on your mind?"

But Alice cried out, "No! No, Charlie, you're not riding off like this! You are going to stay tonight anyhow, and—"

"Can't, Allie," he said good humoredly yet with an easy going sort of determination. "Promised to be up Settlers' Gap before morning, and you know that's a good hard four hours' ride. We'll be on our way pronto. But I'll be turning up again in a couple of days."

"Me," spoke up Nate Briscoe, "I guess I'll stick, and you go 'head without me. You know how I sprained my leg when I come down out'n the saddle and stepped on a loose rock; that leg don't feel like riding a four hour mountain trail."

"I noticed you was sort of limpin'," said Uncle Dick. "Hurt bad?"

Bud said, "Shucks, he ain't hurt at all; just lazy." He spoke lightly enough but for an instant his eyes were hard and angry, as they flashed to a meeting with his cousin's. "You'll come along with me, all right," he said, and again turned to Cass Burdock. "If it's anything private like, Cass, let's step outside," he invited.

Cass nodded and the two moved toward the door. As they did so Jeff Morgan for the first time noted the three dogs; all three were lying under the long table where they had artfully withdrawn, not to be remarked upon and kicked outside. Now as Bud Briscoe passed close to the table end he was greeted by a savage growling, a growling which again made Morgan think of a slavering wolf baring its teeth to rend flesh. Bud, taken by surprise, stepped aside swiftly and whipped out his gun, his eyes blazing with anger, but Alice came running and dropped to her knees by the table and reached and looked underneath, speaking at once soothingly and commandingly.

"Down, Baron!" she said, and did not raise her voice. "Be still, Rufus! You, too, Blackie, *be still!* All of you! Still! Lie down!—That's a good dog."

For though the savage growling continued briefly, it gradually grew lower and softened in the dogs' throats until it was scarcely more than a sort of canine purr, then died away.

Bud Briscoe, his face still red with anger, jammed his gun back into its leather and he and

Cass Burdock stepped along outside. The door closed after them. Jeff Morgan heard the young blond giant say,

"Let's go over to the barn. Injun Pete bunks up out there; I'll make him saddle for us, and then when we get going he can ride out and turn the dogs loose."

"Looks like you thought sure somebody was after you tonight—"

Jeff Morgan stepped softly away from his vantage point, back toward the rear of the cabin, into the thicker dark of one of the biggest oaks with thick branches close to the earth. He thought, I know where they're going; Settlers' Gap. A four hour ride. And one of them will sure be Bud Briscoe, or if not, then he'll be at the Gap. He won't be hard to find—and there won't be a girl there.—Anyhow, not this girl!

And he assured himself further that the thing for him to do now was to make a silent withdrawal, biding his time a little longer, only another few hours, making sure of his man, finishing his business with him. He had no desire to overhear what the two men headed toward the barn might be saying; he had no liking for the sort of thing he had already done tonight, lurking in the dark and watching and overhearing. So the thing was to go back to his horse. And yet for a little while he remained where he was. He found it hard to go without once more seeing the girl in the blue

dress, the girl wearing a murdered woman's gems
. . . the girl who had leapt, launching herself like a
bright, beribboned arrow into the arms of the big
blond, laughing man. "Alice!" He even muttered
her name under his breath.

Presently Bud Briscoe and Nate and Cass
Burdock rode away. When they were on their
horses in the cabin yard, the girl came out and the
three dogs came at her heels; they pressed close to
her, they fawned on her until she put them down
and told them to heel and keep still. The first thing
she did, before the men rode, was to say quietly to
the dogs,
    "Go find Ranger! Go find Big Boy! Hear me,
Baron? Hear me, Blackie? Hear me, Rufus? Go
find Ranger! Go find Big Boy! *Go!*"
    And then she laughed softly as the three dogs
were off like one, like a shot out of a gun, headed
straight down-valley.
    "Now that you boys have made up your minds
to ride," she said, "you'll be sending Injun Pete to
turn the other dogs loose. Baron and Rufus and
Blackie will carry them the word that Pete's
coming!"
    Then the men rode away under the oaks, out
into the moonlight, but whereas Bud Briscoe and
Nate turned straight north toward the upper end
of the valley and the black, lofty mountains
locking it in, Cass Burdock headed south, striking

into the trail which Jeff Morgan had traveled tonight, the trail that led back toward Black Gulch.

The girl, watching them ride, seemed in no haste to return to the cabin. With her hands clasped and raised as high as her breast, with her head tipped back so that her eyes were on the moonbright sky, she passed slowly like one deep in reverie across the clearing among the oaks and just on its farther rim, stopped and sat down upon an ancient stump, one that had served as a seat many and many the time. And now her hands were in her lap, and her face was still uplifted, as she sat as still as the old oaks themselves.

For a little while the rhythmic thudding of hoof-beats disturbed a night otherwise steeped in tranquility; steadily those throbbing hoofbeats diminished with distance presently to die away utterly. And then the night itself whispered its soft secrets, in the faint, scarce-heard stirring of leaves, in the hushed shiver of the tall grass, in the sudden, low bright voices of the insect world. And still the girl sat motionless, brooding in the fringe of shadow edged with moonlight, and still Jefferson Davis Morgan stood irresolute. A dozen times he was on the verge of going to her.

And then there came hoofbeats again, oncoming this time, not loud since the horse approached not at a gallop but at a swinging walk, coming on from the south. And this time no dogs barked.

Young Morgan heard and wondered. The girl, deep in her reveries, did not even hear until she was startled by a rider reining in close to her and swinging down almost at her side.

"Alice!" he said.

It was Cass Burdock returned. All he had done was canter southward a short distance, putting the oak grove between him and the northbound riders, then turn and come quietly back.

Alice Briscoe stiffened, sat looking up at him a moment, then slid swiftly from the old stump and stood stiffly before him.

"Why, Cass!" she said, and her surprise seemed greater than any pleasure she may have felt at his return. "What is it, Cass?"

Again he said, "Alice!" and stopped there. As in the house, he had his hat in both hands and began twirling it slowly.

Jeff Morgan hesitated no longer. Dammit all, he admonished himself, you had to sneak under their damn windows to get a line on the Briscoe layout, but there's no law in the land that'll make you stick here and watch a man and a girl. If he is in love with her, that's his business. If she wants love made to her, that's her business. Jefferson Davis Morgan, it's none of yours, and you high-tail out of here like the devil was after you!

And start he did, swinging around on an angry heel, turning his back on the pair, he headed down toward the creek and his horse. But he didn't take a dozen steps before he came to a dead halt, and again whirled about. He had heard a little muffled outcry from the girl; it sounded as though her voice had caught in her throat—or as though a hand had been clapped on her mouth. He turned just in time to see Cass Burdock sweep the girl up in his arms and move swiftly with her away from the cabin, into the thicker dark in the heart of the grove.

CHAPTER VIII
"KILL HIM! KILL THE BEAST!"

NOT fifty yards from where he caught her up, but well out of earshot from those within the cabin walls, Cass Burdock set his captive down. His horse's reins were still caught over one arm; he kept a firm hand on the girl's wrist.

"I had to talk to you, Alice," he said, and his voice though low-toned was tense and impassioned. "You know—My God, girl, you know! Tonight, on purpose to drive me wild you stand in front of me and show me yourself—and there are lights in your eyes—"

"Cass! You big fool! Let me go. Let me go, I say!"

"Let you go?"

Instead, he swept her into his arms, sweeping her clean off her feet almost as Bud Briscoe had done, and bent down his face to hers, his lips groping for hers. She struck at him; his hat which he had clapped on when he snatched her up from her place near the oak stump, fell off; a long ray of moonlight through a breach in the thick greenery overhead lay across his face and hers; their eyes glittered with the reflected light.

She hammered at his face, but he imprisoned her hands. She strove to scream again, but he put his palm over her mouth.

Then a voice spoke quietly out of the shadows not two steps from them.

"Do you want me to chase this polecat away, Miss Alice?" asked Jeff Morgan politely. "Being a stranger here I'm not sure about things. Sometimes, I've heard folks say, a third party had better keep out."

Cass Burdock, still gripping the girl's wrist, spun about.

"Who the hell are you?" he demanded. "What do you want here? *Get out!*"

"I was talking to you, Miss," said young Morgan, never more mild outwardly. "Do you want that I should throw this gent out, or are you keeping him for a playmate?"

At last, though half choking, she found her voice.

"Kill him!" she cried. "Kill the beast!"

"It would be a pleasure," said Jeff Morgan, and meant it. And in the moonlight she saw him grin! Not a pretty grin, one with a look of murder to it rather. But a grin.

Cass Burdock's hand dropped to his gun.

"Better keep out of this," he said, a cold fury making his voice brittle.

"Better leave your gun alone," Jeff Morgan told him. "Pull it and I'll kill you—"

Already they were standing close together. Young Morgan bit his words off as he leaned forward and drove his clubbed fist into Burdock's face. Burdock went rocking back on his heels and as he did so, balancing wildly, dragged his gun out of its leather. Young Morgan, seeing his intent, was even swifter, had his own weapon in his hand first. He could have killed Burdock then as he had threatened, but instead of firing the single shot that would have ended the affair he used his gun as a club. It was heavy, a Colt .45, and long-barreled. He brought the long barrel smashing down on Cass Burdock's forearm, and Burdock's gun flew out of his grasp.

Burdock's right arm was numb, but such was the man's fury now, what with the two blows he had already taken, what with Alice Briscoe standing there watching him, that he would have been a hard man to handle had that right arm been broken instead of only briefly nerveless. He did not give back an inch; instead he charged his attacker much as a blind bull charges, reckless, his brain on fire, the look almost of a mad man in his eyes when the moon shone full upon his face; and as he leaped forward he struck with his left hand, and caught young Morgan square on the chin and in his turn sent his man reeling back, almost falling.

But Morgan caught himself up short and steadied himself and grinned crookedly again. Again he could have killed his man with one shot; nothing simpler. Instead he took an instant to toss his gun to the girl's feet.

"If by any chance I get licked," he told her, "you'll have a gun to chase this polecat off the ranch."

And then he devoted all his energies, to the last ounce of power within him, to doing a good job and a quick one. The two men came together the third time, battling in the simple, old fashioned, murderous way of any two men who fight to settle the question which can come nearer killing the other with his bare hands. And Alice Briscoe, never stirring after she stooped quickly and picked up Morgan's gun, stood watching them with eyes which grew round and large with a fascinated horror in her whitening face, as the two stood up to each other with each endeavoring to beat the other into a bloody pulp, into insensibility. Cass Burdock was again using his right hand.

He beat with both hands; these men used their fists like clubs, striking anywhere they could with never a man-made rule to hinder them, and when men do not trammel a fight like this one with their artificial rules, the affair may not be pretty to look at but is brutally honest, as fair for one as the other. Every drop of blood was drained out of the girl's face; she went sick from the sound of battered flesh and bone and gristle; the two men in her over stimulated imagination reeled backward through civilization a thousand years so that they were like prehistoric brutes in a primal ooze. She hid her face in her hands and shuddered, but instantly she jerked her hands down again, listening, watching—

"Stop it!" she screamed. *"Stop it!"*

Neither man paid her the least attention; neither even heard her words any more than he heard the oak leaves rustle in the light night breeze; neither would have listened even had he known what she was saying. And before she could call out again the thing was over. And this was the way of it:

Little by little Jeff Morgan was beating Burdock back, and no doubt that initial blow Burdock had taken across the gun arm had done more than a little to lose the battle for him. Inch by inch, despite a grimness of determination grounded in fury so that it was like steel set in cement, Burdock gave ground. He took a terrible beating, he gave a terrible beating, yet he knew and Jeff Morgan, leaping after him, knew that Burdock was beaten. And then, making a queer, animal-like little whimpering noise because his heart was breaking at the thought of being mastered like this with Alice Briscoe looking on, Cass Burdock thought to see his chance. He saw, where the moonlight glinted upon it, the gun which had flown from his hand; saw it lying not a yard from him. As swift as a cat pouncing he leaped for it. He stooped and his fingers closed on its grip and—

But Jeff Morgan saw, too, and again was quicker than the other man by the flick of an eyelash, and before Cass Burdock could straighten up, Jeff was on top of him. The one blow only did Jeff Morgan need to strike now. As his fist crashed into the bone at the base of Burdock's skull, just behind the ear, Burdock went down like a man whose bones had melted in his body, and lay prone and still. His fingers were spread out on the grip of his gun, but they were like the fingers of a man newly dead.

Jeff Morgan stood over him a minute, nursing a bruised fist with the palm of his other hand, narrow-eyed in his watchfulness, ready for anything. But Cass Burdock didn't move. So Jeff, with his back for the moment turned to the girl, did a couple of things which seemed to require being done next. First he took up the fallen gun and hurled it as far as he could, sending it flying high in air over the top of an oak to fall somewhere in the dark of the depths of the grove. That done, and still without turning, he drew out a big bandana handkerchief from his hip pocket and mopped his face with it; there was the salty taste of blood in his mouth and he fancied he was pretty well painted red. Then he picked up his hat which lay on the ground a couple of steps away, and at last walked to where the girl, rigid and silent, white-faced with enormous eyes, stood scarcely breathing.

He extended his hand.

"I'll take my gun back now," he said. "You won't be needing it."

His hand brushed hers as he retrieved his weapon; her fingers were almost ice cold.

"Have you—killed him?" she whispered, and her hand flew to her throat.

He looked at her steadily; he was glad of the moon; they were so close together that he could have stooped and kissed her uplifted, quivering mouth.

"You told me to, didn't you?" he said, and jammed his gun back into its holster.

"Is he dead?"

He shook his head.

"He's out cold, that's all. He'll be coming to pretty pronto. I'll wait until he does, if you say so; then he can get on his horse and ride away from here."

He saw her eyes close tight, then fly wide open again. Her hand was still at her throat, her fingers tight about it, and he could see her ring, the stone like blood.

"Who are you?" she asked. "Where did you come from? How did you happen to be here?"

"Me, my name's Morgan. Jefferson Davis Morgan. I'm from down South. I just got as far as Black Gulch today, riding from the east, across this valley. Then from Black Gulch—"

"You came late this afternoon! You stopped on the ridge, you sat for a while on your horse and looked down into our valley! You were leading another horse—"

"That's right," said Jeff, puzzled. "How'd you know?"

Oh, she had known, hadn't she, from the first sight of him through her spy glass, that he would be coming back! And soon! Hadn't she said so? And here he was already! To herself, looking up at him wonderingly, she said his name, Jefferson Davis Morgan.

Without answering his question she asked again,

"But how did you happen to be here right now? And you called me Alice; you said right off, 'Shall I chase him away, Miss Alice?' How did you know my name?"

Cass Burdock's horse, left to its own devices when the fight started, had whipped back frightened, then with reins dragging on the ground had fidgeted restlessly, not running away, yet withdrawing a score of paces. Now Morgan, before he answered the last question, went for the horse and brought it back; and all the while and even when he was talking with the girl and was profoundly conscious of her nearness as though some emanation from her flowed strongly all around him, tried to keep a part of his mind on the man on the ground. He had the notion that a lot of trickery resided in Cass Burdock.

And while he was taking the few steps to secure the horse and return with it, Alice Briscoe, after watching him wonderingly while his back was turned, had stirred at last and had gone to where Cass Burdock lay. She was bending over him, trying to assure herself that he really hadn't died under that last savage blow, when Jeff Morgan came back to her. Just then Burdock groaned and moved slightly; Jeff could hear the girl's deep breath.

Together, without speaking, they awaited the stricken man's full return to consciousness. Before he turned his head or looked up, his hand started roving, his fingers questing; his first dawning thought was of his gun, just as it had been his last thought before his light went out. His arm swept out in a wider arc; then he lay still a moment, then suddenly rolled over and sat up. He lifted his head and they saw how sick and haggard he looked, with a great dark smear across his mouth and cheek; his eyes, though the moon shone straight into them, seemed dull and heavy. He merely glanced at the girl, then for a long time sat staring into Jeff Morgan's eyes which stared just as fixedly as his.

No one spoke for a long time. Then Jeff Morgan

said, "Your gun's gone, Burdock. Here's your horse."

Cass Burdock rose awkwardly and unsteadily to his feet. He put his hand to his head; Alice saw his hat lying a few feet away and brought it to him. He took it without looking at her; he seemed unable to withdraw his eyes from Jeff Morgan's. Still without speaking he went to his horse, threw his reins over the animal's high-tossing head and climbed heavily up into the saddle.

"Alice," he said, "I'm coming back again. I'm coming back for two reasons. Who this man is I don't know and I don't care, but if God lets me live I'm going to kill him. I'll shoot him on sight or I'll kill him with my hands, I don't care which. That's one reason. The other reason is, I'm coming back again to you. You made me love you; you did it on purpose. You are my girl and I'm coming back for you."

"You are not to come back, Cass," she said, her voice hushed but very, very emphatic and determined. "Never. And you had better go now."

"You heard what I said," said Cass.

He looked at her a long time as though somehow taking her measure all anew; he looked a long time at Jeff Morgan as though memorizing the man. Then he rode away, heading south, down-valley; for a little time hoofbeats came floating back through the quiet night, diminishing, diminishing, dying away at last so that again there was no sound above the quiet breathing of the soft night breeze.

"You have made an enemy who will try to keep his promise," said Alice. A shudder as of cold shook her shoulders. "I know what Cass is like. He has made up his mind that he is going to kill you—Oh, and it is all because of me!"

Jeff Morgan was trying to think straight to the point, and his thoughts meandered like a lazy winding river. It was hard to concentrate the way he wanted to when he stood so close to this girl in the soft moonlight. He thought, here I came out all this way, all this time, to kill Bud Briscoe. That's my one job. So I run into Cass Burdock and now his one job is to kill me. And it's all because Bud Briscoe killed Bob Lane. It sort of seems as though killing didn't settle anything at all, just started up more killings.

He shook his head and batted his eyes and shoved his hat far back.

"You said, how did I know your name?" he said. "I know it's Alice; some of them call you Allie, but I like Alice best. I don't know your last name. The way I know you're Alice Somebody is because while you folks were inside I was outside looking in. I was listening all I could, finding out all I could. It's what you might call spying. That's how come!"

He felt better, having that off his chest. When a man has indulged in a pastime of which he can't quite approve, it's as good as a bath to blurt out the truth, it's that simple confession which is said to be good for the soul.

He succeeded only in further mystifying her.

"But I don't understand! Why? You're a stranger here, you don't know any of us—Or, do you?"

"No. Not exactly.—Say, tell me something: A man by name of Bud Briscoe was here tonight, wasn't he?"

"Of course! If you really spied on us you saw him, didn't you? You must have."

"Does he maybe happen to be the big man with a beard like yellow corn silk? You ran and jumped into a man's arms; you see, like I told you, I saw what went on. Was that Bud Briscoe? Only you called him Charlie. But maybe it was Bud Briscoe?"

He saw her shape her lips to say "Yes." But she held the word back and instead of committing herself asked,

"You say you are a stranger here, that you don't know any of us—Then why do you want to know about Bud Briscoe?"

In his turn he evaded the direct answer.

"I rode back down here from Black Gulch tonight," he said. "I thought a couple of your dogs, chained at the foot of the trail, would eat me, skin, bones and boots. I came on and there were more dogs, chained like the first ones. Dogs that yowl so you can hear them for miles. That's what they're for, to pass the word along that somebody's coming. And now you've sent Injun Pete to turn them loose again. That means that you don't need any watch-dogs on the job any more. Kind of funny, strikes a stranger! Is it just because Bud Briscoe was here and has gone now?"

"You *have* been spying on us, haven't you!"

"What's Bud Briscoe afraid of?" he demanded curtly.

She stiffened at that.

"He isn't afraid of anything on earth!" she flared out at him. "But he isn't a fool, either. He has made enemies; I am afraid that all strong men like him do make enemies. They are a crowd of wicked, lawless, murderous devils! They would shoot him in the back. So sometimes, when he is here and knows that they are following him in the dark, we have Pete put the dogs on guard."

He stared at her curiously.

"You sort of like him, don't you?" he said.

Her laughter taunted him.

"Like him? I love him to pieces! He is the finest man on earth, Mr. Jefferson Davis Morgan."

"You're not already married to him, are you?"

This time her laughter was truly spontaneous.

"Why, don't you know? Charlie—you call him Bud Briscoe—is my big brother!"

"Oh," said Jeff Morgan, and felt like a deflated balloon. He had trouble again assembling his thoughts. Glad, that's what he was to begin with, that the man into whose arms she had sprung so gaily, was a brother instead of a lover. But how be glad that she was sister to the man whom he had sworn to kill, whom he must kill? So all he could say was, "Oh," and thereafter he fell silent for a time.

She was watching him intently, wonderingly.

"You haven't told me why you came here tonight? Why you have been listening to us, spying on us!"

He said, "You go in to Black Gulch sometimes?"

"Why, yes. Sometimes. Not often, but once in a while. Why?"

"You know folks there, then. Maybe you know a man named Jameson? He's the sheriff."

"I have seen him. I don't know him and I don't want to know him. Sheriff!" she sniffed. "He ought to be inside his jail instead! He was put in office by a crowd of crooks, thieves and robbers, and he's no better than they are!"

"But you say you don't even know him! Somebody's told you all this about Long Jim Jameson? Who tells you things like that, I wonder?"

"Why, they all know him! Charlie and Nate and—Yes, and Cass Burdock, too! They all say the same things about him."

"I see," said Jeff Morgan soberly, and scratched his jaw and fell silent for a spell. Presently he asked, "Those other men in the house? One you called Uncle Dick, didn't you?"

"Yes. He's my father's brother. He came to us just a couple of weeks ago; he came West by Panama. He and my father hadn't seen each other since they were boys about six and eight years old."

"And the other man? He didn't open his mouth once. Who's he?"

"My father," she said simply. "He hardly ever says anything. And now you know about all of us, don't you? And I don't know a single thing about you!"

"You'll know sooner or later, Alice," he told her with quiet positiveness. "You'll know all there is to know. I heard Cass Burdock tell you he was coming back. Well, I'm coming back, too. You can count on that."

"I am glad," she said, very frank, her eyes uplifted honestly to his. "I haven't thanked you for tonight, have I? I think I would have rather died than have him—have him kiss me."

"Bud Briscoe gave you that ring and that necklace, didn't he?" he demanded bruskly.

She brushed the ring against her cheek.

"Yes. He always—"

With sudden impulse, his gesture almost brutal, he caught her hand and jerked it down from her face; his eyes just then frightened her and she jerked away from him and whipped back.

75

"Take that ring off!" he commanded, curt and angry. "Take off that damned necklace! Never wear either of them again, hear me? Never so much as touch them again!"

"You—you—Are you crazy!"

He surprised her and he surprised himself. He reached out with both hands, he clamped both of his hard hands down on her shoulders.

"Crazy? No, I'm not! Maybe I am acting crazy right now, but that's only because you don't understand! You listen to me, Alice Briscoe! I never saw you until a few minutes ago, but inside of me I've known you all my born days. I didn't know that I've always been looking for you, waiting for you, going hungry for you, but I have." His hands clamped tighter on her shoulders, hurting her. "I love you, do you understand? I love you now, already, after just seeing you a minute, more than I ever loved anything or everything all rolled together in life. Do you know what I mean?"

"Jeff—Jeff Morgan—*Don't!* You—You frighten me! You don't know what you are saying! You are hurting me—You *are* crazy!"

"No. I am just alive for the first time, and it's all your doing. I love you and I want you all for mine, and that's what you are going to be. And there's going to be merry hell to pay first, and I know that too. Life's a funny game; I found that out when I was sixteen years old. Sometimes it's all like starshine and flowers and slow dance music; sometimes it's just plain genuine hell. We've got to take 'em both the way they come. It's like poker; you got to play the cards the way they fall. Now, I've got to do two things to you: It's going to be my job to hurt you like hell; that's something nobody can do anything about. But then again it's going to be my job to make you happy whether you want to be or not. And I'm going to do that, too!"

He had her terribly confused, excited, eager, frightened. It seemed to her that there was a magnetism in this man that flowed from his hands into her shoulders, throughout her body, and that little sparks were sprinkled through her brain, along her arteries. She wanted to break free and run, and she did not even try to move.

"I love you and I am going to hurt you now," said Jeff Morgan, relentlessly stern, determined to play his cards the way they had fallen. "You love your brother, Bud Briscoe, don't you? And in his damned way he loves you and is good to you, isn't he? Well, he's a dirty crook; he's worse; right now I'd glory in breaking his damned neck. Those jewels he brought you—Your uncle Dick was right! There's blood on them! And you ask why I'm here tonight? Well, here's the why of it, Alice Briscoe: For a long time I've been looking for Bud Briscoe, and now that I've found him I'm staying with him. He's all I've told you and on top

77

of that he's a murdering dog. He killed my pardner, Bob Lane, and I'm here to kill Bud Briscoe. Yes, your brother, damn him! And then I'm going on loving you and I'm going to make you love me!"

She did break free then and struck him across the face with all her might. He stood looking at her, not moving, not saying anything. In her eyes then he was very tall, looming a dark, sinister figure against the clear sky; in his eyes she was a little thing, and easy to hurt. He had said everything already. Slowly she backed away from him, moving measured step by step like one in a trance.

She stopped and stood as still as he was. She wanted to turn and run; she wanted to go back to him and beat his cruel, hard, lying mouth with her clenched fist. She just stood still. A sob caught in her throat and she fought it down. Here was the man whom she had seen through her spy glass! Was that only today, just a handful of little hours ago? She could see him again sitting on his horse up there on the ridge—she could remember the queer little shiver that had run through her, the quick, silly beating of her heart.

Perhaps she was just waiting for him to speak again, to say something, anything. To storm at her for having struck him, to beg for forgiveness for the vicious lies he had spoken, to say that he meant nothing of it all—except that he loved her.

And at last, out of the breeze-ruffled silence, he

did speak. He spoke gently and very softly and yet there managed to be a satin-smooth sternness in his quiet voice.

"There are things you can't get away from, Alice girl. You can't stop the moon from shining up there; maybe clouds might hide it for a spell, but it would keep on shining just the same and after a while the moonlight would come back. You can't keep water from running downhill; you can make a dam if you want to and try to stop it, but after a while it will wash the dam away or climb up over the top and go on. I saw a man not very long ago in a barroom down in Tecolote which is a considerable way from here; he had a little horseshoe shaped steel thing he called a magnet, and he'd put a little needle close to it, and the needle would jump to his magnet just like—just like you jumped into your brother's arms. You couldn't see how the magnet was pulling the needle, but you couldn't stop what had to happen. There's a lot of things you can't get away from, Alice girl. I guess it's always been like that and it always will. I don't want to get away from you, but I couldn't if I did want to. And you can't get away from me. It's just like that, like those other things, mighty simple maybe—and mighty wonderful."

She hung on his every word; her eyes, fascinated, tried to make out every line in his face, the quirk of his mouth that could be so hard and which she just now began to realize could be so very tender, the look in his shadowed eyes. He moved her as nothing in all her life had ever moved her before, he stirred her to some strange new depths, never hitherto plumbed—again she was vaguely frightened as a feeling of helplessness swept over her, as she thought of the magnet making the small thin needle leap to it. She thought, There *are* things you can't get away from—I've seen a twig being carried over a waterfall—

For her, tonight took on all the attributes of a nightmare. Here came a wonder and a glory—and a hideous, unthinkable menace. If only he had said, "I love you!" and there had been no other words, with nothing else needed to say! But he had not stopped there. He had said, "I am here to kill your brother Charlie!"

He saw her standing there looking at him out of enormous, liquid eyes, and again he saw the quiver of her mouth and a throbbing shadow on the whiteness of her throat, and it was given to him to know that he was torturing her even as a present over-masterful destiny was torturing him. Why, in the name of all dark mysteries, did a man always have to hurt the thing he loved? But then, leave love out and would there be any hurt?

He stepped swiftly close to her. An instant he bent over her, his body as rigid as hers. Then he did to her the very thing that he had wanted to slaughter Cass Burdock for trying to do: He gathered her close to his arms and lifted her and held her tight and kissed her. And she kept thinking of the twig she had seen going with the waterfall. She did not know that her arms had crept up about his neck—

He left her without a word.

CHAPTER IX
THE TWIG OVER THE WATERFALL

THE girl was standing like a statue, her hands down along her sides, her face uplifted, her lips slightly parted as her eyes stared straight up into the depths of the sky, her thoughts numbed, agonized, all in a mist of confusion when as from a remote distance she heard a voice calling.

"Alice!" called the voice. "Alice! Where are you? What you up to?"

She might have remained there an hour, hours maybe, but for Uncle Dick's calling to her. Her breast rose higher and higher to a long, lung-filling breath; there was a little struggle in pulling her eyes away from the clear high arch of infinity, in bringing herself down to matter-of-fact earth again and everyday surroundings. She answered, making her voice sound casual, "Here I am, Uncle Dick. I'm coming."

He stood in the open doorway, a small dark figure in the rectangle of pale yellowish lamp-light.

"I was looking at the moon," she told him. "There never was a night just exactly like this, was there?"

"George has already went to bed," he told her. As she stepped by him, going inside, he eyed her in that sharp, watchful, prying way he had. "Me, I was thinkin' about bed, too, but I got to wonderin' about you."

He followed her into the front room—they called it the parlor—and closed the door, shooting home the iron bolt that served as a lock.

"You didn't have to wait for me," she told him lightly. She didn't look at him; she didn't want him looking at her. "It was nice of you, though. You can go to bed now, and I guess I'd better."

She patted a fictitious yawn and then busied herself with winding the clock on the mantel.

"Let me see your gew-gaws again, Allie," he said abruptly. "I didn't get much of a look at them. They're sure mighty pretty, ain't they?"

The stranger's words, the words so curtly spoken by young Jeff Morgan, began to echo in her memory: "Take that ring off! Take off that damned necklace! Never wear them again. . . . There's blood on them!"

She stripped the ring off her finger in haste and handed it to Uncle Dick. She unfastened the necklace and placed that in his hand, too. She was thinking of a man who had a magnet and a steel needle, and how the needle leaped to the magnet

82

like a girl going into a man's arms. She was hearing Jeff's plain and simple, yet vehement words, beating back against the sounding board of her memory. She thought of the twig going headlong with the waterfall. She had been the twig tonight while a strange man was the waterfall. He had kissed her, and no other man had ever done that. And her arms had gone up around his neck—she knew it now—and she had let him kiss her as he wished—And she had kissed him!

And he had told her, "I love you!" And he had said, "I am going to kill your brother." Yes, he had said those things before he kissed her. And she, even after he had said them, was the twig running with the waterfall!

"Yep, mighty pretty, mighty pretty," said Uncle Dick. "Hm. Bud didn't say exactly where he got 'em, did he? Nor exactly how much he paid for 'em?"

She pretended to laugh.

"You know how Charlie is! You haven't known him very long, of course, and you don't know him very well, but you do know how he is! He'd never think of things like that."

"I'll tell you what I think," said Uncle Dick. "I've saw gems and jew'ls a-plenty in my time. There was a feller, a high-tone gam'ler he was, down to New Orleans where I hung out for a spell; I knowed Jake Devlin like I know my own boots. He had him an awful fancy mist—missis,

83

an' he liked first rate to hang bright and shinin' colors all over her, an' most of all he went in for greens and reds, and the greens was em'ral's, and the red ones was rubies, an' they cost more'n plain di'mon's."

"I don't know what you mean, Uncle Dick!"

"You all are my folks," he said, the red gems cupped in his palm, his eyes brooding over them. "Jus' the same I don't know you awful well, do I? Me bein' a Johnny-come-lately out here. Take Bud, now. Maybe he's awful rich?"

That set her laughing. She was poised on the heights that were a borderland between laughter and tears. To laugh was better; anyhow it asked less explaining.

"Charlie? Rich? He owns half a dozen lovely saddle horses and—and—Well?"

"Me," said Uncle Dick simply and in a way solemnly, "I ain't got very much money myself. But I've got some salted away, and I know where I can raise a few bucks more. You wouldn't sell these gew-gaws, now, would you, Allie?"

"Sell them? Sell Charlie's presents?"

"Not if I offered you, say, five-six, maybe seven thousand dollars?" And now he was eyeing her in that fashion of his which was like shooting flint-tipped arrows into your heart.

Alice sat down limply; there was a bench conveniently situated and she dropped to it with a gasp.

"What on earth are you saying?" she asked in a

small voice. "Why, Charlie never had any part of that much money."

And again echoes resounded in her mind; words that a compelling stranger had spoken so bluntly.

"You ain't exac'ly a fool, are you?" demanded Uncle Dick. "Or are you?"

"I don't know what you are talking about! Are you just trying to tease me tonight? Oh, I'm tired, Uncle Dick. Good night."

She jumped up and hurried to the door leading deeper into the cabin. The adjoining room was the dining room; she could slip out through a side door there, pass several doors of the long dwelling, slip into her own room without disturbing her father or going through any other room whatever. But Uncle Dick's voice was calling after her.

"Hey! You're fergittin' your gew-gaws!"

"Keep them for me until tomorrow morning— Good night," she called back, and the door slammed.

Outside, she did not go straightway to her own room; instead she stopped a moment under one of the oaks. She pressed the back of her hand against her mouth. She had just now been kissed. It was the first time in her life. And the man who had kissed her had said never a word thereafter but had gone swiftly, leaving her alone, leaving her torn and uncertain, lifted into an ecstasy, plunged into an inferno. And she didn't even know where he had gone.

She knew he must have a horse somewhere nearby; he would have gone straight to his horse. But where? Hidden somewhere, of course. In the oak grove, then—or down in the dark by the river. Leaving her he had turned riverward, hadn't he? And he couldn't have gotten far while she was returning to the cabin, while she had a few words with Uncle Dick. Even yet he must be somewhere near!

She picked up her skirts and ran, passing under the low-drooping boughs of the oak, under still another oak, into the clearing beyond, stopping half in shadow, half in mellow moonlight. From here she could see the long wavering dark line of the river growth, willows and poplars with a white-barked, noble sycamore here and there—and she was just in time to see a man on horseback riding out of the dark of the river woods and into the full moonlight. And she knew it was Jeff Morgan, and she watched, scarcely breathing, to see what way he was going, whether he was being drawn back to the cabin and her, whether he was turning south and into the trail which led back to Black Gulch—whether he rode north and toward Bud Briscoe.

She saw him turn in the saddle. He did not check his horse's gathering speed, but he did look back toward the cabin. And then he rode on north.

She ran to her room. She lost a tiny blue slipper on the way, stopped automatically to turn back and snatch it up, ran with the slipper in her hand, and flung herself into her room. Her hurrying fingers struck a match and lighted a candle. She ripped off her pretty blue dress and let it slide from a bench to the floor. A piece of calico tacked across a corner made a closet; she whipped the calico aside and lifted a little riding suit from the nail on which it hung; she had made it herself from a picture she had seen in an old copy of the *Atlanta Constitution* on the Ladies' page. It was of blue-gray cloth, a jacket with a wing collar inlaid with red velvet, a pair of riding breeches, very full and modest. And there was a pair of black leather boots to go with it, and a broad blue-gray hat with a small pale green plume.

She was still buckling on her belt as she blew out her candle and ran out and went dodging through the sturdy trunks of the grove, headed toward the barn. She hoped that Injun Pete was back, to rope and saddle a horse for her, but as soon as the wish was formed it was abandoned; there could be no such luck, as Pete couldn't be back, leisurely buck that he was, for a full hour yet. But there was luck left for her. In the corral were half a dozen horses and she had but to take her pick. She sped into the barn, groped for the rope which she knew would be coiled on the peg just at the right of the door as you went in, and was making her loop as she came out and opened the corral gate. She chose the long, lean black with the white nose and four white stockings; that was Apache Kid, young and swift and in a way dependable, though not over tame, a horse that at least would stand to be saddled and would not jerk its nose sky-high to avoid the bit.

She threw a pretty rope, did Alice Briscoe, dragging the long loop on the ground behind her until the right moment came, then making the thing come alive as it slithered through the air and settled unerringly; Apache Kid, starting to bolt, came to a quivering halt at the familiar command of a rope about his neck. She saddled and bridled him, she buckled on her spurs, she had the gate shut after them and was up in the saddle all in a flash. She leaned forward and patted the horse's lean, hard shoulder.

"We're going places tonight, Apache boy," she said softly. "So let's go!"

After a while, far ahead in the open valley she saw a horseman drifting northward. He was following the main trail which, at his present rate, would bring him to Settlers' Gap in four or five hours. She said to herself, "I wonder what you would say, Mr. Jefferson Davis Morgan, if you knew that I was following you! What would you think? You kissed me just now, didn't you, after half killing another man, one that I know a lot better than I know you, for trying to do the same thing! What would you say? What would you think? *What would you do?* But you don't know, do you? Now suppose I just rode up to you and asked you a question, suppose I said, 'Tell me, which one of us is the magnet and which is the needle?' What would you say then? And suppose you knew where I was riding, and why: What would you say? And what would you do about it?"

Now she felt no need for haste. She knew where Jeff Morgan was going, and how long a time it would take him to get there. He was a stranger in these mountains, and she knew the trails within a radius of a score of miles as she knew the palm of her own hand. All she needed do now was drift along in his wake, keeping out of sight yet from time to time making sure that he still rode on ahead, until such time as they passed beyond the narrowing confines of upper Green Water Valley and entered Daylight Pass and struck into the rugged country beyond. Then it should be very simple for her to strike into a spur of the main trail, speed on for all that Apache Kid was worth for three or four miles, cut back into the main trail again, ahead of Jeff Morgan, and come up with Bud Charlie Briscoe in ample time to give him her few words of warning: "A stranger, a man who calls himself Jefferson Davis Morgan, says that you killed his friend, Bob Lane, and that he is coming now to kill you." All very simple.

Time ran by smoothly like sand through an hour glass, like the river slipping down along its well worn channel, like the stars sweeping through their endless courses, and after a while time stood still. That was when, long after she had swerved from the main trail and had used her spurs and knew that she had shot ahead of the man she had at first followed, she stopped on a ridge rimming the upper end of the valley, where it pinched down so that it was only half a mile across from ridge to ridge, and sat there, still in the saddle, and watched and waited to see whether Jeff Morgan still rode north, whether he would soon cast a long shadow across the highland meadow through which the main trail led.

Sitting in the dark where a high, knife-edged granite cliff threw its shadow down into the meadow's rim, she heard at first nothing but the beating of her own heart; her heart felt ready to burst. She dropped her reins on the saddle horn and clasped both hands, pressing hard, against the tumult within her breast. Until tonight she had never truly loved anything, anyone, but Charlie—Bud Briscoe. And now, since that first glimpse through her spy glass, no matter how crazy it all was, she loved somebody else. What could you do about a thing like that? What could the needle do, what could the twig do? And, when you thought of the magnet and of the waterfall, were they to blame? Look at the river down yonder. Look how it sped through the mountains, leaping down in many a cascade, winding and twisting through many a ravine and valley, racing headlong to the

90

sea. It couldn't help it. It didn't know where it was going, or why. It just had to go.

She didn't know what cosmic forces were. Even today do we know whether they are truly cosmic or merely comic forces? All she knew was that she was riding with her heart in her throat, riding to tell Charlie that the young man whom she had discovered only today through her new spy glass was coming, close behind her, to kill him.

So she waited, and after a time she saw, down in the narrowed valley and well behind her, the patiently advancing horse and rider. They didn't hasten and they didn't loiter; they just pressed steadily on and made her think of the eternal commonplace phenomena like the measured passage of the seasons, like day giving place to night, like sunrise at the appointed time and sundown in its turn. Like the beating of her own heart which grew steady again. It could beat and beat and beat, the same way until it stopped.

She pressed ahead again, still keeping to the high, dim trail, hardly more than a deer track, on the ridge, touching Apache Kid with her spurs, speeding through the dark silent pines like a shadow through a realm of shadows. She told herself, Now I do know where he is going. For a while, although I knew, I hoped I was wrong. But he keeps straight on; he told me what he means to do. Come on, Apache! We've got to get to Charlie first!

The mountains closed in on both sides, and the valley was choked by them so that its narrowed neck was scarcely more than a steep-walled, black ravine, a sort of devil's playground, from the bleak and sullen look of it, with black, lava-like boulders frowning against the skyline, with broken lava rocks strewn along steep slopes, with an ink-black, froth-flecked river running wild in its deeply gouged runway over embedded stones grown glassily slick and slippery with wear of eons and a slimy lichenous growth. The moon smote the racing stream in places, turning it into gleaming quick-silver, leaving it in places as black as bubbling coal tar, and mysterious with profundities of depths.

Where the river was wide but not deep, where there was a chancy ford which she knew, she put Apache Kid to the water. He snorted and flung up his head and rebelled, but she raked him with her spurs and Apache struck into the stream. The water frothed over his fetlocks, up to his knees, it raked his belly, it grew shallower again as his mincing hoofs neared the farther side. And then Apache Kid slipped on a treacherous, hidden, slippery rock and his fore-feet shot downstream while his struggling lean body was thrown upstream, and Alice Briscoe found herself in the drag of the river, water well above her knees, and saw her horse lying on its side with the scurrying black current pouring headlong over it. Apache Kid was down on his side, and even his gallant head was under water. And he did not rise.

The girl steadied her footing; she still had the reins in her hand; she strove frantically to jerk the horse up, to get his head above water before he drowned. And the submerged beast, struggling wildly, managed in time to get head and pumping throat above the smooth black surface of the river. He struggled mightily, did Apache Kid, to find his feet and stand on them, but only flopped back, unable to rise, barely able to keep his flaring nostrils some three or four inches above the strangling waters.

She thought—No, she wasn't exactly thinking but impulses and instincts exploded throughout her mental processes—He is dying terribly! It's a broken leg, his shoulder is broken against the rocks. He can't get up; he is going to suffer and drown! Why, oh dear God, why haven't I strength to pull Apache Kid out and somehow save him? He has carried me so many and many and many times—he has been so good to me!

She knew she was growing hysterical, overemphasizing things, being a little fool, but she did not care! "I don't give a darn," she cried out loud, smudging her eyes, her cheek, with a wet sleeve. "Apache, you've been good to me; now you're in trouble and I can't help. If I only had a gun, maybe I could shoot you, and save you all this agony."

She thought then in a strangely explosive sort of

way of Jefferson Davis Morgan. He was riding this way, wasn't he? She had been spying on him, following him, pressing ahead of him, avoiding him at all turns. But now there was no one in the world to help poor Apache Kid but young Morgan, headed now to kill her brother.

She forgot everything but Apache Kid's tragic dilemma and the leisurely oncoming Jeff Morgan. She waded against the stream, out through treacherous boulders and through its pebbly strand to the dry shore. And the first thing she saw, seeming very far away, slowly drifting black figures making a combined centaur shadow-shape under the bright moon, were Jeff Morgan and his horse.

She snatched off her hat and waved; she ran out into the full moonshine and kept on waving; she began calling at the top of her voice:

"Jeff! Mr. Morgan! Oh, Jefferson Davis Morgan! Help! *Jeff!*"

He was following the north trail which led through these narrow defiles straight on to Settlers' Gap, and at this time of night in this silent bit of highland wilderness had no thought of being seen or called by anyone. Yet through the stillness he heard a far-away call, as fine and dim as those ancient horns of Elfland faintly blowing, a voice as unreal as a voice in an almost forgotten dream, calling over and over, "Jeff! Jefferson Morgan! Help, oh, help us!"

And then, somehow, he knew it was Alice

Briscoe calling to him. Strange that he knew who it was, since he had thought her so far away, back there at the old Briscoe cabin, since he scarcely heard her voice; but he did know. And he raked Dandy's lean sides with his spurs and came flashing down across the meadow lands to the creek, and found her there, and came down out of his saddle in a rush and caught her two hands in his, saying:

"Alice! Oh, my dear!"

A foolish sort of thing to say, he thought by the time the words were out. But she didn't seem to notice anything wrong about them. Her hands, surrendered into his, gripping his strongly, were as eloquent as her following words.

"Oh, Jeff! What are we going to do? My horse— it's Apache Kid, Jeff, and there never was a finer horse in the world and I love him the way you love—I don't know what you love, but you have loved a horse, haven't you? Or a dog? Or maybe a friend of one kind or another? Apache Kid slipped in the water and has a broken leg; he can't get up and he is drowning; and I—I haven't even a pistol and—and—Oh, Jeff, I can't bear it—all alone— Will you—?"

He put his arms about her and held her tight. And for a little while she was grateful, glad to be in his arms, warmed there and heartened, like a little child. Tears were streaming down her face, her lashes were thick and heavy with them, and he felt her breast throb against him. He did what any man, young or old would have done, men being at crises like this without imagination but with a tender tendency toward fatherliness; he patted her on the back and muttered, "There, there; it's going to be all right," and things like that.

And then he strode into the current and to Apache Kid. He watched the animal struggle, strive to rear up and scramble to its feet, then fall back until almost, though not quite, the water was over its head. Slowly Jeff Morgan dragged his gun out. Alice watched him, then turned her back and went down on her knees on the pebbly shore, her hands pressed tight against her ears.

But after a time, a longish time it was, she knew that no shot had been fired. She dreaded to turn, to remove her hands, lest she do so just at the wrong time. But in the end she had to look. And she saw that Jeff Morgan had again holstered his weapon, that he had moved so that he was downstream from the no longer struggling horse, that he was bending low, both of his arms lost to the shoulders in the creek. And then she heard a mighty and somehow heartening shout from him, and he came running, splashing water so high that she, on the ground, could see bright iridescent drops in the moonlight.

"There's a chance!" he called to her, and the next moment she watched him and wondered as he stripped his small, tight bed roll from behind the saddle of his own horse. He got the thing down, unrolled and spread out, and she made out that he had a small, bright bladed hand ax in his hands as he dashed back into the stream. And so, of course, she wondered more than ever! Was he going to kill the poor brute with a hand ax? To save powder and lead, maybe?

He began chopping, under water, like a man chopping wood. The grisly, shuddersome thought came to her that he was chopping off Apache Kid's broken leg! She screamed at him and came running back into the swift, swirling stream. He looked up and grinned at her.

"Take it easy, Alice girl," he said casually. "The way I said, we've got a chance! I wouldn't be a mite surprised—You just wait and give me a show to make a try!"

For once the way things seemed was the way they were. He was chopping wood under water. His exploratory arm had found the whole trouble; he whacked away with a will, finding his work cut out for him since it is no simple task to do your chopping with the blade of your ax glancing through a swift current, but he kept unremittingly on, and then there was a brief time during which he heaved and strained and the girl was at utter loss to understand—and then he had Apache Kid by the bridle and had slapped the horse's shoulders smartly with his riding quirt, and breaking through froth and great crackling bubbles Apache

Kid stood up, stood steadily on four feet! And Jeff Davis Morgan, his grin never broader or more triumphant, led Apache out of the river and to high, dry land. And there was never a limp!

"You see," explained Morgan, "there was a small log, not over six or eight inches thick, and water-logged it was and jammed tight between boulders. And when your horse slipped and went down, he shoved a front leg under the log, there being just room, clean up to the shoulder. And there he was!"

The moonlight made diamonds of the drops of water on the girl's face, and some of the drops might have been tears. She began to tremble from head to foot. She said, accusing herself,

"If only I'd had a gun, any sort of a gun, I'd have killed him! And he wasn't even hurt! Jeff!"

"You're soaked to the skin," said young Morgan. He gave his own shoulders a jerk against a sudden penetrating cold; summer it might be, but up here, at night and at these altitudes, it grew chilly enough without the aid of wet garments plastered tight to their bodies.

"What are you doing up here anyhow?" he thought to demand. "Why is it you're not home and in bed? Where do you think you are going?"

But he didn't have to ask; he knew before the words were well out of his mouth. On her way, of course she was, to warn her murdering brother, Bud Briscoe, that a stranger, a certain Jeff

Morgan, was at last riding him down. He said angrily,

"I wasn't going to shoot him in the back! You would have done better to keep out of this, Alice girl. This is no girl's business anyhow. And now you're going to scoot back home as fast as the Good Lord will let Apache Kid run with you!"

"I'm not! I won't!"

But her passionate denial lost some of its force because her teeth were chattering. Partly nerves, maybe, troubled her; but there were her cold, wet clothes, too.

"So you're not? So you won't?" he said after her, and there was a hint of mockery in his voice. He added, piquing her, "If that's what you said! Your teeth are chattering so a man can't be sure whether you're thanking him or scolding! Hm, let's see. It'll take you an hour back home, won't it? Or three-four hours to skedaddle on to where your precious Bud Briscoe is—longer, if you trip your horse up again. Darn it, girl, what am I going to do with you? I don't want you getting your death of cold the first night I find you!"

This was all new country to him, and while he spoke with her his eyes roved up and down the narrow ravine-like valley with its broken hills on one side, with the ragged bulwarks of the mountains stabbing at the sky on the other—and of a sudden in a moonlit meadow, at its very edge that was darkening under the shadows running out from a bit of pine forest, he made a discovery. There was a tiny cabin, as sure as you were born! Not over a couple of hundred yards away, a half-hidden and utterly dark abode of sorts, yet a thing of four walls and a roof. At least it seemed from where he stood to have a roof, and he was dead certain of a rock chimney.

"Now!" said Jeff Morgan in a tone that might have been Columbus' at the time when land swam unmistakeably into his ken. "There's a cabin. We're going to wake 'em up; they're going to build you a good hot pine fire; you're going to dry out and then go home. Come along, Alice."

"We're going to do nothing of the kind," she informed him tartly. "There are two excellent reasons—It's an old deserted, tumbledown place and no one has lived there for years in the first place, so we can't wake 'em up. On top of that I have somewhere that I want to go. Thank you for helping me with my horse, but—"

She sneezed.

"That settles it!" said Jeff Morgan.

He waded back across the stream, took his own horse's dragging reins and without mounting returned to her. But already, thinking to see her chance for escape in full flight, she had scrambled up into her saddle and started upstream. But Apache Kid, though unhurt, was stiff and his legs numb and heavy, and within twenty yards Jeff Morgan, mounted now, had overtaken her. He let the two horses run along side by side; and that was because they were headed straight toward the ruin of an old cabin. Then, with the cabin close at hand, he reached out and caught Apache Kid's rein close up to the bit, and brought both horses to a stop.

Alice Briscoe, lifting her own quirt as though she would strike him across the impudent face, exclaimed hotly,

"If you think for a minute that—"

And then she ruined it all with another sneeze.

"Down you come," said Jeff Morgan and dismounted and lifted his arms for her to come down.

And she saw how that grin of his had come back.

CHAPTER X
"GIVE ME A FEW DAYS OF LIVING!"

THE cabin wasn't as far gone in ruin as at first it appeared. To be sure, one room was a jumbled pile of debris, rotted logs, warped gray planks and slivers of an old shake roof. But once upon a time there had been two rooms, and the main room, the sturdier built, though without floor and with but half a roof, did offer walls and, best of all, a rock fireplace. In no time at all young Jeff Morgan had a fine fire blazing.

"Now," he said, "you get good and dry. And while—"

"You're as wet as I am," she reminded him. "Wetter, even, from being half under water all that while."

"Take off some of your clothes," he cut in. "Wait a shake; I'll hang up my tarp over the door; then while I'm taking care of the horses you can undress and dry your things. I'll whoop before I come barging in on you."

"Of all the things!" gasped Alice.

But he only grinned at her and went away, and presently fastened his piece of canvas over the door and went away again; she heard the jingle of his spurs, the clank of bridle chains and slow thud of hoofs, all receding. She ran to the door, pulled the canvas aside and called:

"I'm not going to stay here—You don't think—"

"You get good and dry, then we'll talk. You don't want a red nose and watery eyes, do you? You dry out the best you can, first of all." And then his whistling—he could whistle like a bird, Jeff Morgan—floated back to her loud and clear but diminishing with distance as did the other sounds of his withdrawal.

"Of all the nerve!" the girl flared out.

But there was comfort in the crackling fire to which she slowly and thoughtfully turned, and already steam was rising from her clothes. She said, "Darn it anyway," and then shrugged impatiently and said, "Well, at least he isn't going on right now to where Charlie is!" She pulled off her

102

boots and poured the water out; it glistened upon the small area of stone hearth, trickled away to make a dark pool on the dirt floor. She hesitated a moment; she could still hear the whistling: it was "Her Bright Smile Haunts Me Still." It sounded even farther away.

Hastily she slipped out of her outer garments and hung them before the fire from the stone ledge of the mantel, fixing them in their places by setting a couple of loose stones, handy by the hearth, atop of them. Then, scantily clad as she was, she began a slow turning before the blaze.

"Just like roasting a chicken on a spit!" she told herself, and smiled a little. After all, she was not afraid of Jeff Morgan now, though she had feared him for a few electric moments both before and after he had sent Cass Burdock on his way. And she needn't fear for Charlie at the moment.

Reassuringly, "Her Bright Smile Haunts Me Still" came to her from wherever Jeff Morgan had betaken himself with the two horses. She had a picture of him staking the horses out, very leisurely about it, rolling a smoke, looking up at the moon and maybe figuring what time it was, how long before he would come up with his quarry at journey's end. No, she wasn't in the least afraid of him right now—With sudden impulse she stripped to the skin, hastily wringing out her underclothes and then bending toward the fireplace, holding them to the blaze. And she kept her head tipped to one side, so as to hear better—and stiffened the instant the whistling died away, and breathed deep and went on with her task when the clear notes came back again.

She thought, "After all he is every bit as wet as I was. And if it hadn't been for him I'd have let poor Apache Kid drown! I wouldn't have thought to feel under water, and even if I had found what was the matter I couldn't have done anything about it! And he *is* being—nice."

She tiptoed back to her canvas curtain and shyly peeped forth. It was lovely out there with the moon making a glory across the narrow strip of valley, making both silver and, in the shadows, fluid ebony of the river. She listened and heard the whistling, and she smiled, and it was a queerly tender smile, as soft as the moonlight itself. He was being good to her! And then, through a screen of brush and river-side growth of willow and alder she saw sparks shooting skyward, and then the glow of his fire!

She returned to her own fire entirely without fear; she began singing softly:

"Oh, 'tis years since last we met,
    And we may not meet again,
I have struggled to forget,
    But the struggle is in vain!
Oh—La la la lala—(Darn it, how does it go?)
    And her spirit comes at will,
In the moonlight on the deep
    Her bright smile haunts me still."

and was as methodical about her drying out process as though she were in her own room at home.

So unhurrying in fact was she that when his voice shouted, still thank goodness at a safe distance, saying, "Here I come, Alice girl!" she had to scream back at him, "No! Wait a minute! Please, Jeff. Just a minute!"

And she heard him laughing, a chuckling sort of laugh like a boy's.

"Let me know when you're at home to callers, lady," he said from quite nearby.

"Just a minute!—All right. Come in, won't you? And you'll forgive us if we're a bit upset here? You see, there was a party—there must have been a party! Look how things are strewn all over—"

He came in and stood looking at her, looking at her surroundings, and he started laughing again. He surprised her by catching both her fluttering hands in his purposeful ones.

"Alice! *Alice!* You are the only girl in all the wide, wide world! Did you know it?"

Of an old mangled wreck of a bench he provided a seat for two; he propped up the broken end with a rock and a couple of bits of board on top of it to make the thing fairly level; they sat in front of the fire.

"You have been good to me tonight, Jeff Morgan," she said quite simply. "Two times.

When you took care of Cass Burdock; when just now you saved Apache Kid for me."

"Let's get acquainted, what do you say?" he returned quite as simply. "Me, I've told you my name. I've told you why I'm here. I'll tell you more things about myself in case you'd like to know. And I'd like powerful well to know a lot about you. I'd like to know all about you, Miss Alice."

They were sitting close to the fire and he had thrown on fresh dry wood; she saw little pale wisps of steam rising from his knees, as vague against the firelight as cigarette smoke in the sun.

"You didn't get yourself very dry," she said. She stood up. "I'll go outside for a while; you could get dry here before the fire the way I did. I'm as dry and warm as toast."

"You might run away," he said, smiling at her.

"No, I wouldn't." She was serious about it. "When you were dry I'd come back and we'd talk a little while. I think," she added very gravely, thinking of many things, "that it might be a good idea if we did sort of get acquainted."

Most of all she was thinking about Bud Briscoe, her big brother Charlie, and the errand which Jeff Morgan so frankly admitted had brought him this way. He read all that in her eyes.

"Yes," she said very softly. "We don't really know each other yet, even after a night like tonight, do we? Or, do we?" She laughed a little

106

nervously. "You say let's get acquainted. All right. Let's. You can call me when you are ready."

"Good girl," he said. He wanted to put his hand on her shoulder, to pat her tousled curly head, but didn't. "But you don't have to go; I'm not very wet; I'll dry out fine this way. Let's see. How'll we get started. We know each other's names, that's about all. Well—you just sit down again."

Alice sat down again. He grew silent, staring into the bed of rich red coals forming in the maw of the fireplace. Damn it, he got to thinking about rubies, and if ever before he had wanted to kill Bud Briscoe, he wanted now to do the job with his bare hands, to strangle the big blond handsome devil. That Bud Briscoe, loving this little sister of his after his own damnable fashion, should bring her jewels from Big Belle of Nevada City, newly murdered—

"You see, I'm from way down South," he began. "When the War started I loaded up my old rifle and got on a horse and said good-bye to mama and papa and brother John and sister Annie and my cousins, and I rode—and I had the luck to fall in with a party of Morgan's Men—"

Then he told her of their old southern plantation, of his folks, of their negroes, of life as it ran, large and simple and generous. And of some parts of the War that would not shock her too much. There were things he had the grace to leave out. And he had to tell of Bob Lane, his friend, and of the two

107

of them drifting West. And then, just before he got around to speaking of the late afternoon when he came back to camp with a young buck deer slung over his saddle, and found Bob dying,—just before he got to that he pulled up short and managed a grin at her and said:

"Whoa, Bill. Here I'm going hell-for-breakfast, since I crawled out of the cradle to almost until I found you—and never a word out of you telling me! Now I'm listening, Alice, for a spell while I roll a cigarette and you talk!"

You know how it is: When anyone, especially a stranger or a person you've only half way known for an hour or so says, "Now you talk," you can't for the life of you think of a single word to say.

"I feel just like I was sitting here sucking my thumb!" Alice flared out at him, and immediately set him laughing at her. She pretended to fly into a small fury. "You poke your finger at me and say, 'Talk!' That would make anybody go dumb, and you know it."

"Tell me about Bud Briscoe; you call him Charlie. He's your brother, so you think you know him pretty well! But just how much do you know about him?"

"I know that he's fine!" she cried warmly. "He's the finest man I know. Oh, I have two other brothers; they're younger; they're Hank and Robert and—Well, they're not at home most of the time. They like to go places." She laughed, but

Jeff Morgan thought that in her voice he detected a note of uneasiness which she was eager to cover up. She hurried on: "And there's my father, the silent man; George Briscoe his name is. Oh, he's fine, too, but he's older and life has been hard at times—And he never quite got over it when my mother died; that was six years ago. Then there's Uncle Dick; you'd love him. He just joined us a few days ago. So you see I've got lots of fine folks, but I guess Charlie is the finest man in the world!"

Jeff didn't look at her for a while but, with his head down, sat staring into the glowing bed of coals; and he didn't even look up when he said soberly and with marked deliberation:

"I've seen a good many girls in my time, Alice; I've even been to a few dances and picnics and things. And I've seen a few mighty pretty girls, and mighty nice, but I've never seen a girl anywhere near like you. I sort of gave you that idea, didn't I, down at your place in the valley?"

Then he did look up, and then she turned a warm rose-pink. Her eyes wanted to run away and hide from his, but there was a sort of courage within her that held them unhidden upon his.

"I guess it's love all right, Alice," said Jeff, as grave as a judge. At the moment he didn't sound or look overly happy about it; he was simply face to face with a tremendous fact. He might have been a man who had been hit with a club.

"I guess it maybe is, Jeff," said Alice, her voice not raised above a whisper, and how her rose-pink cheeks flamed red.

"And here's the hell of it—" he began.

"Please, Jeff! I wish you wouldn't use swear words. Especially—Oh," and she twisted her hands in her lap, "when we are talking like this!"

"I won't," promised Jeff. "Honest, Alice, I won't after this. But right now those are the only words I know: Here's the hell of it—I'm out to kill Bud Briscoe and it's a job I've got to do."

She didn't say a word. For a short time her agonized hands kept twisting, then they lay still. All the bright color went out of her face; her eyes were enormous as she stared at Jeff's face, hard and bleak and relentless, with his jaws bulging under the stress he set upon them; then her eyes drifted back to the fire and of a sudden closed tight and the tears squeezed through and hung on her cheeks like morning dewdrops. And still she didn't say a word. She knew these pioneer men, them and their codes; hard codes and without mercy so many a time, yet frequently just, too. Anyhow, they were men as little to be moved as a great granite cliff with a girl's soft palms against it.

"You see how it is, Alice girl?" said Jeff steadily and dispassionately. "You see how I wasn't really cussing. It's just hell on wheels and that's all there is to it. I'm going out and kill Bud Briscoe; maybe tonight. Then I'm coming back for you. You're my girl, sweetheart, no matter if the stars fall down and the whole damn world busts wide open."

"You know that couldn't be, Jeff! How could I ever be your girl, really and truly and with everything that is in me, if you killed Charlie? Oh, Jeff!" She shot out her hands to him. "Won't you, for my sake—"

"Can't," said Jeff, and wouldn't touch her hands with her thinking he might be softening, might be turning traitor to Bob Lane, the best friend any man ever had—killed by a laughing devil, Bud Briscoe, just for forty dollars and the fun of it!

So for a space neither said anything; a deep silence pervaded the old cabin set in the heart of a great sweep of wilderness country, a silence only softly set throbbing by the small sounds of the fire in the fireplace. Jeff Morgan spoke first.

"We start saying one thing," he said, "and first thing we know we have switched clean off and to something else. I asked you a while back just how much you really know about Bud Briscoe. You said he's fine. But what do you *know* about him? He goes away a lot, maybe? And stays quite a while? The way you say your brothers Robert and Hank do."

"Suppose he does?" she retorted with spirit. "He's no stick-in-the-mud, if that's what you mean."

"Those dogs, now, that are chained up and bark when anyone comes into your valley so that they send the word ahead half a dozen miles that company is coming; Bud Briscoe's dogs? Sort of a funny thing, a set-up like that, especially way out here in the woods."

"I told you already! There are men, gunmen, highwaymen, who would kill my brother—"

"Bud's dogs?"

"We-el, they were. He gave them to me though. You see—

"Yes, I saw," he said dryly. "I saw that those wolfish devils love you and are as gentle with you as a herd of kittens; I saw too how they'd like nothing better than to pile on Bud Briscoe and tear his throat out; I saw the way he grabbed at his gun—"

Her eyes flashed at him; she grew scornful or made convincing pretence of scorn.

"You mean, I suppose, that a dog can look into a man's heart and soul, can tell a good man from a bad one!"

"Well, I've heard folks say that," he said in a slow, measured voice. Again there was nothing to be added for a moment or two, then he said in the same quiet, measured voice, "Did you ever hear of a woman they called Big Belle of Nevada City?"

"I don't want even to speak of such a person!" And then, all without logic, she flung at him, with an edge to her voice, "You know her, of course!"

"I never heard about her until this evening. They

told me in town who she was. They told me she had been robbed; she screamed and fought, and so got killed. They said she wore the only real rubies in California—a couple of blood-red rings, and a necklace to match. And they said that the sheriff was looking for Bud Briscoe."

She sprang to her feet, a small fury with clenched hands and blazing eyes.

"You are trying to tell me that my brother is a murderer and a robber!"

"Yes, ma'am," said young Jeff Morgan regretfully. "That's exactly what I'm aiming to tell you, Miss Alice girl."

"You—you—you horrid beast! You liar and cheat and—You dirty coward!"

He didn't even stand up. He kicked a burning coal back into the fireplace. Then he sat still on his bench until the next words suggested themselves, and he spoke them with his characteristic unruffled mildness:

"You heard what your uncle Dick said, Alice. He told you those stones cost a whole whale of a lot of money."

"And you! A man to sneak up in the dark to another man's house, and peek and pry, and spy and listen! Do you think I'd ever believe a single word a man like that said to me? Yes, you're all the things I've called you, and a spy besides!"

He only lifted his shoulders wearily and wearily let them down.

She went to the broken door, walking swiftly, and passed outside. He did not stir to follow her; he said to himself, it's hell, that's what it is. But she won't go like this; she'll stop and think and come back. And I'd better leave her alone a minute or two anyhow.

And Alice did exactly what he somehow knew she would do. She stopped when well away from the cabin and lifted her face toward the serene sky; she saw the softly bright glory of the moon, its shed beams seeming to drip from the still leaves of the trees, and she saw the sparkle of the stream, and she listened to the vast, infinite silence and to a small voice within her breast. Slowly she turned and retraced her steps. When again she stood within the frame of the doorway he had not moved; he sat with his back to her, his shoulders hunched forward, his eyes sombre on the fire. If he heard her step he gave no sign.

"Jeff!" she called softly.

"I knew you'd come back," he said quite simply. His shoulders squared like a soldier's as he stood up and faced her. "Here we just found each other tonight, Alice, when it seems like I'd been hunting high and low and all over the world for you since I was born. So we can't just turn our backs on each other and walk away like that."

"I am glad that you knew I would come back." There was enough light for them to read what there was no attempt to conceal in both their faces; a girl as young as Alice Briscoe and a man as young as Jefferson Davis Morgan are rarely as honest with each other as were these two at that moment. "I guess," she went on in a hushed voice that with all its quietness was rich with frankness and sincerity and a deep earnestness, "that, come soon or late, most folks have their troubles. Ours has hit us like a sledge hammer, hasn't it, Jeff?"

"Yes, dear, it has," he said.

She tried to smile but he could see how her lips trembled. Yet she said with no tremor disturbing her words:

"I love your fire that you made for me, Jeff. I loved looking into it. But outside there is a great big round moon that God put up in the sky for people, for people like us, Jeff, and I love it better even than your fire. Let's go out and watch it a little while; let's listen to how quiet the world is—and how peaceful."

He stepped swiftly to her side and took her hand in his; he could have put his arms about her and kissed her again, but he didn't. Her fingers squeezed tight about his as together they walked through the old doorway out into the moonlight.

For a little while they did as she had asked, they looked at the moon, at the clear sky with its widely spaced stars, then at the black forests and the barricades of the mountains and the flash of running water, and they were silent and close together both physically and in their troubled thoughts. Then he said, after a deep breath:

"I know what you mean, Alice."

Hers was a long, quivering sigh; he could see the rise and fall of her breast; he could even see once more how there were tears on her cheeks.

"Yes, you know. I knew you would know! It's funny, isn't it?" Her sudden smile was radiant, tear-splashed as it was. "Men and girls are not the same, are they? But then the sun and the moon are different, and a pine tree is different from a flower, and dogs and cats are different, and so is a wolf different from a tree squirrel. They can't help it, can they, Jeff? And you can't blame any of them, can you?"

"I know," he muttered. "Alice girl, I'm so sorry that—"

"Shush, Jeff!" She hugged his hand with hers harder than ever; for a still instant, while she was getting a renewed grip on herself, he saw how her lip was caught between her pretty, white teeth. "Let me talk just a minute; I've got to! See how clear the moon is? And that one star 'way over yonder? Well, I see things just as clear as that shining moon and star. You mean to kill my brother. You have told me; you have been honest; you don't see any way out of it. But—do you have to hurry, Jeff? After you have your way, after you—after you kill Charlie, can I ever talk to you again? Can I ever stand like this, my hand in yours, and look at the moon with you? Can we ever again look into each other's eyes even? Or what if Charlie kills you? Can I ever see him again? Can't you see—Oh, Jefferson!"

"Alice! With all my heart—"

"I haven't quite finished. Almost, though. You see, it won't be just each other or one of you that you two are killing; it will be something in me; it will be me, Jeff! Now wait! I'm young, Jefferson Davis Morgan, and I am terribly in love. First of all I learned to love this great big mother world of ours; I've loved it until it seemed to me that my love for it was too big for any one girl's heart to hold, that my heart would have to break all to pieces because of it. And I love Charlie. And now you come, and everything has to happen all at once. And I've got to tell the truth, Jeff. I love you! And I'll tell all the truth! I don't know why and I don't understand, but I love you more than I love the great big round mother world and more than I love my brother Charlie—No, Jeff; you've got to wait a minute yet; you've got to listen to me. You see, Jeff, I'm sort of a Johnny-come-lately to this country; we've been here only a few years; it was like coming straight to heaven when I got here. The nights here, the mountains, the daybreaks and sundowns, the stars and running river with its lights and shadows and a fish breaking up through bubbles, those leaping fish and the deer standing shy in the woods, the songs of the birds in the early morning and their sleepy songs in the evenings—Oh, Jeff! *And then you came!* Don't you see, don't you feel what I am trying to say and can't say at all?—Jeff—"

"Say it, Alice dear. I think I know—"

"Give me a few days of living and loving before the darkness has to come!"

He clamped his lean jaws hard down; his whole body stiffened—and yet she saw that, cruel and hard and relentless that he was making himself, there were drops now as of dew on his high cheek bones.

"Alice!"

He opened his arms and she came into them like a bird into its nest.

And then, before their lips touched, while only their eyes met, filled with the moon glory and still another glory far greater, the night's stillness was broken by the rude clang of iron shod hoofs upon a rocky trail. A dream was torn, a celestial moment shattered; they whirled about and saw, clear in the moonlight, a mounted man coming down-valley, and could make out plainly his big dark bulk in the saddle, and even the markings of the horse he rode; for the horse was ink-black splotched with snow white—

"It is Charlie!" cried the girl. "He is coming this way, too! He has seen the sparks out of our chimney—"

Then Jeff did kiss her.

"You go back inside," he told her.

She clung to him.

"Jeff! Will you promise me—"

He didn't mean to speak sternly when he said:

"You know there are times when a man can't promise anything. We love each other; that's settled. Now we'll have to stand by and see what's in the cards, what's coming up next."

CHAPTER XI
AT THE FIRST CHANCE IN SETTLERS' GAP

NOTHING could have been more abrupt. Yet it remains that in lives there come moments that shut down as sharply, as fatefully as any guillotine, no matter whose the head under the blade.

Jeff Morgan stood out in the clear moonlight, his thumbs hooked into his belt, his old black hat jammed down so that it came down to his scowling eyebrows, his frozen attitude that of a man who simply awaits his destiny. Much hung on the next moment. Perhaps everything.

The rider upon the grotesquely marked palomino came racing headlong and, even before plucking his horse to a standstill, began roaring out incoherent curses along with the clear cut words,

"Hank, is that you? Robert? Which one of you, you damn dirty cowards? I knew you had run out this way, you dirty rats. Now, damn you, give me a hand or I'll break your damn necks for you; you left me all shot up, like the yellow dogs you are, maybe bleeding to death. Get a move on, will you, and help me down!"

"Quite a speech," muttered Jeff Morgan to himself, and then Bud Briscoe leaned out from the saddle, beginning to slump and spill earthward, and automatically Jeff Morgan caught the great bulky body in his arms and eased it to the ground.

Bud Briscoe was wearing his right arm in a hammocky sling made of a couple of big bandana handkerchiefs knotted together; whether his wound was in arm or shoulder Jeff Morgan had no way of telling. He only knew that here, for the third time within only a few hours, he and Bud Briscoe were close together—and that this time he had Briscoe in his arms, and that Alice, Bud Briscoe's sister, was only a few yards away, watching, listening—

Bud Briscoe was briefly unsteady on his legs, then braced himself to stand squarely and unswayingly planted, and muttered growlingly,

"I tell you, Hank—Hell, you're not Hank! Robert, you—" He took a backward step and steadied himself again. "Not Robert either, by God! Who the hell are you anyhow, stranger?"

Jeff Morgan was in no haste answering. He had to think of two things: Here, at his mercy, was the man he had traveled so far, so long a time, to find and kill; it was a very simple matter, look at it one way, to slide a six-gun up out of its leather, set the blunt barrel to a man's temple, blow his brains out and so end it. The other thing was that Bud Briscoe was again weaving uncertainly on his feet; he was hurt; no matter who a man was you couldn't shoot him like a dog. Not though he deserved to be shot like the dog that he was. You couldn't quite do it.

"Me," said Jefferson Davis Morgan, "I'm no friend of yours, Bud Briscoe. We don't even know each other. But I've been looking for you for a long time. There's nothing on earth I'd like better than to fill you so full of lead that you'd sink through your boots—plumb to hell where you belong. But it's kind of hard work shooting a sick dog—even a sick yellow dog."

"Why, I know you!" cried Bud Briscoe. "I remember your face! You're the crazy kid that kicked in on our fight tonight in the alley in Black Gulch!" He shoved out his hand. "Put her here, pardner!"

"And I made a mistake," said Morgan sourly. "I wanted to be in on the other side of that fight. No, we don't shake hands. Maybe you didn't get what I just said to you, that I've been a long while looking for you and I'd rather shoot you than find a million dollars."

"Yes, you did say something like that." Bud Briscoe pushed back his hat with his available hand, the left, and mopped and scrubbed at his forehead, and while so doing regarded young Morgan with slitted eyes. He affected to laugh, though his laughter did not ring true. "Here I've already been shot up once tonight, and I'm not hog enough to ask for any more. Besides, there's no quarrel that I know of between you and me. If I ever even saw you before tonight or heard of you, I'm double damned if I know where or when. Not drunk, are you?"

"Listen to me, Briscoe," said Jeff Morgan, his voice flat and deadly. "I was on my way just now to Settlers' Gap to overtake you and to burn you down. Get this straight: The way I said, I can't bring myself to shooting a sick dog, not even when it's you. But I'll tell you this: I'm still looking for you, and there's a reason. Maybe you'll remember being in Tres Robles about five months ago, and maybe you'll remember murdering Bob Lane. He was my pardner. I've been on your trail ever since. I reckon you'll know me when we meet up again, won't you? Well, then, go for your gun."

Bud Briscoe was briefly silent. Then:

"You're crazy!" he snapped. "Tres Robles? I've never been in Tres Robles in my life. And I never heard of your pardner, of any Bob Lane. You've got my word for that. Want to call me a liar?"

"Yes," said Jeff Morgan in his still way. "A liar and low-life and a sneaking killer that will even

122

shoot a woman down—a woman like Big Belle of Nevada City—if she screams and makes trouble when you try to rob her of her ruby rings and bracelet."

Briscoe jeered at him.

"You jump me when you make sure my gun arm is all shot up, and then you start in working on me! Why, you son of a—"

Very neatly, almost dispassionately, Jeff Morgan slapped him across his full-lipped, sneering mouth.

"Keep your words in your face," he said quietly. "I'll jump you again when your gun arm is well, and I'll kill you as sure as taxes, unless you kill me first, which I doubt. And I can tell you're not hurt bad; so I won't have to wait long to get you. Now you stay right here where you are for a minute; I'm going into the shack and out, and then you can—"

But Alice Briscoe, who had missed never a word, came running and she and Jeff Morgan met after the effect of running into each other's arms.

"Charlie is hurt—"

"Don't worry, Alice girl," he said, and took her by both elbows. "I'm running out on you now, leaving you with your brother. But I'll be back as sure as God lets me live. I'm going to see you, and it will be soon. And I've got to see him, as both Bud Briscoe and I know. Good night—" He stooped close to her hair, tumbled over her ear, and said softly: "I love you so much that it hurts, girl. And you're going to love me the same way."

She let him hold her a second, and she held him. They drew apart then, with one mind. She said, in a queer, hushed voice,

"I heard everything! Jeff, I am afraid!"

Bud Briscoe called out sharply,

"Hey, what the hell? That you, Alice? Way out here? With this man?"

Before answering Charlie "Bud" Briscoe, she said, and her voice was tremulous, uncertain, frightened,

"Jeff, I feel as though the whole world had just started rocking and swinging and dropping away under my feet! Yes, see me soon. Yes, go now. Is Charlie terribly hurt?"

"You talk with him," said Jeff, and released her. "He'll take a lot of killing, will your Charlie."

And then he left her and went, straight as any string, back to his horse.

And she, for a moment, watched him going his purposeful way, then ran on the few steps to Bud Briscoe.

"Charlie!" she gasped. "What is the matter? What has happened?"

He was always gentle with her, one thing to be said for Bud Briscoe. But tonight, for the one and only time in his life, he was as rough as sand paper.

"What the hell are you doing up here with this

man?" he demanded, forgetting his own problems. "Who is he and where did he come from and where did you get to know him? And how does it happen that you and him, this time of night, are way up here all alone, just the two of you?"

"I'll tell you," she said. "But I asked you first: what is the matter, Charlie?"

For a little while he was as awkward, as lost for words, as any small school child before an austere teacher. He shifted and cleared his throat, and was all at sea. It was crystal clear to her, as it could not help being, that he was asking himself just how much she had overheard, how much she had taken in. He had called for Hank, for Robert, and he had damned them up hill and down dale—and he had—or hadn't he?—admitted to being shot up?

He said at last, "I was going to meet Hank and Robert down here. I saw the light of a fire so I guessed they were here ahead of me. Have you seen them?"

"Charlie," said Alice, and put a hand as gentle as a rose petal upon his shoulder, "you are hurt. Someone shot you. Is it very bad, Charlie?"

"Your voice sounds sort of funny, Allie," he said. "What's happened to you?"

"We are going to have a good talk, the two of us, Charlie," she said, and tried to sound light-hearted. "We are both asking questions! I'll tell you anything you want to know. Are we going to be honest with each other tonight, Charlie? Come

125

on inside; there's a fire; let me see your hurt."

He went with her, though reluctantly. She saw something of his troubled face in the moonlight; in the brighter light in the cabin, what with the moon filtering in and the blaze in the fireplace, she saw his tell-tale biting of his heavy lips, his obvious endeavor to get himself in hand. Her presence here had taken him by surprise and utterly off guard; on top of that his wound was irking him; for the first time he found it hard to make his eyes lift to her enquiring ones. But he did manage a sort of grin.

"Tell me, Charlie!" She began untying his sling for his arm, rolling up his sleeve, terribly anxious for him. But she did want to know.

For another moment or two he was at a loss for words, what to say, what he could tell her that would fit into the pattern of himself as she knew him; what would not contradict whatever he had said just now to the stranger and that she might have overheard. He said,

"Shucks, Allie, it's nothing to worry about. You see, like I told you when I headed for Settlers' Gap, I had promised to be up there tonight. Well, you see, it's like this—"

Still he couldn't think of just exactly what to say, not being a brilliant liar though a thoroughgoing one, and knowing that his sister's wits, when sharpened by as keen an interest as now, were far shrewder than his. So he broke off with a

126

convincing "Ouch!" as she uncovered the wound half way between his elbow and shoulder.

"Oh, I'm sorry! Oh, Charlie!" She had seen the raw, ugly gash that a bullet had made, tearing through the flesh of his outer arm.

He was as tough as a saddle leather, was Bud Briscoe, and now his short laugh was convincing. And he began to get ideas. She had heard everything he had said to the stranger, he would bet on that. Well then,

"You see, Allie," and now he had the sights of his imagination lined up on his objective, and so began to feel sure of himself, "Robert and Hank, they met me up there. There's a big cattle spread, a ranch up in the hills about sixty miles from here, that I've had my eye on for quite a spell. Well, I was letting Hank and Robert in on the deal; and I was letting a few other boys in on it, too, it being too big for me to handle all by myself. Then there's that other crowd, those jaspers I told you about, that I had a hunch was following me into our valley tonight. Well, they are out to get the same ranch. And we had a—Aw, Allie, you know, or maybe you don't know how it goes? Nate spoke up pretty sharp, and I stuck with Nate, and pretty soon we got into a sort of fight. That's all it is. And, like you see, Allie, all I got was just a scratch in the arm."

"Yes, I see," said Alice, but her lips tightened.

She saw that he really wasn't badly hurt. Then

127

there was something else: she had heard him say to Jeff Morgan that he was shot in his gun arm. Well, Alice knew that Bud Briscoe was left handed. And it was his right arm that was wounded. And, too, she had seen Jeff Morgan slap Bud's mouth to stop its spilling curses. And then there was that terrible woman, Big Belle of Nevada City—

"You just wait a minute, Charlie," she said, and ran outside. Almost immediately she was back with a strip of clean cloth; she had torn it from her underskirt. She did as well as she could, binding up his arm.

"You're coming straight on home with me now, Charlie?" she asked.

He shuffled and hesitated and scratched the back of his head.

"You go along," he said. "Likely I'll show up real soon. If I don't—"

"Why didn't you tell me Robert and Hank were up here?" she asked. "I didn't know they had got back from Yellow Jacket or wherever it was they went this last time."

Again, though for but a second, he checked back his words.

"I didn't know either," he said. "I ran into them up at the Gap."

She knew that he was lying to her tonight, perhaps, lying in everything he had said. She asked, quiet but insistent,

"Tell me about Big Belle, Charlie. I heard Jeff say something to you about her. Did you know her? Is she dead now? Did somebody rob her?"

To gain time he hid behind a name and a counter question.

"Jeff?" he demanded, though he must have known. "Who is he?"

"The man that just left us. Jefferson Davis Morgan. He—"

"Where did you get to know him, Allie?" he cut in sharply.

"Tonight. In our valley. He was looking for you. And you know what he wanted. He wants to kill you because of something that happened months ago in Tres Robles, wherever that is."

He chuckled. "Kill me? That tramp? I'd slap him down like a mosquito!"

He shouldn't have used the word "slap." She remembered what she had just seen—and heard. The sound of Jeff's flat hand on Bud Briscoe's face had been like a pistol shot. And he hadn't answered her question about Big Belle of Nevada City.

"Charlie, I'm going now. I'm sorry you won't come home with me—"

"Wait a shake! You haven't told me how you happened to be way up here with that man Morgan!"

"No, I guess I haven't. And there are things you haven't told me. Well, he told me, back at our place that he was riding to the Gap to kill you. And

I rode ahead to get to you first. And Apache Kid slipped in the river, with his leg caught under a log that I didn't know was there, and I saw Jeff coming and called to him to help. And—" She lifted her chin; her eyes darkened and were inscrutable. "And he helped, and he was fine to me, Charlie."

"Huh!" Something within him, a native jealousy or perhaps just a sense of craft, made him exclaim, "And he didn't grab you? Didn't make love to you, didn't try to make you pay—"

Somehow, right then and for the first time in all her life, Alice could have slapped him just as she had seen Jeff Morgan slap him.

She said steadily,

"I told you that he was fine to me. I am going now, Charlie. Won't you come?"

"You go ahead, Allie," he said, "I'll wait here a spell. I'll try to look up Robert and Hank; they will most likely show up pretty soon. If they don't, I'll know where to find them. You go ahead; me, I'm all right."

"Yes.—Yes, I'll go, Charlie. Good night."

She whirled and hurried out; she ran to her horse where Jefferson Davis Morgan had tethered it beyond a screen of willows. She stood a moment, first looking down at the black charred sticks where he had made his little fire, to semi-dry his outer clothing; to think of how he had given her her own fire, her privacy. Then she looked up at the sky with its full moon, with the big bright star, so many and many millions of miles away, and thought in a spirit of awe how her eyes and his eyes had run out across those vast distances to see together the same bright spot in infinity. She patted Apache Kid's satiny shoulder.

"You are alive, old boy," she said. "That's because Mr. Jefferson Davis Morgan came our way at the right time."

She tried not to think too much, not too deeply. She went swiftly up into the saddle and with never a backward look struck across the little river again, heading back into the trail which would lead her southward and so home. But, when Apache Kid, as tense as violin strings, as nervous as a cat, had crossed the stream which had come so close to being his undoing, she let her eyes rove as they would—and they turned across the narrow slit of a valley, and northward. And so she saw, silhouetted on a high ridge against the sky, a horseman pressing steadily on in the general direction of Settlers' Gap. She remembered an old song, and began humming it softly as she turned south:

"Oh, you'll take the high road,
And I'll take the low road—"

And so she took the low road, back to Green Water Valley, and as she rode she kept wondering and wondering why Jeff Morgan should go on to

Settlers' Gap, knowing that Bud Briscoe was not there. The moon looked down on her, very bright and gay, very impersonal, and had no message for her. That bright star gleamed beautifully and triumphantly, somehow like an ancient knight in glittering armor, she thought, and yet had no word for her. And when she looked again northward, over her shoulder, she had the last glimpse of a man on horseback forging on toward the Gap.

And as for Jefferson Davis Morgan, northward he had started and northward he decided to keep on going. For one thing, it was a good long ride back to Black Gulch, and when he got there what did he have? Just an extra horse in the stable that he did not right now require, that could stay there until Kingdom Come or until Morgan wanted the animal; for another thing, Settlers' Gap was not only nearer but newer, newer at any rate to him. He would see what it was like, having once or twice heard of the place. And it looked to him as though perhaps Bud Briscoe might have a bit of unfinished business there.

So he shook out his reins and headed on toward Settlers' Gap—and did most of his thinking about Alice Briscoe.

Settlers' Gap! He had wondered what sort of place and now he knew. There were those who called it Three Fools' City—which the greater fools, they who had been tricked by fools' gold, or those who, jeering at them, called it a city? It was hardly more than a crossroads. Down out of a snaky, black ravine came turbulent Settlers' Creek. There was a bridge across it, one of those old roofed-over bridges; Jeff Morgan's horse's hoofs made a light little staccato song upon the loose planks.

It was late at night; for a time, even when right on top of it, he couldn't see the "City." Under the high, sharp cliffs squatted a half dozen unlovely buildings; there was, he came to see presently, the customary General Mercantile Store; in its windows, which would have been dark but for the moon's kindly light, were, it would seem, all of the necessities of a well ordered life together with most of the luxuries; saddles and thick slabs of bacon, coffee and sugar and flour, miners' picks and shovels, beans in bulging bags, rifles and shot guns and revolvers, scales to weigh your gold in if you had any gold to weigh, bolts of calico, coiled ropes and boots and bottles of hair tonic. Then he saw, too, other places which asked no help from the moon; the saloons of Settlers' Gap, still wide open though pretty quiet tonight. They would have been noisier, busier, had Bud Briscoe and his merry men tarried a while.

Jeff Morgan figured it was growing pretty late, that he might as well bed down here as anywhere. Still, first, it might pay to look around. He swung down from the saddle in front of the First Chance saloon, threw Dandy's reins over the hitching pole, slapped his horse friendliwise upon the shoulder, and stepped across the plank sidewalk and into the long, lamplighted room.

The place was attended by but few patrons, not more than a dozen in all. The first one of them that Jeff Morgan noted as set apart from the rest was a girl. She was young, she was a dusky brunette beauty, she was dressed flamboyantly. Her dress was a flaming scarlet, cut very low over a full white bosom, her sleeves were short and she wore long black kid gloves and an enormously wide brimmed hat with a scarlet ostrich plume, and fine black stockings and tiny high-heeled shoes. And she was very pretty in a daringly provocative sort of way, what with her big eyes and long shadowy lashes and small, smiling, full, red-lipped mouth. There were two or three other young ladies; this one alone caught his eye, he did not know why at first—and then he did know why! The girl was pulling off one of her long black gloves as he came in; on her milk-white finger he saw a blazing, blood-red ring, a ring that was a dead ringer to the one he had commanded Alice Briscoe never to wear again. And he remembered that Alice, with her necklace, had had but the one ring—and Long Jim Jameson, sheriff over at Black Gulch, had spoken of Big Belle's "rings." Was this the other one? Was this ripe beauty a friend of Bud Briscoe's? Not that he cared; only that in this consideration no doubt lay the explanation of the girl having arrested his roving glance. With Alice Briscoe in his heart tonight, in his blood, no other girl counted for so much as the snap of finger and thumb.

The girl looked tempestuous, like a small gathering tornado, a young volcano masking itself under curving hills, a sultry, passionate, reckless and perhaps desperate creature. At any rate as she stripped off a glove, her high-heeled slipper was tapping impatiently; her eyes flashed to the newcomer, she took him in from bootheel to the high crown of his hat, and she molded her pretty face into a welcoming smile.

"Hello, Big Boy," she said in a softly pleasant, deep throated voice.

He lifted his hat gallantly and kept on toward the bar. But, half way across the floor, he changed his mind. He came back to her corner table.

"I'm a stranger here, Miss," he said, and sounded apologetic. "But as long as you've said howdy, maybe you'll let me fetch over a bottle?"

She let her smile drift away. She looked tired, he thought. She said listlessly,

"Sure. Come ahead. Let's drink to better days."

"Thank you, ma'am," said Jeff at his politest, and went to the bar for bottle and glasses and promptly returned to her. His spurs which he hadn't troubled to remove jingled musically as he came tiptoeing so as not to drag the rowels.

"Don't you ever take your spurs off, even to have a drink or something?" she said.

He sat down, put his hat on a vacant chair, ran his fingers through his hair and grinned at her.

"No ma'am, not as a usual thing," he said. "When I go to bed some nights I have nightmares. I can ride 'em out better with spurs on." He poured the two glasses. "Here's hoping you always keep right along riding pretty, Miss."

They clinked glasses. Jeff, tasting each drop because he was tired and thirsty, disposed of his liquor; the girl gulped hers, then set her glass down sharply.

"I don't know why I gave you any high-sign to come over and sit with me," she said petulantly. "Thanks for the drink, Big Boy." She began drawing on her glove. "And good night."

Yes, the ring, covered now, was a dead ringer to that Alice had worn.

Jeff eased back in his chair.

"I know," he said. "Tonight you saw a friend of yours—he got into a little trouble, maybe? And went hightailing out? And you've been won-dering—and you have sort of been waiting while you did your wondering—"

"You've seen Bud?" she said eagerly. "You know where he is and—Oh, tell me, won't you?"

"Mind if I roll a smoke, Miss?" asked Jeff Morgan, very polite.

CHAPTER XII
IN THE BARROOM MIRROR

JEFFERSON DAVIS MORGAN had a smile which was warmly pleasant and friendly without being obtrusive. He lighted his cigarette and remarked in his best society manner,

"It's real nice to have met up with you, Miss. Being a stranger here I'll make bold to make myself known, shall I? Me, I'm Jefferson Davis Morgan, late of the South, now meaning to abide out here in California." He finished with a nod over his lifted glass.

The girl had really lovely eyes; they were big and alight with spirit and expression; her features were almost flower-like, retaining an intriguing sort of youthful innocence; she tended toward voluptuousness sheathed in her flaming gown and great plumed hat and costly stockings and French shoes, but it remained that she was very young.

She regarded him curiously; he saw a flicker of shadows across her face; her eyes closed and opened again, wider than ever, and he was sure that her mouth had trembled.

She shrugged elaborately.

"You're a gentleman, Mr. Morgan. Anybody can see that much. From the South? A rebel soldier? Uhuh," she went on when he nodded. "Well, the War's over; let's forget it. Me, I'm from right here; but I was born in Georgia, raised in California not far from where we are tonight, not far from Dry Town. My name is Georgia Hill. If you'll pour me another drink I'll drink it to knowing you better."

He obliged and she took her glass between restless fingers, twirling it on the table, spilling a few drops. She watched the liquor spill over and again shrugged her graceful shoulders. Then she lifted her eyes to his; there was something very appealing in her look.

"Tell me about Bud," she said.

He twirled his own glass but spilled never a drop; he didn't drink much, but he did hate to see good liquor squandered.

"Where are Hank and Robert?" he countered. "Where did Nate Briscoe go?"

"It seems to me, Mr. Morgan," she retorted rather sharply, "that for a stranger you know a good many folks up here!"

"I know precious few, Miss Georgia Hill," he told her. "These three men I've just asked about, I don't know a man of them; not one of them ever heard my name even. But I have heard about them, and I know there was some sort of a mix-up up this way tonight, and that Bud Briscoe got hurt, and they all scattered. That's all I know."

"Then, if you don't know the boys, why are you asking about them?" she asked suspiciously.

"A man can have his reasons, you know," he

reminded her, his smile replaced by a noncommittal gravity.

"Yes, that's right." She lifted her glass as though to down it like the first, but changed her mind before it touched her lips and sat twisting it again. "Well, maybe we can swap news; I don't know much about anything, though. Sure, there was some sort of trouble; there always is with those boys. But I don't know much about it; over at the old shack in Long Ravine, by the bridge. There were the boys you mentioned, Bud Briscoe of course, and Nate, and Hank and Robert—and some others. They seem to have gone out of town in a cloud of dust." She shoved her glass aside. "You might tell me what you know about Bud; I was sort of thinking he might come back."

"I met up with him heading south, between here and Green Water Valley. I had a word or two with him. You could tell he had been in a fight; looked like a bullet in his right arm, shoulder maybe. But I'd say it's nothing to keep him in bed. Where he's going, I don't know."

She listened avidly, then leaned back in her chair and he saw her go limp; it was as though she had been taut for hours and only now relaxed. He judged her age at something less than twenty years. Eighteen or nineteen maybe, hardly more. And Bud Briscoe's girl? There was that ring on her finger; she couldn't get the glove all the way on over it.

"I am glad you told me," she said. "Thanks. And

I'd answer your question if I knew how. I saw Hank Briscoe and his young brother Robert in here early tonight; they both were drinking more than they ought to, seeing they can't drink much and walk straight. I saw Bud a minute; Nate Briscoe was with him. Where they all went—"

She broke off; her eyes roved beyond him to the door. She said,

"You asked about Nate Briscoe, didn't you? Well, here he comes now and, if you ask me, he looks like a man that had been eating something that didn't taste right. I hope he chokes; I hate the rat anyhow."

Jeff Morgan did not turn, but out of the corners of his eyes he could see Nate Briscoe crossing the room toward the bar, brushing up the ends of his small neat blond mustache, his speculative eyes taking in everything, quite as though he had never been in this place before, as though he were interested in it though and meant to ferret out every shadow in every corner. For a second longer than elsewhere those crafty eyes of his lingered with Georgia Hill, with the stranger sitting at her table. And suddenly Jeff remembered how in the cabin down in Green Water Valley he had seen Nate's eyes turned covetously upon Alice—or had it been upon Alice's new finery? Certainly now the same look stamped itself upon his face—directed at Georgia Hill, or at the ring which even yet her glove did not hide.

"He's looking at you," said Jeff. "Or he's looking at your ring. By the way, did you ever hear of a woman they call Big Belle of Nevada City?"

"Belle? Why, of course! She runs a boarding house, or anyhow she did. I stayed with her a while, and I love her. Everybody does. And— *What do you mean?*" she hardly more than gasped. "Nate looking at my ring—Big Belle—"

"Did you ever know her to wear a ring like yours? A necklace to match?"

"Tell me," the girl demanded feverishly. "What are you driving at?"

"You know that she is dead now? Killed yesterday, or maybe it was the day before. Robbed of her jewels, and—"

"Oh, my God!" whispered the girl, and her face went white. She stared at him, she sat staring at the blood-red stone on her finger. Suddenly she pulled off the ring and let it tinkle against the glass on the table. And her eyes, wide with a sort of horror, still clung to the bright blood-red stone.

Nate Briscoe, long-legged and loose-jointed, came swinging over to their table. He had stopped midway to the bar, then turned and made a bee line to their corner.

"Hello, Georgia," he said.

The ring lay gleaming like a burning coal on the table; steadfastly Nate Briscoe kept his eyes away from it and upon the girl's.

141

She looked at him but didn't say a word of greeting. His eyes crept from hers to Jefferson Davis Morgan, a man so far as he knew whom he had never seen. Jeff Morgan paid him not the least attention. Nate Briscoe looked again at the girl's unsmiling face, appeared for a moment to be weighing balancing considerations in the scales, then jerked out a chair and sat down.

"Mind if I have a drink with you?" he said coolly.

This time Georgia did answer. But that was only after a level look into Jeff Morgan's inscrutable face, only after her subsequent white-shouldered shrug.

"I'm with Mr. Morgan," she said. And to Jeff, "Mr. Morgan, this is Nate Briscoe. If you want him to visit with us, he's ready. If you don't want him I guess he'll get up and go 'way."

Nate Briscoe laughed at that, and a peculiarly nasty sort of laughter was his. He made as though the girl were merely being facetious, teasing as girls liked to be. He lifted his brows, keeping his mouth still humorously smiling, as he asked as though sure of himself and his reception, being slightly sarcastic at the same time,

"How about it, Mr. Morgan?" He stressed the "Mr." He was already reaching for the makings of a smoke as he added, "Glad to know you and hope you don't mind."

Jeff Morgan did not trouble to look at him. To the girl he said indifferently,

"It's for you to say, Miss Georgia. If you'd rather talk with this gentleman, I will step along to the bar."

"Oh no!" said Georgia. "Don't go so soon. I wanted—"

Then Jeff Morgan turned in his leisurely style to their uninvited table companion. He said in his politest vein,

"You heard what the lady said? Let's leave it this way, shall we: If we want you we'll know where to send word for you to drop over and see us."

Nate Briscoe's fingers froze upon his unfinished and now forgotten cigarette.

"Say it again, stranger," he said. "Maybe I didn't get you right."

"You got me," said Jeff, and moved only very slightly, merely shoving his chair back a few inches.

Nate Briscoe had horned in with a purpose. His low-lidded eyes were still hard with his purpose, the covetous look was still aprowl within them: Either he wanted Georgia Hill, just a girl, or he wanted the thing on the table, just a red ring. He slashed his eyes across to a meeting with Jefferson Davis Morgan's.

"New in this country, ain't you?" he said evenly.

Jeff regarded him as from a far distance, and didn't say a word.

Nate Briscoe, unable to stare him down, transferred his look, piercing and cold and angry now, and perhaps even threatening, to the girl.

"I wanted to talk to you, Georgia," he said. "I had word for you from Bud."

A bright eagerness sprang up in her eyes; then of a sudden it died away. She knew Nate, she knew that he was just building up for something, that he lied. She said listlessly,

"All right, Nate. Spill it. What about Bud? Maybe you know what happened to him and where he is right now and where he's headed, and why? I'm listening fine!"

Nate bridled. Obviously he was in no pleasant mood on coming into the place and had grown no more lighthearted on arrival. He spat out his words, saying,

"You're getting over your shoe tops, Georgia Hill; take it from me and watch your step. Bud sent you a message; if you want it I'll give it to you when we're alone together. It ain't for publication from hell to breakfast, not amongst strangers."

Jeff Morgan thought, He's lying. He's got no message. He just wants to get this kid off all alone. Or just her and her ring.

He did his thinking for his own benefit and kept his mouth shut. Georgia Hill moved restlessly on her chair; she didn't know what to do or say. It might be true that Bud's cousin had some word from him; somehow she didn't believe it. And, as she had already told her new acquaintance, one Jefferson Davis Morgan from the South, she had no particularly great liking for a certain Nate Briscoe.

She looked at Jeff. He looked at his whisky glass. Nate Briscoe looked at them both. Georgia Hill, having sent her eyes traveling across the faces of the two men, dropped them to her glass and said at last,

"No, Nate. Not tonight. I'm with Mr. Morgan. Bud will bring me his own messages when he gets ready. See you some other time, Nate."

Nate Briscoe was a hard man to put down. He seemed pretty sure of himself. He grinned at her and said,

"Aw, quit the queen stuff, Georgia. I'm telling you—"

Jeff Morgan cleared his throat. He managed to make the sound as that of sand paper on old iron.

"You heard what Miss Hill said, Briscoe? All right; good night then."

He seemed very inoffensive, very gentle, very mild. Nate Briscoe looked him up and down. Slim, young Jeff Morgan, seated and slouching as he was now, loose in his chair, gave the altogether fictitious impression of a callow and inadequate youth. There were times when he liked to give such an impression. So there are times when a man likes to put an angleworm on his hook.

Nate Briscoe, fashioned largely in the form of

Bud Briscoe, but never so effectual, never so strong of muscle and will, was of the order of the old fashioned bully who won most of his battles before going into them. He had a way of lifting the corners of his mouth under his small mustache which resulted in showing his small white teeth and gave the effect of a wolfish snarl. He had allowed himself to be tricked by this stranger's look: at the moment Jefferson Davis Morgan would have given any stranger the impression of being a very futile boy still fumbling along in his 'teens. Maybe seventeen, maybe nineteen at most. Surely not grown to man's estate. Perhaps only about sixteen! So mild and innocent did he look!

But it remains that one couldn't have been one of Morgan's Men during the War without having been toughened. You rode and you raided, you killed or were killed, and if you went in as a boy of fifteen you were a seasoned man within one or two years. And you could ride pretty nearly any horse that had four legs, and you could shoot the eye out of a coon in the dark in a tall tree. But these were facts which Nate Briscoe, regarding the young man across the table contemptuously, was in no position to take into consideration.

Nate Briscoe, speaking from the depths of that mistaken contempt of his, said out of the corner of his mouth, held loose and crooked,

"Good night? That means you're on your way. Make it lively, you young billy goat or—"

Already Jeff Morgan had shoved his chair back; he had one thumb hooked into his belt. There was a trick he knew; he hadn't tried it for a long time; no better time than now, he thought. He said mildly,

"I don't like your heels, Mr. Nate Briscoe. They're too high. Mind if I trim 'em down?"

He didn't seem to move a muscle; he didn't seem even to have glanced down, and certainly neither Nate Briscoe nor Georgia Hill saw his trigger finger move. Yet there was of a sudden a double blast of sound; he hadn't drawn his gun out of its loose-fitting holster, yet Nate Briscoe leaped to his feet as though bee-stung, and looked down wonderingly and saw that one of his high cowboy heels had been shot off, the other scarred.

The bartender ducked down behind his bar and when he peeped over its top again he had his own gun in his hand; the several men in the room whirled and made themselves small while figuring out what it was all about.

Jeff Morgan did his level best to grin sheepishly.

"My gun went off," he apologized. "It does that sometimes. I didn't happen to burn you, did I, Mr. Briscoe? The way you got up—"

Georgia Hill, as nervous as a cat tonight, began to giggle. Nate Briscoe's face went flaming red. The bartender and the others caught on; they saw what it was all about. A man laughed; they all laughed. And the girl in a paroxysm that was near hysteria clapped both hands over her mouth.

"Morgan—" began Nate Briscoe, furious.

"*Mr.* Morgan to you, Briscoe," said Jeff, and seemed to mean it. "Now move along and give us more room. Know what I mean?"

He was still in his chair; the chair was tilted back, balanced on its hind legs. His thumb was still in his belt. His eyes were not quite so young now.

This was the first time Nate Briscoe had ever been publicly laughed at. The new experience rankled. It was easy to mark in his eyes how his decision was being balanced. With all the joy in life he would have killed this quiet Jefferson Davis Morgan, and the onlookers would have said that he acted within his rights, with due provocation. Yet, when it came to killing, it was always well to remember that any man may get in the way of a wild bullet—and the soles of his feet still tingled.

"Morgan—" he said.

"I told you to say Mr. Morgan. You do it," said Jeff quietly, "or so help me God I'll shoot you dead."

All could see how Nate Briscoe's fingers itched for his gun. Likewise it could be seen that he was still using his head; if he moved a muscle he was as good as dead.

He twisted his face into what went for a smile, a

148

grin like a man's with a stake driven through him. He said, with all the sarcasm he could muster,

"*Mr.* Morgan! Now if you'll—"

"Bully!" cried Jeff. He swung up easily to his feet. "Now I'll step over to the bar for a minute, and you and Miss Hill can have your little talk." He smiled at the girl; his eyes drifted to the ring on the table. He said, "If I happened to be in your pretty little shoes, Miss Georgia, I'd keep my eyes on that ring of Big Belle's."

He went tiptoeing, like a cat in wet grass, to keep his spurs from jangling as he stepped along to the bar. He bethought him to say over his shoulder, "There's a bottle on the table; have a drink, Briscoe. Later I'll ask you a question or two: what happened to Hank and Robert, and why Bud went running. Squat and be happy."

Barrooms have always had their mirrors. Barroom patrons like to pull their mustaches or pick their teeth while admiring their battered or bloated visages in a long glass which shows them theirselves from hat crown to bootheels. There was a mirror here behind the bar which had cost the proprietor many a golden dollar to freight up from San Francisco. Jeff, with his back turned to Nate Briscoe, had already located Briscoe in the mirror.

And when Nate Briscoe, infuriated beyond any controlling, went for his gun, Jeff Morgan saw his hand run down to his hip. If any faster man than young Jefferson Davis Morgan ever came into

Settlers' Gap, there is no record of the happening. He spun on his heel and as Nate Briscoe clawed his gun up out of its leather, Jeff Morgan fired from the hip. He didn't want particularly to kill Nate Briscoe, for young Morgan, with all he had gone through was not a killer at heart; he did want to save his own hide and he did want to put Briscoe in his place. So he sent three shots, the three linked together so that they were like chain lightning, and very neatly broke Nate Briscoe's right arm, and spilled Nate's gun to the floor before it had sped a single shot. And, then again tiptoeing like a cat in the grass, muffling his spur jingles, Jeff stepped along to the bar.

"A cigar, pardner," he said to the bartender.

He got his cigar and paid for it and lighted it. Nobody laughed this time. He could see in the mirror how Nate Briscoe stood, rocking on his heels, his face a dead, pasty white, his left hand clutching his right elbow; he could see Georgia Hill staring at him wild eyed. He pretended to see nothing.

He set his elbows on the bar and asked quietly of the man behind the bar,

"Being as I'm a stranger here, maybe you can tell me: Where can I get a room over night, and where can I bed my horse down, and is it so that somebody killed Big Belle of Nevada City?"

CHAPTER XIII
VICTIMS OF A BRISCOE FEUD

ALERT as Jeff Morgan was, he couldn't in the nature of things have his eyes everywhere at one and the same time, and thus he did not see the man just entering through the swing doors from the street, but he recognized a familiar voice as the sheriff from Black Gulch remarked tartly:

"You and your gun seem to be making a lot of noise, Mr. Morgan. What right have you got to be shooting up innocent bystanders?"

Jeff turned and looked Long Jim Jameson up and down; he thought, "The old fox must have hung back, watching from outside. And from the slant of his eye he has got something up his sleeve." He said coolly:

"Howdy, Sheriff. I'd be proud to buy you a drink."

"Sounds reasonable," said the sheriff. He advanced, stepping close to the wall, skirting the wall all the way until he arrived at the near end of the bar where he stopped several feet from where Jeff stood. Jeff saw that the man's swift eyes were taking stock of every corner of the big room, of every individual in it, and readily understood why Sheriff Jameson elected to have a wall conveniently at his side or back. "What's the occasion of all the shooting?" he asked mildly when Jeff had moved over to join him at his strategic place at the bar's end.

Jeff shook his head and lifted his shoulders apologetically.

"It was just one of those things, Sheriff," he said. "I'm powerful sorry. You see I am just getting used to carrying a gun, and the darn thing went off sort of accidental like. I guess it didn't do any real damage though."

The bartender, his face an absolute blank, set forward the sheriff's bottle. Long Jim Jameson poured his liquor, snapped his head back and shot the draught home, snorted and reached for a cigarette. He said tonelessly:

"Well, be careful after this, young feller. A kid like you oughtn't to tote a gun until he gets the hang of the thing." Then, without turning, he called, "You Nate Briscoe, step up and have a drink. It might do you good."

"Thanks," growled Nate, nursing a wounded arm, looking sick and bewildered. "I guess I don't want anything, Jameson. I'll be moving along."

"Like hell you will! I said come have a drink. First, you sure need it; second, I dropped in for a chat with you—with you and Bud. Step up, Nate."

Nate Briscoe stepped along, having no choice, since the sheriff's voice had sharpened and rang with authority. Jameson poured a full whisky glass for him, a thing that one man didn't ordinarily do for another, but no one could resent the act which was so obviously a kindness to one newly crippled. Nate gulped his drink; he swallowed the second which Jameson obligingly poured.

"Where's Bud?" the sheriff demanded.

"I don't know," said Nate. "Haven't seen him for a long time. Now I've got to go.—Damn it, man," he flared out, bucked up by his double shot of forty rod liquor, "can't you see I'm bleeding like a stuck hawg? Let me out of this."

"Speaking about Bud Briscoe," said Jeff Morgan, "it's a funny thing: I saw him an hour or so ago, Sheriff. He was heading south and, just like his cousin here, he had a dose of lead poisoning in his gun arm. Maybe it runs in the family?"

"All right, all right, all right," snapped the sheriff. "I'd rather grab Bud than Nate, but I'm lucky to get my rope on either one of them. Nate," he said, and was very curt and stern, "you're under arrest for murder. And don't worry about your sore arm; I'll get you a doctor and the county will pay for it. Now let's get going."

"Murder? You're crazy!" cried Nate Briscoe, and began edging away.

The girl, Bud Briscoe's girl Georgia, had been listening and watching; now she slid out of her chair, scooped up her blood-red ring and started to the door. But though the sheriff had given no hint of having even seen her, he now called to her sharply.

"Step up this way, Miss," he commanded. "And

don't try to chuck that ring in a spittoon on your way. I want it."

She stopped, hesitant, a vivid picture of uncertainty in her big hat and high heels and flaming dress and black gloves; she was as still as a carved bit of marble, save for the tremor of her ostrich plume.

"I—I don't know what you mean—"

"Come ahead, like I said," the sheriff invited. "Maybe a drink might do you good too. If our friend Mr. Jefferson Davis Morgan won't pay for it, the county will. Come along and make yourself welcome."

"No! No! I am going—"

"It might be a good thing if you do the way I say," remarked Long Jim Jameson. "Likely it would save you being put to considerable bother in the long run."

The girl looked desperate, all but ready to break into full flight. She even looked appealingly to Jeff Morgan who just now had seemed so nice and friendly. He lifted his shoulders ever so slightly; he made the suspicion of a gesture with his head, beckoning her forward. Reluctantly, one small half-gloved hand shut tight, she came to the bar, clicking in her high heels.

The sheriff lifted his hat to her; he even regarded her in a tolerant, faintly admiring yet quite fatherly sort of way. At the same time he put out his hand.

"Better slip me that ring for safe keeping, Miss," he said. "Oh, I saw it the minute I came in. Where'd you get it? Nate didn't give it to you, did he?"

She kept her hand frozen tight.

"You've got no right! It's mine and I'm keeping it!"

"Well, maybe you can, at that," said the sheriff. "I'd sure hate at my age rough-housing a pretty young girl like you, just to grab a ring off her finger. But seems as though I'd seen you some place; seems as though I almost knew who you were. Not the little Hill girl, are you? Hm. Never stayed with Big Belle over at Nevada City before you came up here, did you? You, along with Lady Kate and a few others? Hm. Never noticed the red rings Big Belle wore, did you? Didn't know that a couple of boys tried to grab her rings off, did you, day before yesterday, with Big Belle singing her song and walking high on the champagne trail? Didn't know she put up a fight and yelled her head off—and got killed? The killing was done by your friend Bud Briscoe, along with Nate here. If either Bud or Nate gave you that ring and anything else, you better hand it over to me. If you're thirsty, like I said, Mr. Morgan will buy. Or even I will. But let's get this ring business over with."

The girl looked more than ever terrified. Again her eyes traveled everywhere, and she was like

155

some small helpless animal in a snare; again she looked appealingly at Jeff Morgan.

"I'd do the way the sheriff says," he advised her gently. "You'd never get any fun after this wearing that ring, would you?"

She flung the ring to the bar, picked up her skirts and ran. No one moved to stop her as she raced the length of the room, broke through the swing doors and vanished in the cool outside dark.

And Jeff said, "Well, good night, Sheriff. You're heading back to Black Gulch, maybe? I'll be hoping to drop in on you one of these days. Meanwhile, do me a favor? I left a horse at the livery stable; suppose you tell them to take good care of it for me, and if I don't ever show up— Well, it's a gift to you. Do that?"

"Sure, sure," said Jameson. "Me and Nate here will be riding right along; we cut back through the mountains up here so we don't have to go poking down through Green Water Valley where they say right now the climate ain't over healthy. What about you, kid? What are you up to, anyhow?"

"Me?" said Jeff. He rolled a slow cigarette. "I kind of like this country; first time I clapped my eyes on Green Water Valley I must of fell in love with it. I'm going some place right now and squat down on a stump or a rocking chair, and do me a mite of thinking."

"Pays to think sometimes, kid," conceded Long Jim Jameson. *"Adios, compadre."*

"*Buenas noches* yourself, old timer," said Jeff, and went his way.

His way led him to an old shack down by the covered bridge over the river, a place mentioned to him by Bud's girl, Georgia Hill. He had an all overpowering urge to know all that could be known of Bud Briscoe, Nate Briscoe, Bud's two brothers Hank and Robert—all of them. That they had foregathered here in Settlers' Gap tonight, that they had had something up their sleeves, that things had gone wrong, so that they fled one way and another with anyhow Bud Briscoe wounded, he knew. Well, then? It was just barely possible that at the shack down by the covered bridge he might come upon some decipherable "sign."

He stopped in the dark, twisting road and tied his horse among the buckeyes fifty yards this side of the noisy stream. It was growing late; it was a pleasant night filled with moonlight and roofed by a lovely clear sky and haunted by ineffable memories. Was little Alice Briscoe at home by now, sleeping with her cheek cuddled against her rosy palm, her hair a stilled cascade down along a white pillow?

He chose to think of her like that, safe at home in her own room. Still he wondered about her and did some worrying, too. All that he knew was that he had left her with that scoundrel, Bud Briscoe, whom she loved so blindly. Or, was she still blind?

He hung his spurs on his saddle horn and stepped along where a short-cut trail led through the blackberry bushes edging the river; he saw the long, dark blot of the shack, and there was not a light in it and no sound came from it. Well, he had just taken the long chance; it wasn't likely that anyone would be here now.

An essential part of young Jefferson Davis Morgan's makeup was his stick-to-it-iveness. Once that he had made himself a plan, no matter how sketchily, he was apt to go through with it. Be the place dark or bright, deserted or housing a full company, he would do what he had started out to do, and look it over.

And so he moved on toward the dark house, the black blot of a place down at the river's edge, with the dark silence only gently ruffled by the river's chuckling murmurs.

Better, he decided judicially, if he had gone to a room somewhere and to sleep. There was nothing here to help him in any direction. Better if he had gone along with the sheriff. Better if he had headed back down the valley, to the long lone cabin where now he envisioned Alice Briscoe asleep. But still, hounded by his thoughts, he kept along toward the dark and empty shack hiding itself in the dark of the deep ravine.

A sharp little wind came whispering down through the aspens, and an owl hooted, and take it all together the moment was a black and dismal one. He thought, My horse is hungry, and has got a right to be. Me, too. And all I'll find is an empty house. And why did the good Lord make idiots anyhow?

He stepped gingerly on the porch of the crazy, swaybacked place he was invading. The owl hooted again, as though deriding him; an owl in a tree just across the laughing river. Somehow this insistent derision stepped up his determination, and he went along in search of a door. Groping, he found it; it stood wide open, a door inviting to dark and empty silence.

Well, this wasn't the first dark door he had ever taken stock of. When with Morgan's raiders, when younger than he was now, he had gone with another dozen men to raid a cross-roads settlement; they needed food and wanted horses. With an ax he, young Jefferson Davis Morgan, had attacked a door. He remembered the things that so swiftly afterwards had burned themselves into his soul.

On the porch, he listened to the quiet dark house; it didn't pay always to take silence at its face value. But when, though he waited, there was no sound, no glint of light, he stepped softly through the door, then to one side so as to have the wall at his back, and listened again and even sniffed the air. He was about to strike a match when at last he heard a first faint rustling sound. It could have been made by a pack rat dragging at a scrap of paper but then, in the dark and uncertainty it could have been pretty nearly anything. His hand dropped to his hip; he stood very still, forcing his narrowed eyes to make what they could of his surroundings. But though he waited and frowned into the dark, he still could not analyse the sound which he heard a time or two, which then surrendered to the oppressive stillness.

"Anybody here?" he asked.

And he got his answer. A voice said, very faint and dim and hard to understand:

"Make a light. For God's sake, make a light. It's so damn dark—"

"Who are you?" demanded Morgan. "Why don't you make a light yourself?"

But this time there was no answer, though he was patient. He thought, There's somebody here mighty sick or shot to pieces.

He swept a match along his thigh and did it with his left hand, having his gun out in his right. He saw a man lying on the floor almost at his feet; rather something that had been a man, a little while ago, a dead thing now. He saw two other bodies, whether living or dead men he could not at first tell. He saw an overturned table, a broken coal oil lamp that had rolled into a corner and that glinted in the flare of his match, reflecting its thin flame weakly.

On the floor near the overturned table was a candle end. He let his match burn down, lighted the second, again took swift stock of the dreary, tragic room and stepped to the bit of candle. He lighted it, uprighted the table, stuck the candle in its own grease on the table and reviewed the evidences of an evening of tumult.

Two dead men, as dead as door nails, one man still breathing but even so looking more dead than alive.

The one living man of the trio stirred uneasily; his eyes flew open and he tried to pull himself up against the wall. He was very young, scarcely more than a boy, possibly nineteen or so—and instantly Jeff Morgan knew who he was. He was a Briscoe; one of Alice's brothers, either Hank or Robert.

There was blood on the floor, dull and heavy and already thickened. There were three guns; and there were dim blood tracks in the dust showing where other men had gone their hurried ways, leaving the dead and dying to take care of themselves. Here without a doubt, Bud Briscoe had come by his wound, and here his brother who, he had thought had run out on him—

His brother? His brothers, rather. One of the dead men, looking even younger than the living one, was unmistakably one of the Briscoes, like

Bud, like the cousin Nate, like the young fellow trying to pull himself up against the wall.

"Well, kid?" said Jeff, as the boy's haggard eyes stared at him.

"Get me a drink, will you?" the boy said huskily. "Oh, my God, how I've wanted a drink!"

"Water do? Wait a shake, kid. I'll get it."

There was a door in the rear wall, and Jeff went through it, using another match. Here was a sort of store room, as bare now as Mother Hubbard's cupboard; but there was an outside door, and a small porch there and a basin, dipper and keg of water. He filled the dipper and brought it back; he put an arm about the wounded man's shoulders and helped him with his gulping of water. The young fellow sank back with a long satisfied sigh, his mouth and downy beard wet.

Jeff noted a narrow bunk against a wall, its old ragged blankets half on the floor, and straightened them after a fashion. Then he picked the wounded man up, a light bundle for him to handle, and made him a degree less uncomfortable than he was, sprawling on the floor.

"I don't suppose there's a doctor anywhere near?" he asked. "Looks like you might need one."

"No." The boy's fever-bright eyes stared at him. "Dead, are they? Both Hank and Rawlings?"

"They look pretty dead to me, kid. The young fellow is Hank? Then I guess you are Robert Briscoe?"

"Yes. But it don't make much difference now who I am." The young, bitter mouth twisted. "Guess I won't be anything by morning. Anyhow, damn him, I got Whitey Rawlings while Hank was still alive to see me; I bet old Hank died happier. Say, where's Bud? Him and Nate?"

"They're all right. Bud made his getaway, heading back to an old shack in a ravine down toward Green Water Valley; he got hurt, either in the side or arm, but nothing much. Nate is here yet; he didn't get hurt here but just now he got into trouble at the saloon and got shot in the arm." He paused a moment, then added, "The sheriff just blew into town; he's got Nate in tow, headed for jail over at Black Gulch."

"He's a dirty cold-decking dog, Nate is," groaned Robert Briscoe. "I hope they tie a knot under his left ear and jerk him to heaven. And Bud run out on us, did he? I'll kill him if ever I live long enough. Him and Nate always was two of a kind."

It was an ordeal for him to talk; he lay back limply, his eyes closed, his lax-muscled jaws letting his mouth sag half open, his face white save for the grime upon it and a blood smear that had come from his bloody fingers.

Jeff Morgan wanted to ask what the affair had been about, who was responsible for the two dead men and Robert's wound and Bud's, and all that. But he realized that it was no particular business of his, and that this Briscoe boy was near the end of his tether; Robert might flop over and die in two minutes.

"Anything you want, kid?"

The boy looked puzzled.

"I don't know you. Who are you anyhow? You a friend of Bud's or of Nate's?"

"Me, I'm Jefferson Davis Morgan. I'm a stranger here, a Johnny-come-lately. I'm no friend of Bud Briscoe's or of Nate Briscoe's, just a stranger. The way any man would do, I'm asking if there's anything you want? In a minute I'll look you over and see how bad your hurt is and if I can lend a hand with it. I've got nothing much on my mind tonight; I'll see about a doctor if you want one; I'll do what you say."

For a time Robert Briscoe didn't say anything. Again his eyes were closed and he seemed to have sunk into a coma. Yet a keenly observant Jefferson Davis Morgan saw how the boy's hands were clenched hard, and presently in the uncertain light he made out a little, tense ripple along the hard, stubborn muscles of his jaw. Robert Briscoe, though with but little strength left in him, was trying to gather that strength.

"Listen you, stranger," he said, spacing his words. "You don't need to plug up the hole Rawlings made in me; I fixed it up pretty good myself—that must have been a good many hours ago, and I've stopped the bleeding. A doctor, yes, if you can get me one but I don't reckon there'll be time."

"I'll get busy," said Jeff. "And while I'm away I'll send somebody over here to give you a hand."

"Keep your shirt on, Morgan. Said your name was Morgan, didn't you? Know where Green Water Valley is?"

"Yes. It would take me three or four hours to get down there, as long to get back. And—"

"I know. Maybe I'd be dead long before you could make it. Listen, Morgan: Bud is a yellow rat; so is Nate, maybe even worse than Bud. They both run out on us when trouble started. Now, listen—Say, give me another drink, will you?"

Jeff obliged. Again he supported the young fellow's shoulders, steadying the dipper, while Robert Briscoe gulped his water. Then:

"If I'm going after a doctor—" began Jeff, but young Briscoe cut him short.

"Keep your shirt on, can't you?" he said irritably. But he spoke painfully, with labored effort. He said, "There's a girl down there—"

"Yes, I know." Jeff wanted to help the boy save his strength and so spoke the words he knew Robert Briscoe was straining to utter. "It's Alice Briscoe, your sister. And she has seen Bud; she knows that he is hurt; he didn't tell her that you and Hank had been hurt too. I don't think he even knew, because—"

"No, Bud wouldn't!—Say, will you ride down there for me, Morgan? With word for Alice?"

"Yes." The answer came emphatically, without hesitation. It would be hard to refuse this boy anything right now.

"That's good. Thanks, Morgan. Now, let's see: First, I'm feeling kind of sick and weak in the head; got it? It's damn hard thinking straight. I'll tell you some things; you won't tell her everything, maybe, not to hurt her too damn much. You see, the kid thinks Bud is God and Santy Claus and all that sort of thing. Here, lift me up, will you?"

Jeff folded one of the ragged blankets and rolled it into the shape of a rough and ready pillow; he bolstered Robert Briscoe up with this behind his shoulders.

"We were all set to rob the bank over to Yellow Jacket," said Robert. "It was a pet idea of Bud's; he's been working on it a long time. Next Saturday, late afternoon; they'll have a hell of a lot of money in then, ready to ship out to the Black Jack Mine Monday, for the month's payday. You see, Whitey Rawlings used to be one of Bud's gang—that was before—"

"Look here, kid," said Jeff sharply. "Maybe you're speaking out of turn. Maybe you're saying things you'll wish you hadn't. All this is no business of mine."

In heavy silence Robert Briscoe half sat, half lay propped up against his blanket roll.

"Give me a cigarette," he said.

Jeff Morgan rolled and handed him a Durham cigarette, and lighted it for him.

"I guess you're a square guy, Morgan," Robert said after the first lungful of smoke. "Well, anyhow, I'd take my chances, because maybe I won't be hanging around here long." His eyes drifted to the floor; the candle light flickered fitfully upon two dead faces, the man Whitey Rawlings, the youngest Briscoe boy.

"Wait a shake," said Jeff.

He meant to move both bodies out of the boy's view, but Robert shook his head and said:

"Leave 'em be. Poor old Hank, he's company and he knows I'll be seeing him soon. As for Whitey Rawlings," and a queer, crooked grin distorted his good looking, boyish features, "it does me good to look at him the way he is!"

"Get along then with what you wanted to say."

"Sure. And don't think I've gone off my head and don't know what I'm talking about. Only it's sort of hard to draw it short. I said as how Rawlings used to work with Bud. They had a row a year back. But before that Bud had hid a lot of swag up here close in to the Gap; it was to be split when there was a full pot, and he cheated Rawlings out of his share. That's Bud for you; I bet he'll be damn glad to have both me and Hank out of it so there'll be the more for him to hog. Well, Rawlings got wind of the bank hold-up for next Saturday; he horned in here with a couple of bums that are playing in with him; that's how the fight started. Now some of all this you can tell Allie; maybe not too damn much. Anyhow, I want her to know what's happened to me and Hank; I want her to know the sort Bud is; I tell you she thinks he's a tin god. Got it, Morgan?"

"I think so," said Morgan slowly.

Robert slumped lower down on the bunk.

"Maybe I'm pegging out pretty pronto; maybe I can stick it a few hours," he said huskily. "I'd sort of like to see Alice. You tell her?"

"I'm going right now. I'll send someone over to lend you a hand while I'm gone. Luck, kid."

"Sure," mumbled Robert. "Sure, Morgan. And thanks."

Jeff Morgan went out softly and softly closed the door.

CHAPTER XIV
A LITTLE MAN LIKE A
QUESTION MARK

AFTER that night it was a full week before Jeff Morgan saw any of the Briscoes or their friends. Leaving the badly wounded Robert, he had gone straight to the Settlers' Gap saloon, had told the bartender of Robert's desperate condition, his need of help right away and a doctor as soon as one could be located, had added only, "There are a couple of other men got shot; the Briscoe kid can tell you more than I can," and then struck south, headed to Green Water Valley again. It had been late that night, the dark hours of another early morning rather, when he had come to the long, low cabin. No dogs barked; that was because Injun Pete had them shut up in the barn. Jeff pounded at a door and small, brisk Uncle Dick came in his bare feet, carrying a rifle. After a word with him Alice had been routed out.

Her eyes were heavy with sleep, her hair in lovely disorder, her cheeks faintly pink, and she clutched tight about her a sort of Mother Hubbard thing within which she was very young and very sweet.

Uncle Dick listened to the few words Jeff had to say, then chirped up, "You get ready, Allie. I'll get dressed in a jiffy and have the horses ready. I'll go 'long with you, of course."

Jeff hadn't gone into details; better let Robert do that for himself, if Alice got to him in time. Anyhow, with the girl in possession of the essentials, that both Hank and Robert were badly hurt and might not live—he didn't have the heart to tell her that already Hank was dead—the rest could wait.

He saw Alice and Uncle Dick ride away, hurrying. Then, making it easy for his horse, he rode on slowly down-valley and up the old Rim Trail and so into Black Gulch. With Dandy stabled, with his other horse looked to, he went to the hotel and upstairs to a room, and to bed.

And in Black Gulch he holed up a few days. He had told Alice where he was going, where he could be found were there any occasion to look him up, and he felt that this was no time for him to go to her. She had found her troubles all of a sudden pouring down upon her as thick as rain drops in a thunder storm, what with the death of one brother, perhaps of another, too; what with her first inkling that big handsome Bud Briscoe, her girlhood hero, was what he was instead of what she had dreamed him. Jeff wanted to see her, to put his arms about her—but already he knew that she was the sort who would not want to be comforted. She would want to be alone, all alone with her grief.

During these first few days Jeff and the sheriff came to know each other pretty well; they had a drink or two together when they met on the creaking wooden sidewalk of Black Gulch's one street, they chatted once or twice in the sheriff's bare little office. Jeff considered the things Robert Briscoe had told him, and had to contend with the natural impulse to pass the word along to the duly constituted representative of the law. But he judged the affair was not exactly his, that Robert Briscoe had spoken to him man to man, that there was no hurry. So, beyond giving the barest sketch of conditions as he had found them in the old shack by Settlers' Gap's covered bridge, he kept his mouth shut. The shrewd Long Jim Jameson may have suspected that he was holding something back: Long Jim knew that most men at most times held back some little thought or knowledge or suspicion of their own, circumstances building up so many reasons for a still tongue. On his side, however, the sheriff talked freely.

Nate Briscoe was in jail in Yellow Jacket, charged with having a hand in the murder of Big Belle, and Long Jim remarked complacently that he wouldn't be a bit surprised if some of the boys busted into the jail and strung Nate up from old Hangman's Tree, a noble and experienced poplar at the edge of town. As for what he termed the fracas in Settlers' Gap,

"A good job all 'round," he said in his mild way. "It was a fight between two cutthroat gangs, Bud Briscoe's and Whitey Rawlings'. Maybe it's too bad that both the young Briscoe boys got killed; Hank died fighting and Robert cashed in the next day. Maybe they're better off, too, seeing as how both of 'em was being headed hell-wards in tow of Bud. It would have been nicer if Bud had got killed instead, but you can't have everything just so in this life, ever notice? As for Whitey Rawlings, they ought to have shot him the day he was born."

He explained about Rawlings. For a time he and Bud Briscoe had been inseparable, were known to have been out on many a wild rampage together, were something more than merely suspected of having been in cahoots in more than one bit of law-breaking that had a pile of easy money for its object.

"About three years ago there was half a dozen men like that trailin' their luck with Bud and Whitey, mostly with Bud because he always had a way with him; he didn't take orders easy, but he was in the way of givin' 'em, and makin' 'em lively. Everybody knows they rustled cattle and saddle horses, and that they stuck up stages, but nobody could ever get the low down on them. They got away with a lot of money and they sure spent a lot, gamblin' and drinkin' and raisin' hell in general, but folks have a notion they've still got a hell of a lot hid out somewhere, and it's supposed that Bud and Whitey had a ruckus about splittin' it. Anyhow, they did split up their gang; Bud dragged the Briscoe kids in on his side along with another killer or two; Whitey started out on his own. Well, that sort of thing can't be very well helped; sooner or later some of the solid citizens, kind of cool of head until they get mad, and steady of trigger finger, will get 'em, unless," he chuckled, "they do like over in Settlers' Gap and get themselves first, which them sort of boys does kind of frequent."

This was one of their chats in Jameson's office. He had gotten just this far when a man riding into town, riding lazily, slouching not ungracefully in the saddle, caught his eye through the uncurtained window.

"There's another one of the same outfit now, or I'm a liar," said the sheriff.

Jeff frowned out at the loitering figure, finding in it something troublingly familiar. The man was young and tall and lean and dark; there was a dash of dandyism in him with his fancy boots and dove-gray Stetson with its silver buckle, his showy holsters and belt and spurs. He was a man who looked hard and yet overlaid with silk.

Suddenly Jeff knew who he was: Cass Burdock, the ruffian he had half beaten to death that night in Green Water Valley for laying a hand upon Alice Briscoe. Jeff merely said,

"He looks and he rides like he thought he owned most of this part of the world."

"That's Cass Burdock. A rich man, some folks say; a four flusher, say others. He does flash money at times; never works but does some fast thinkin'. He owned three minin' claims over at Yellow Jacket last year; bought 'em and sold 'em and bought a ranch somewheres. A good hand at poker, too, and damn the limit. Yep, he's been with Bud, and maybe they've worked together and maybe they haven't, and he's been runnin' with Whitey Rawlings of late. Oh, we got us some nice neighbors around here, Mr. Morgan."

Jeff nodded absently, stared out into the street for a meditative moment, then remarked casually,

"You're kind of nice and friendly, telling me things like all this."

Long Jim Jameson grinned.

"Meaning that you wonder why I talk my head off to a man that's pretty nigh a stranger to me? We-ell, let's see. I liked the way you tore into that fight in the alley, even if you did chip in on the wrong side and come damn near shootin' my head off." He removed his hat and pursed his lips, looking again at the hole in it. "And you told me that you thought you was shootin' Bud Briscoe, and somehow I believed it. I notice that you are stickin' here; most likely before long you'll be runnin' bang up against some of our distinguished citizens. Well, a man can't ever tell, but it might come in handy some day to have you on my side."

"Thanks," said Jeff Morgan.

He could tell Jameson about the Briscoe crowd's plan to stick up the bank in Yellow Jacket, or he could keep his mouth shut. Well, after his way of thinking, a man was lots of times sorry for shooting off his mouth too soon and mighty seldom sorry because of keeping it shut. Then, after the fracas in Settlers' Gap, no doubt the plan had either been discarded or postponed for a happier day. Also, there was time yet before the date set. He said,

"I like it here, Sheriff. It's kind of big and comfortable and a man might fit into it nice and easy. I've got a little money put away; I'm apt to get me a ranch something like Green Water Valley sometime."

"You don't look to me like a man that's loaded down with money," said Jameson, and eyed him steadily and then, blunt with his words, said, "How'd you come by it?"

Jeff Morgan laughed softly.

"Beginning to wonder if maybe I'm one of the Rawlings or Briscoe crowd? Nothing like that; I'm a lone rider, Sheriff. Well, it's a long story and me, I'm not much good at spinning long-winded yarns. After the War I worked a couple of months for forty dollars a month; so did my pardner, Bob Lane. We felt rich then and quit. We dropped down to a little Texas town and bought us some beans and tomatoes and boots, and a beer or so, and we got into a game. We hit luck that night; we rode out with about four hundred dollars."

The sheriff leaned back and smoothed down his black and white cowhide vest.

"Four hundred dollars don't go awful far when it comes to ranch buying," he said.

"I tell you we hit a run of luck, Bob and me. We bought a freight team and hauled freight, and then we sold out, and doubled our ante. We sure rode high, wide and handsome for a spell; brand new clothes, horses, saddles, everything. And we dropped into a new gambling house that Rawhide Williams opened up down in El Paso last year. And we made us some money. No horse stealing, mind you, and no stage robbing; just honest money picked up at a few whirls at faro and a little fooling around with draw. And we kept running in the luck right up to the time—"

His eyes clouded.

"Then they killed your pardner," nodded the sheriff. "But seems as though you said they bush-whacked him just for fun and forty dollars?"

"Forty dollars is all he had on him, and they knew it; they followed him out of town where they had seen his roll. Our main stake—Well, we kept it cached."

"Like you do now, maybe?" said the sheriff. "Or maybe you've got it soaked away in a bank some-wheres."

Jeff Morgan thought of the bank over at Yellow Jacket, due soon for a raid, and he remembered other banks. Some just blew up of their own accord. He shook his head.

"No banks for me," he said.

Again Jameson nodded. "Me, too, kid; I'm that-away. Maybe it's safer carryin' it around with you, maybe diggin' a hole for it with a rock on top. I dunno." He cleared his throat. "But the stake you two had was half yours, half your pardner's?" he suggested.

"You're a nosy old party today," said Jeff, but with a smile. "It was, but Bob and I had a deal: if anything happened to one of us, the other took the pile. You see neither of us had any folks left to think about. What the War didn't wipe out, the troubles and hard times did." He rose, shook out his legs, pulled down his hat and moved toward the door. "If you happen to know of a ranch something like the Green Water Valley place, might let me know. *Adios, compadre.*"

"Addyose, kid," said Long Jim. Then just as Jeff's hand reached the door knob, he added, "Since you seem sort of to like the Green Water, and if you think you could swing it, whyn't you buy it? Most likely it'll be for sale, and dirt cheap, real soon."

Jeff halted. "Tell me," he said.

"Well, it ain't altogether paid for yet, to begin with," said the sheriff. "And the part that is paid for has got a blanket on it, mortgage being held by old man Parker, Lute Parker over at the bank in Yellow Jacket. Bud Briscoe maybe has got money salted away in the hills, but it looks like Bud was on the run. Most likely Lute Parker will gobble the ranch in, lock, stock and barrel, unless the gent that just rode by does the gobblin' act; everybody knows that Cass Burdock is dead set on gettin' Green Water Valley—and maybe a girl to go along with it. So long, kid."

"So long," said Jeff absently, and went out, pondering these matters.

He knew well enough that Cass Burdock wanted the girl at Green Water Valley. He felt that he knew that Burdock wanted her red ring and bracelet, too. And now the valley itself? A young man who struck high, this Mr. Cass Burdock, whether rich man or four flusher.

He saw Cass Burdock's horse at a hitching rail in front of a pair of swing doors; passing, he looked in and saw Burdock at the bar, his attitude arrogant, his hat back, as he reached for bottle and glass. A moment Morgan hesitated; that night in Green Water Valley Cass Burdock had said to Alice Briscoe, "I don't know who this man is and I don't care, but if God lets me live I am going to kill him." Yes, he had said that, and that he was coming back to the valley; he seemed to have just two thoughts in his hot head that night: To sweep the girl off her feet; to kill Jeff Morgan on sight.

Jeff sighed and shook his head and passed along without turning in; it struck him that with other matters on his mind, Mr. Cass Burdock could wait, and hell take him. But before he had gone a dozen steps Jeff Morgan stopped, shrugged, turned back. Might as well get the thing over with one way or another; might just as well know what Cass Burdock was like.

He shoved one of the swing doors open and went into the barroom. It was late afternoon and there were only four or five men beside Burdock at the long, dusky bar.

Jeff ordered his drink, standing half a dozen feet from Burdock, with no one between them. He gave no one the impression that he was interested in Cass Burdock, that he was even looking at him or conscious of his presence. But he poured his drink and lifted his glass with his left hand. He knew from his brief experience with the man how swift he was.

Burdock glanced at him as at any stranger and glanced away with not a flicker of an eyelid. Well, Long Jim had said that the man was a poker player; there was no telling whether or not he recognized the newcomer. Morgan took into consideration that his meeting with Burdock had been at night, and though a night of full moon, still shadows were tricky and a man but once seen, though in the grip of a fight, might not be identified at the next unheralded meeting. Yet he had the electric sense that Cass Burdock did know him and might strike as quick as a rattlesnake or might choose to let the moment go by. He might even wait for Morgan, with his drink finished, to turn his back.

No, there was no reading anything in Cass Burdock's lean, hard face. But it remained that Jeff felt that Burdock had recognized him; it had been a bright moon that night down in the valley and as keen a man as Cass Burdock, his senses keyed up to awareness of all details as the two men stood up to each other, would be pretty sure to know his antagonist when he saw him again. Inwardly Jeff shrugged; might as well get the thing settled, he thought.

He finished his drink, having taken ample time

about it; he rolled his cigarette and lighted it, very leisurely. When still there was no sign he said to the bartender,

"Anybody been in here asking for me? My name's Morgan, Jefferson Davis Morgan."

"Not that I know of, stranger," said the man behind the bar.

And Cass Burdock didn't even glance up from his glass. But startling Morgan, the quick voice of a small man spoke up from the end of the room.

"Hello there, Morgan," said the small man. "I just got to town; was just about to ask where you might be."

He came forward, walking jerkily. All the while Cass Burdock had never batted an eye or twitched a finger. Jeff Morgan laughed; here, chirping up at a pregnant moment like this, came the smallest, dryest, most furtive and alert of all the Briscoes he had seen, Alice's crafty looking uncle Dick.

"Have a drink, Briscoe," Jeff invited.

"Don't mind if I do," said Uncle Dick. "Thankin' ye kindly." He poured a full glass and shot the fiery liquor down his throat. "Luck to you, and sudden death to all your enemies," he said affably, and added, "I've been thinkin' about that horse of yours and am ready to talk turkey if you're still of a mind to sell it."

Jeff's expression did not change as he looked down into the little man's innocent face. There had been no talk between them of any horse and for an instant he was all at sea. But he was swift enough to realize that Uncle Dick did have a word to say to him, no doubt wanted that word in private, had possibly really been looking for him. He rejoined carelessly,

"I'm just on my way for a little ride. Walk over to the stable with me if you like; both my horses are over there."

"Suits me," said Uncle Dick, then bethought himself to suggest a return of hospitality with Jeff having a drink on him. When Jeff shook his head the two went out, Jeff thinking that Cass Burdock, even though murderously and treacherously inclined, would scarcely go so far as to shoot him in the back with Alice's uncle a witness.

"Is it on the level that you were really looking for me?" he asked as they made their way stableward.

Uncle Dick carved himself a sizeable hunk of plug cut, stuffed it into a cheek that he made bulge with it, hitched up his jeans which always seemed about to slide off his lean hips, and answered characteristically,

"We-ll, you might say yes and you might say no. You see, I had to come in town on some other business. Likewise, I knowed you was here, I got to thinking about you, and I reckon I might have looked you up if you hadn't showed up when you did."

"You didn't waste time answering when I asked the barkeep if anyone was asking for me."

"No, I didn't. You see, I know about you and Cass Burdock having had a scrap that night down in the valley. Allie told me; she was considerably shook up and riled by all the grief coming her way so sudden-like, and busted out with a lot of things. And I reckoned if I spoke up sharp enough it might stop you and Cass from starting shooting then and there."

"Any particular business of yours?" asked Jeff mildly.

Uncle Dick chuckled.

"Me," he confessed with a twinkle in his bird-like eye, "I never did hanker to be what they call an innocent bystander, meaning I'd a heap ruther not have two gents shooting wild, with me in the same room."

"What did you want to see me about?"

Uncle Dick spat far out, then rubbed his chin.

"You know that both Hank and Robert is dead and buried," he said. "Robert wasn't dead though when you saw him seeing how he sent you for Allie; he must have done some talking. I got to wondering if he'd said anything about—Oh, shucks; about things in general?"

"What things in general?"

"How'n tarnation can a man say what things in general, seeing as how they are in general? Just—just in gen'ral, dammit!"

"You've got something on your mind," said Jeff, very cool with him. "Either spit it straight out or keep it to yourself."

"Shucks, it ain't anything in partic'lar. Like I said, just in gen'ral. We-ll, for one thing, Robert mought have said where Bud was headed for. I reckon Allie would sort of like to know."

"You mean you haven't seen him from that night?"

"Neither hide nor hair. We do know the sheriff caught Nate and drug him off to the calaboose down to Yellow Jacket. We don't know where Bud went to."

"I don't either. I haven't seen him since I left him and his sister together. And you can tell her that I know that Robert didn't know where Bud was or where he was going."

"Hmf. Thought as much. Bud's a bad egg, like we both know; like pore little Allie ought to be figgering him out for herself by now. We-ll. Hmf." He spat farther this time, rubbed his chin harder. "Anything else Robert said?"

Jeff Morgan felt pretty sure the circuitous old rascal was dead set on some particular scrap of information and wondered what it could be; before answering he even cast back in mind, checking against the few things a dying Robert had told him.

"He didn't talk a whole lot, you know," he said. "Hurt so bad I didn't think he could stick it out long enough for his sister to get there from Green Water."

As they neared the stable down at the end of the street, Uncle Dick began dragging his feet. He peered sideways at his companion, spat and rubbed his chin.

"You don't talk so goldarned much either, do you?" he said with a hint, only a hint of tartness.

"All folks talk too much," said Jeff.

"Allie told me about you and Bud, anyhow how you was looking for him; how there was bad blood between you—"

Jeff didn't say anything. Leading the way he reached the stable; the boy who was lazily on duty there came inching out of the harness room as he caught sight of them and said howdy. Then Uncle Dick spoke up briskly, saying to the boy,

"I'm wanting my horse already; saddle him for me and I'll give you two bits."

The boy disappeared into the big, dusky building that was so fragrant of hay and horses and saddle leather. Uncle Dick's lean fingers snagged Jeff by the arm; speaking in a lowered voice he said,

"I've had me my hunch for quite a spell that Bud was no good. He's a robber and a killer and a horse thief. Right, am I?" When Jeff merely shrugged, Uncle Dick came pretty well out of the underbrush: "Did Robert give you an idee where Bud and his gang had their hideout?" he queried.

In a flash Jeff thought he had the explanation of the old fellow's string of questions, of his insistence. He remembered how Robert had spoken of a place, not far out of Settlers' Gap, where a lot of loot was cached. Did good old Uncle Dick know of that loot, did he figure there must be a place somewhere not too far away where it was stored for safety—and did he judge it was as much his as anyone else's if he could come at it?

"I'm taking a ride," said Jeff. "So long."

"Which way you going, young feller?"

Jeff shrugged. There was no reason for refusing an answer. "Over to Settlers' Gap," he said.

Uncle Dick must then have established a record for long distance spitting; he rubbed his chin so hard that you could hear the rustle of his scrub of a two or three days' beard. He chuckled pleasantly as he exclaimed,

"Now, that's a funny thing! I was heading over that a-way myself before riding back down into the valley. Wait a shake; I'll poke along with you."

Jeff Morgan's was a rather grim smile, still there was amusement in it and no great resentment. The little man was in his way a likeable little scalawag; not a man you'd trust out of sight or in sight, for that matter, but a fellow you might come to sort of like—after a fashion. Jeff said,

"Sure. Let's ride."

But as he shoved his toe into his stirrup his face was sober. He was still asking himself questions about Uncle Dick—how much the devious little man guessed and how much he knew—and why he should be riding so far out of his way as to pass through Settlers' Gap—

185

CHAPTER XV
DOWN THE DEVIL'S CHUTE

"THERE was a man name of Throgmorton," said Jefferson Davis Morgan. "How he got a name like that, I wouldn't know, but—"

"Did they hang him?" asked Uncle Dick. "And was that why?"

He poked up the fire, settled the pot of beans, placed the coffee pot accurately and cozily withal in a nest of glowing coals, set the newly browned bacon in a tin pan atop a convenient flat rock and reached for that doubtful looking mess, ready in a tin pan, whereof flapjacks are made. Jeff sat on a log on the bank of the wild little creek, rolled a morning cigarette and watched alternately his busy companion and the streak of light showing against the pine crested ridges that announced the sunrise.

"Anyhow," he said, "this was Throgmorton's place, not much of a place maybe, unless there's gold on it the way he thought, or unless you just like a spot where you can get off by yourself and let the world roll by, or unless plenty of fish and all sorts of game, big and little, are worth fooling with. Not worth much, I guess, and Throgmorton one unlucky night gambled it away right down there in Settlers' Gap, lost it to a halfbreed who'd sell it for a saddle and a bottle of red-eye—and that same night somebody did make an end of this party Throgmorton. Shot him, so I heard it said, instead of hanging him."

"I've often noticed, Mr. Morgan," said Uncle Dick, pulling his hat brim to fend off the heat and smoke as he squatted by his fire, "as how you use a hell of a lot of words when you ain't got nary a thing to say, and how when a man asks you a question, your words all dry up and blow away before you get around to wrappin' your tongue around 'em."

"If you ever get so low down on your luck that you'd even work for a living," observed Jeff, sniffing the warm aromas floating to him from the pine wood fire and looking at Uncle Dick Briscoe approvingly, "I might give you a job as cook."

"I thought we was talking about a man name of Frog-martin."

"Throgmorton. No, not about him; just about his place. I rode through here not long ago; kind of liked it. I found the halfbreed last night. It's my place now."

"Along with the stone house? *And* the log cabin? Both?"

"Both. And you can keep right on sleeping in the log cabin after you go to work cooking for me."

Uncle Dick snorted like an old horse. "What'n hell have I been doing these last two-three days? The only thing I notice is that I ain't been getting paid for it."

"You've been getting your grub free, old timer, and a place to sleep."

"We-ll, there's something in that. But—"

"*And* a chance to do your snooping around. Come on any sign of what you're looking for yet?"

"Me?" said Uncle Dick in that innocent way of his. "I don't know what you're talkin' about. Do you?"

This bit of wild land that Jeff had just made his own, with its beetling iron crags at the back of a broad crescent of green mountain meadow, with its flashing streams, three of them, its dense forest growth, was on the slope of the wilderness slightly lifted above, slightly withdrawn from the disreputable little crossroads cluster of ramshackle buildings known as Settlers' Gap. Under the cliffs was an old stone house of two rooms, a room and a half, rather, since the second was a dug-out into the mountainside, windowless, dark and damp, good for nothing on earth, so far as he could see; not even a store room. The front room was entered by a wide, sturdy door; there was a square window in each wall; the prospect was not unpleasant since from this vantage point one could look out over his own wilder acres, across a shadowy hollow down through which glanced the head-waters of Green River, and beyond that, could see Settlers' Gap looking picturesque in the brief distance. Then, a quarter of a mile from the stone house was the old log cabin. Jeff had dropped his bed roll at the more pretentious habitation; had had no desire to dwell with another man squeezed in with him, had made Uncle Dick at home in the log cabin. They were breakfasting outdoors, at the nearby creek.

"I like it here," said Jeff, "while I'm sort of looking around. Better than the hotel at Black Gulch. A place for my two horses, too. Maybe I'll go out and get us a fat young buck today."

"And maybe, you think, if you squat here long enough Bud Briscoe might show up?"

"He hasn't showed up in Green Water Valley yet?"

Last night Uncle Dick had ridden southward. "Going to poke down and see how Allie is getting along," he had said. What time he had returned, Jeff had no idea; he only knew that here was Uncle Dick again, dry and spry and cricketlike, ready to build a man's-sized breakfast and to help destroy his own handiwork.

"Nope," he said. He squinted his eye, turning his head sidewise, whether to shut the smoke out or to peer at young Morgan. "I saw Allie though. She's all right, that girl; as pretty as a picture, she's brave like a couple of Injun chiefs. She mentioned you, Morgan; said something or other about you."

Jeff looked at him steadily without saying anything. He knew right well that Uncle Dick, if he had anything he wanted to say, would go ahead and say it without prompting. But at that moment he would have liked to choke the old reprobate: he would give a lot to know all that could be told of Alice and, if she had mentioned him, he would have given a lot to know what she had said, how she had said it.

"Look out or you'll burn those flapjacks," is what he said, after a silence long enough to give Uncle Dick reasonable time to go on, were such his intent.

The old man indulged in one of his characteristic snorts. He attended to his cooking and then, without bothering to look up, knowing full well that he'd get no change of expression on the other man's face, he said a mite spitefully,

"Cass Burdock was down there. Said he came to see Bud or to ask where he was. But I noted how him and Allie took a little short walk outside for a little while. Cass Burdock sure has got an eye for a pretty girl, or anyhow so I hear folks say."

Of course Jeff didn't say anything. They breakfasted and then Jeff stood up and stretched and patted his midriff.

"You sure can cook," he said.

"And, man, you sure can eat!"

"Both of us," agreed Jeff.

"Looky here," said Uncle Dick, and snapped a dry stick in his leathery hands and pitched the broken ends into the fire. "You just said you bought this Godforsook goat ranch; you just said it's a good place to hang out while you're looking around. Well, dammit, what are you looking for anyhow?"

"Not the same thing you are," said Jeff. "Me, I'm just figuring on getting me a ranch around here somewhere; this place, I don't count. A real place, something like Green Water Valley, if I can find it."

Uncle Dick slapped his leg.

"Say! That's the first time, I bet a man, that you ever got down to a real answer to anybody's question! A ranch like the Green Water, huh? We-ll, whyn't you buy that one? Got any money? George would be damn glad to sell out."

"Would he?"

"Would a mouse sink its teeth into a hunk of cheese? George has got a belly full of Green Water Valley, you just believe me. Sell? He'd almost throw it at you. But, on the side, kid, tell me this: Got any money?"

"Would I tell you if I had? You'd cut my throat in my sleep."

So Uncle Dick licked his spoon and eased up his old bones and went down to the creek to wash the dishes. When he came back to the camp site Jeff was striding down into the meadow, dragging the loop of a rope after him, headed for his browsing horses.

Uncle Dick scratched his head and asked himself a few questions: Why, he wanted to be told, had young Jeff Morgan established himself here in the dark narrow valley in which Settlers' Gap nested like an evil bird in a darksome place? And how much had the dying Robert Briscoe told him? And where in the devil's name was Bud Briscoe's hideout? These and other questions a very inquisitive Uncle Dick asked himself.

He kicked the last dying brand back into its place in his rough and ready fireplace; he dumped a bucket of water on the glowing sticks and, under his breath, said with solemn emphasis,

"I'll eat a bug if I can make him out."

He watched the young man rope his horse, saddle it and strike south. "Going down to Green Water, I bet a man," grumbled Uncle Dick. But Jeff Morgan didn't go all the way to the long cabin down in the valley that day; he stopped at that other cabin, the old ruin of a place where he had made a fire for Alice Briscoe to dry herself, and looked the place over. Here he had last seen Bud, and he had it in his mind that if Bud had come this way once he might repeat. Taking his time, he cast about for some sign but found none. There was nothing to indicate that the spot had been visited since he had ridden away and left the girl here. Well, then, where had Bud Briscoe taken himself?

Not back to the valley, if any credence were to be given Uncle Dick's words; not to Settlers' Gap, and most certainly not to Black Gulch where Sheriff Jameson was pop-eyed in eagerness to catch a glimpse of him. A hideout somewhere in these mountains until a wound healed? Very likely. And so young Morgan spent some two or three hours casting about, hunting some likely trail which Bud might have ridden to his lair. He did find a couple of dim trails, little used; he did follow one and then the other a two or three miles; they led nowhere in particular, one to a rutted county road, used little more than the trail itself, the other to the tiny crossroads village of Red Rock, neither to any trace of Bud Briscoe.

The best part of his day came when he rode to the top of a ridge and looked down into Green Water Valley. He saw the oak grove, the gently rounded knoll, the river sweeping by, and a corner and chimney of the long log cabin.

And, too, it was the best part of Alice Briscoe's day. He was not above three miles away and sat his horse out in a clearing with the sun yellow about him, and she gasped when through her spy glass she found him. Her heart leaped when she was sure that it was really Jefferson Davis Morgan! It seemed like magic, to be at one moment sweeping the silent and empty forest lands and bare slopes, all of a sudden to have him in the small round of her glass. He looked so near! She could see his horse toss its head, she could see the bright flash of a silver buckle. "Jeff!" she breathed softly.

She *knew* that he was coming to her! It seemed so endlessly long since they had had their few moments together. To her he was like something that had stepped boldly out of a dream; he had come into her life abruptly, just as now of a sudden he bulked tangibly upon the empty circle of her glass. She *knew* that he was coming to her as straight and swift as any arrow, and her heart beat harder than before and her breast tightened and the blood flushed her cheeks.

But he did not come. He was thinking about her; she knew that, and in this knowledge she was right. But he could not tell that she was thinking of him at the moment, could not guess that she was even looking at him, holding her breath for his first move toward her. For he had another thought too, and that had grimly to do with Bud Briscoe. He had to find and kill Bud Briscoe first of all. After that? He could only shrug, set his jaws and swing his horse about, vanishing from her pleading eyes, so that a moment later all that she could see was the ridge with the golden pools of sunshine on it and the black splotches of shadow—and again for her the world was as bleak and empty as it had been during these last tragic days. She went listlessly back to her room and threw herself down on her bed and wept. She was very young, very sad and lonely, very deep in love, and life seemed as black and terrible as midnight in a storm. Even little old Uncle Dick, whom she had begun to love, had failed her, staying away on some mysterious business of his own.

George Briscoe was a sad man. Heavy-thoughted, lugubrious, mournful, a man whose light had gone out long and long ago. There was something very fine in old George Briscoe that most folks didn't know anything about, didn't even glimpse. He harbored in the depths of a strange, lonely soul a tremendous capacity for love. There had been a girl in George's life, just the one girl whom he had watched flower into lovely, tender young woman-hood, whom he had made his wife, who became the mother of his children. Until she died his love had flourished like a banyan tree, spreading out even to encompass them. But she had died. A light went out along with her. And what joy had his neglected offspring ever brought him after that? He knew full well about Bud, his eldest, the silky-bearded Charlie Briscoe. And he knew how Hank and Robert were drifting downstream, over the rapids, along with Bud. And even Alice, who had for a time been a sweet gleam through the dark-ness of his days, who shone even now like a slim young moon, only made his sorrow the deeper, reminding him so poignantly of another slender young moon of an Alice. And now—Hank and Robert, two sons, dead; and Charlie, God knew where.

"Me," said George Briscoe to himself, "I'm digging out of here. I'm pulling stakes and going home. I'm taking Allie with me and going home."

"Home," was old Virginia where he had been born and raised, where he had married the girl he loved and had started to make what he could of life, something fine and warm against his heart. And look at the damned thing now! Yes, soon he would clear out and head back with what life had left him, back to the rising sun.

He went into the quiet house. Lonely, it was. The boys dead or away; Uncle Dick prowling off into the mountains; Alice always vanishing. He went as far as her door; he heard her sobbing, and tiptoed away.

"Me," said George Briscoe the second time, more emphatically now, "I'm taking Allie with me and pulling up stakes and going home."

He sat on the front porch in an old rawhide-bottomed chair and smoked his pipe and brooded. Then through the mystery of the brushy riverside all spotted with light and shadow he saw someone on horseback coming on toward where he sat. Well, callers here were rare: Bud, maybe and maybe Dick, possibly Cass Burdock—

It was a girl in a long riding skirt, perched high upon a side-saddle, hurrying yet riding gracefully. A mighty pretty girl, he saw as she drew nearer, wearing a floating veil which did not hide her prettiness, a big pale blue hat with a plume drooping over its broad brim.

She reined in, close to the porch, and looked at him a while in silence. Then she said in a breathless sort of fashion, as though she had traveled hard and her heart were in her throat,

"Is Bud here? Bud Briscoe?"

George, bethinking him of long forgotten manners, rose slowly and knocked out his pipe.

"No ma'am," he said. "Not here."

"This is the Briscoe place, isn't it?"

"Yes ma'am, this is it," said George. "But Charlie hasn't been around lately."

"You know where he is?" She sounded eager and earnest, impatient, too.

He shook his head.

"I wouldn't know that. Nobody has seen hide or hair of him for a week, about. He might be most anywhere, Charlie might."

"I've got to see him! I've just got to see him— Say, who are you anyhow? You're Bud's father?"

"Yes. I'm George Briscoe. But, I tell you, I don't know a thing about Charlie, where he is or anything." He hammered his pipe against his heel and jammed it with unusual savageness into his pocket, and said, sounding angry, "And I don't know that I give a damn." Then, again remembering his manners, he added more quietly, "Asking your pardon, ma'am."

Alice heard them and came outside, wondering, onto the porch. Her eyes widened to take the new girl in. She had never seen her, didn't know who in the world she could be, but she had heard a girl's worried voice demanding Bud Briscoe.

The two girls looked each other up and down, frankly probing from top to toe; they had in common only their femininity and youth and prettiness. Beyond that they were set as far apart as opposite ends of a lode stone, as far as the north pole from the south. Out of a brief, suspicious silence Alice said in a quiet voice which sounded as from a distance,

"What is it about Charlie?"

The girl on the horse sat there looking steadily at her a long, investigating moment. Then she demanded bluntly,

"Who are you? Do you know where he is?"

"I am Alice Briscoe. I am his sister. No I don't know where he is. Do you?"

The girl on horseback made up her mind; she gathered up her skirt and slid down from the saddle, dropping her horse's reins to the ground.

"I want to talk to you," she said to Alice. "Please let me."

George Briscoe said, "You girls don't need me. I'm going over to the barn. You two can sit here on the porch and visit."

The two girls stood on the porch, looking straight into each other's eyes, appraising each other.

"I am Georgia Hill," said the visitor. "Bud and I go places together. We're old friends. We—" She stiffened, ready to grow defiant, then she laughed and sounded and looked embarrassed and yet determined. "We're maybe going to get married sometime," she said.

"Oh!" said Alice. She looked at Georgia with a new and different interest; then suddenly she smiled and put her hand out. "I'm glad you came, Georgia," she said. "I think you are nice."

Georgia gave her hand with a queer sort of reluctance. Nice, was she? Well, maybe and maybe not. She knew instinctively that she wasn't nice in the way this wild rose Alice Briscoe was, and she knew that Alice wouldn't think her nice if—Oh well, why did she have to get started thinking of a lot of things that didn't matter.

She said quickly, giving Alice's hand a quick warm grip then pulling away from it,

"Tell me about Bud!"

Alice shook her head so that her curls whipped against her cheeks.

"I can't. I don't know anything. I haven't seen him since the night—the night Hank and Robert were killed. You heard about that, didn't you?"

"Yes, I know. It was hell, wasn't it? And Bud was hurt too, wasn't he?"

"Yes. Not very bad though. He rode away; I don't know where. He said he would be back before long. That's all."

Georgia began biting her nails which already were ragged from biting. They were, Alice thought, like the Lady Glyneth's in the fairy tale. She felt sorry for Georgia though not altogether knowing why.

"I'm worried," said Georgia. "I'm terribly worried. About Bud. He's running hog-wild lately. Alice, can't you tell? Hank is dead now, isn't he? And Robert, too! I didn't know them so well but—Oh, there are a few things I do know, and I'm scared for Bud! Where is he? Why can't I find him and make him stop!"

Alice began to see that though she had loved Charlie Briscoe so deeply in her way, so tenderly, another girl could love him too, and fiercely. She forgot some of her own sorrows, sorrowing for this strange girl.

"I am mighty glad you came to see us, Georgia," she said quite simply. "I even wish you had come sooner! You had better tell me some things, hadn't you? Tell me what do you mean when you say you want to make him stop. Stop what, Georgia?"

Georgia jumped up and lifted her long trailing riding skirt and walked up and down the small porch like an angry young tigress in her cage.

She came to a sudden stop in front of Alice.

"What'll I tell you?" she cried hotly. "You know, anyhow you ought to know; I guess you know him a whole lot better than I do, you being his sister and knowing him all your life, me never having seen him until three months ago! You know how sweet he is, Alice; you know how wonderful he is—and you know what a devil he is, too! And you know he don't care for God or the devil when he's running wild! And you know how he gets his money, you know the things he does—Oh, Alice!"

She was very young, was Georgia Hill, very loving and warm blooded and impulsive. She let herself go. She dropped down on her knees before Bud's sister and stretched out her arms, not meaning to be dramatic, not helping it; drama and melodrama were in her blood, and her heart was beating so that it was a pain in her breast.

"Alice! You love him too, don't you? In your way, I mean, just the way a sister does, not the way I do, but anyhow you do love him. Let's save him, Alice! You and me, let's save Bud from—from being the way Hank and Robert are right now."

Alice shivered. Those dear boys, Hank with his broad grin and a dimple at the right side of his mouth, Robert with his warm eyes and warm heart and the funny cowlick in his hair. Dead now; so young and yet dead. And Charlie?

But there was Georgia on her knees before her, Georgia loving Charlie with all her heart, and terribly concerned about him.

Alice put both her hands on the other girl's shoulders; she said softly,

"Tell me, Georgia. You are so worried about Charlie—you call him Bud but I call him Charlie. It doesn't matter. Tell me. Why are you so frightened?"

Georgia opened her lips to speak, but her small white teeth were close clamped together and she didn't say anything right away. Then she sprang to her feet, stiff and tense, and exclaimed,

"Because I love him so! Because he is sliding down the devil's chute clean to hell! Because, if we can't stop him, I tell you he's going to be dead like Hank and Robert soon! That's why I'm scared."

She paused a moment; her deep breast rose and tightened; she said explosively,

"You know all about Big Belle, don't you? You are not just a blind little fool, are you? *You know!*"

Alice's hands twisted in her lap.

"What is it? What am I supposed to know?"

"But you do know!"

Alice mutely asked herself, Do I know? Am I just hiding from the truth? And she said to herself, Oh God, *don't!*

She said to Georgia,

"Tell me. What about Big Belle?"

"She wore rings and bracelets that everybody in California knows! Those red rings and that bracelet of hers are known from Nevada City to Monterey! Bud gave me a red ring, a lovely red, red ring. The sheriff came and took it away from me, the same time he took Nate Briscoe, the same time a man named Jeff Morgan shot Nate's heels off and shot Nate's gun out of his hand—he could have killed him, I guess, for that man Jeff

202

Morgan is like sudden death. Oh, why am I telling you all these crazy things? I am trying to tell you about Big Belle of Nevada City, that's it. You see I used to live with her; she was like a mother to all us girls. She was great. She's dead now. They shot her down because she yelled her head off when they tried to grab her rings and bracelets. And—and Bud gave me a ring, and I know—Oh, God!"

Georgia was trembling; she broke down and began to cry. Alice sat as stiff as a tiger lily on its stalk. Her eyes stared straight ahead, cold eyes that were unseeing as a confusion of images shimmered like heat waves in her brain—and with apprehension for Charlie came thoughts of Jeff Morgan, that same Jefferson Davis Morgan who had shot Nate's heels off, who had shot the gun out of his hand; the same Jefferson Davis Morgan who had gripped her so tightly in his arms, who had kissed her, who had said "I love you! I am going to kill your brother and then I am coming back for you! You can't get away from it!" Or something like that.

And she thought of the magnet and the steel, of the twig going down over the waterfall.

She gripped Georgia's hand. She said, her voice low and stilled,

"Georgia, I guess there are a lot of things we don't know. Don't cry, Georgia. I have cried my head off all this week; it doesn't do any good, does it? Let's see what we can do. Can we do anything? If Charlie—you call him Bud—is in trouble, can we help him? I don't know where he is. Tell me what his trouble is, tell me, if you can, how we can find him. And then we—"

"We?" cried Georgia. "What can we do? There's Nate Briscoe; he's as crooked as a stake and rider fence down in Georgia; that's where I come from. They've got him in jail now, haven't they? They're going to hang him, you'll see, and serve him right. But Bud—They can't hang Bud! But they will—unless—Oh, I am going crazy!"

"Georgia! You don't mean—"

Georgia sat down on the edge of the porch and buried her face in her hands.

"I don't mean anything! I just know that Bud has a gang with him that will do whatever crazy thing he says; I know they are going to rob the bank in Yellow Jacket when already Bud has enough money hid away in the hills to last a king a thousand years! And I know that Hank and Robert knew, and Rawlings knew, and I guess everybody knows by now, but Bud don't know that they know—and they will grab him down—and they will hang him the same as Nate—*and I can't find Bud to tell him to lay off!*"

Alice thought of the dogs which were guardians of the trail when Bud came down into the valley—how always he was living in the foreboding of being followed and of how he

204

always had to keep looking back over his shoulder.

The two girls sat very still and the valley was still all about them. The world itself seemed to stand still.

CHAPTER XVI
WHEN THE STAGE CAME IN

THE down grade stage, its horses at the final dead run and pounding up yellowish puffs of dust, swept into the little town of Yellow Jacket. It was late afternoon and the tiny settlement drowsed under a genial summer sun. Men pushed their way out of one and another saloon door, out of the Silver Mirror and out of the hotel and other places, to watch the stage come in.

Jefferson Davis Morgan came out of the Silver Mirror along with the rest; he had been in Yellow Jacket a couple of hours, looking the place over, finding the bank, sizing up its location with regard to certain outside vantage points. Today was the day that Robert Briscoe had said Bud meant to rob the bank. Every chance, judged young Morgan, was against the carrying out of Bud Briscoe's plan. Since its inception he had been wounded, if only slightly; his two brothers had been killed; there had been the general mess created by Rawlings trying to horn in. Yet there was always the off chance: The possibility resided within the

205

undealt cards that Jeff Morgan might have a rendezvous here today, appointed by fate, with Bud Briscoe.

He watched the passengers alight in front of the hotel, three men in their linen dusters and an old woman with a bundle; he saw them go into the hotel. He saw the baggage removed from the boot and dumped on the plank sidewalk; he saw, too, that with the stage driver on the high front seat there was a guard with a Winchester, and he noted that the guard stayed in his place. Then the stage drove on down the road and stopped at the bank. Two men came out; they and the guard carried a box into the bank.

In front of the bank there was the usual hitching rail and at the rail several saddled horses. One of them was Jeff's. Jeff strolled along the street, his eyes everywhere at once though his attitude was that of a chance loiterer. He stopped to roll and light a cigarette; he saw that the stage had gone on its way to the stable and that men who had surged out of saloons had gone again about their business, either returning to the bars or going to their horses or wagons and starting home. Yellow Jacket, ten minutes after the arrival of the stage, slept in the mild summer sun.

Jeff looked carefully at every horse along the street, especially at the horses near the bank, trying to find one he might recognize—Bud Briscoe's horse. But there was none that he knew.

He strolled along, passed the bank, glanced in, kept strolling on to the corner. His cigarette went out; he stopped, scratched a match on the sole of his boot, looked down the side street. It was empty, flat with silence.

He thought, I was pretty sure he wouldn't show up today, but a man never knows; I'm not sorry that I rode twenty miles to find out. No hurry, though; there is always the off chance.

He turned down the side street, meaning to square the circle about the bank, to have a look at the place from all angles. Behind the bank was a narrow, still street; call it an alley. He saw a man on horseback jogging along lazily, head down, seeming half asleep. He couldn't see the man's face; he didn't know the horse. He turned the corner at the rear of the bank and kept on. He saw another man riding into the narrow street; this man, too, looked half asleep. And so Jeff Morgan, his senses alert, looked after him suspiciously. And he quickened his step: His own horse was tied at the hitching rail in front of the bank, and he might need a horse in a hurry. For, while he was doing his measured thinking, he saw the third rider and then the fourth drifting slowly through the alley; he cast a quick glance over his shoulder and made out that the first of these four had stopped and seemed for a moment at loss whether to turn right or left. And Jeff Morgan knew that here was Bud Briscoe's gang and that they were going to strike through the bank's back door—through back and front, both, perhaps—and he dropped his leisurely stroll and walked swiftly, back to the front of the bank, back to the place where his horse was. And his thumbs were hooked into his belt.

He came to the main street, turned the corner, saw the drowsing horses at the hitching rail, his own among them—and a sudden start along his tense nerves like the plucking of a tight wire, a violin string, made a little ripple of expectancy vibrate through him.

He saw Cass Burdock.

He knew it was Cass Burdock, but when you came right down to it he couldn't have lifted his hand and sworn on the Bible that it was Cass. A funny thing, you might see pretty nearly all of a man, his hands, his body and note his carriage, and yet unless you saw clearly that small portion of him, his face, his eyes and nose and mouth, you couldn't be what you call dead sure. And he didn't see this man's face. In the first place, Cass had his hat brim pulled down, like those other drifters in the quiet alley; on top of that, he was mopping his face with a big red bandana handkerchief exactly as though it were full mid-summer, as though in a terrific heat, his face was streaming with sweat.

And a frowning Jeff Morgan grunted to himself, It's not as hot as all that, my boy. You're in on this with Bud's crowd, or you're cutting in somehow;

and you are nobody in the world but Cass Burdock.

The man swung down from the saddle, threw his horse's reins over the hitching rail and went into the bank. As he did so both hands were lifted to his face; he snapped his bandana up into place, swiftly tied its ends behind his head and thus made himself a mask that would do well enough, a mask such as most bandits used.

And now, Jeff Morgan advised himself, all hell is due to break loose—and Bud Briscoe doesn't seem to be any part of it.

Inspiration visited him; he stepped swiftly to Cass Burdock's horse and said to himself with a pleasant though faintly sardonic chuckle, Here's playing a dirty trick on somebody, and I sure do hope I've got the right man! He pulled the horse's bridle off; he knotted the ends of the reins about the animal's neck, he dropped the bridle itself with its heavy Mexican bit over the hitching rack. He thought, If Cass Burdock comes out on the run and jumps in the saddle for a lively getaway he is going to have him a time!

And a voice said, almost in his ear:

"Hello, Kid Morgan! Playing games, huh? Well, I was young once too, damn if I wasn't."

It was that little evasive dried-up man, Alice's uncle Dick. How he happened to be here just now was something that Jeff Morgan didn't have time to figure out. Perhaps Uncle Dick had, like himself, come by an inkling that there was to be trouble at the Yellow Jacket bank; possibly he had followed Jeff; it could conceivably be that he had arrived by chance. The arm of coincidence is long.

"Have you seen Bud Briscoe?" Jeff demanded. "Is he in town, do you know?"

Uncle Dick squeezed his eyelids together. But before he got around to saying the first word in any answer which he might have bethought him to make "all hell broke out" as Jeff had felt it would.

From within the bank came the reverberating thunder of a shot gun; that deadly instrument, when of the sawed-off variety, can be smuggled in under a man's coat and, loaded with buckshot, can come close to blowing a hole through a brick wall. There was a shout of command, a yell of desperation, three or four quick pistol shots—and then a heavy silence even more ominous than these vicious explosions. A little wisp of acrid smoke, bluish and turning gray and feeble in the sunlight, drifted out through the front door.

Before a man could snap finger and thumb twice, racing figures came plunging out of the bank. There was a tall man with a small canvas bag clutched tight in one hand, a smoking Colt in the other—a red bandana hanging askew over his face yet managing to make a mystery of his features. Cass Burdock, for a bet, carrying a fat percentage of the loot. At any rate he ran to the horse at the tying rack which Jeff Morgan was so sure was Cass Burdock's; he flashed up into the saddle and caught at his reins as his spurs raked his horse's sides—

There were so many things happening all at once, so many men moving as swiftly as men could move, that it was hard to keep the entire picture clear cut and definite:

Out of the corner of his eye, only half consciously, Jeff saw a small rigid figure on horseback across the street—a girl. Later he would know who it was, Alice Briscoe—but right then with his mind divided he couldn't fasten on details which seemed to be on the rim of happenings instead of an essential part. He saw two men dash out at Cass Burdock's heels—they too leaped into their saddles. Some man, weaving queerly, unsteady on his feet, came out as far as the sidewalk just in front of the bank door, fired twice after the fleeing men and then folded up, dropping as limp as a half-sack of flour. There was the sound of other pounding boots within, sounds diminishing; other men were running back to the rear door.

Jeff took to his heels, his gun in his hand, headed toward the alley where he knew the rest of the bandits were bound toward their getaway. Right now he was looking for Bud Briscoe; there was every chance, he decided at last, that Bud was one of those who had attacked from the rear. He was only vaguely aware of the fact that Cass

Burdock was having trouble with his horse, that other men were yelling and racing down the street, that Uncle Dick on foot and the girl on horseback were speeding along after him.

He swung the corner, dipped into the alley, saw three horsemen raising great clouds of yellowish dust—and saw Bud Briscoe.

Bud Briscoe ran staggeringly. He stumbled, almost fell, caught himself up and ran on to his horse. A man within the bank, coming to the door, had a long barreled revolver in his hand and fired; Bud staggered and began to sag, then with a desperate effort, a final explosion of all the strength left within him, steadied himself and plunged on.

A burning red rage seared through young Jefferson Davis Morgan; here he had come so long a way to get Bud Briscoe and some infernal fool in the bank was killing Bud right before his eyes! Damn it, in the name of all that counted on earth, in the name of his murdered pardner Bob Lane, Bud Briscoe belonged to him!

Bud Briscoe made his lurching way to his horse. There was blood on the hand he put up to the saddle horn, there was blood smeared across his face that, save for this high coloring, was as white as a dead man's; he didn't seem able to find his stirrup with his heavy foot.

Jefferson Davis Morgan, shaken with his anger, boosted the man up into his saddle.

"Get the hell out of here, Bud Briscoe," he said,

"and keep going—and go get yourself healed up—and let me kill you. *Ride, you fool!*"

Bud Briscoe didn't consciously hear a word of it. But in the saddle, still clinging to the pommel, he jammed his spurs home *and rode!* He went out of town enveloped in the dust cloud of his own making. And Jeff Morgan, noting neither the girl at the mouth of the alley, nor Uncle Dick who was goggle-eyed not ten steps behind him, sped back through the alley, raced around the corner and toward his own horse at the hitching rail.

And then he burst into joyous, unfettered laughter.

It was Cass Burdock all right! His bandana had been whipped from his face and hung about his neck; his hat was gone; he was having the devil's own time. Why his horse hadn't bolted you wouldn't know unless you knew more equine psychology than any horse does. At any rate there sat Cass Burdock in the saddle, clutching his small canvas bag, never thinking to let it drop—and there already were some forty or fifty interested onlookers gathered—and the horse, raked by vicious spurs, with no bit in its mouth and only the silly reins about its neck, was devoting all its rarest energies to such bucking, sidewinding and sunfishing as it had not remembered to do for many and many a day. And Cass Burdock's long lean body was being snapped back and forth, this way and that, like a cracking bull whip in the

hands of an able mule skinner. He pulled leather—
it did him no good. Jeff Morgan was not the only
man who laughed: Cass Burdock shot high in the
air and landed, sitting down and briefly bereft of
his sense of location, in the thick dust of the road,
and at last his horse departed.

Cass Burdock saw Jeff Morgan, and Jeff nodded
and said:

"Yes, sir, Mr. Burdock. I had the fun of taking
your bridle off. And it's kind of nice to see you
squatting right where you belong, down in the dirt
under other men's heels."

What Cass Burdock said then is no longer of
record, but his words were crisp and vigorous,
short Anglo Saxon words for any man to understand. And, leaping to his feet, he went for his gun
and started shooting.

Jeff Morgan fired just once, not seeming in any
great hurry, and shoved his gun back into its holster. And Burdock, looking bewildered, sat down
again, and this time he did not curse nor did he
rise; he rolled over and lay flat, the small canvas
bag in the dust at his finger tips.

"You sure can shoot a gun," said a voice admir-
ingly, Uncle Dick's voice.

"Yes, I can shoot," said Jeff. "I didn't kill him,
you'll find. But he's safe for the good folks of
Yellow Jacket to take home with them."

"But you let Bud Briscoe go! You helped him
get away! Dammit, I saw you! Are you crazy?"

"Crazy? I guess so."

He stalked away, going for his horse. He didn't even remember the girl on horseback. He was thinking wrathfully, "Every time I see that damned murdering dog, Bud Briscoe, he cheats me. I'll get him yet if I have to follow him round the world, if I have to wait for him until I'm bald headed and have shed all my teeth."

From the hitching rail he looked in through the open front door of the bank; he saw a man lying on the floor, the manager perhaps, probably dead. There was another man badly hurt, down on his hands and knees, trying to get up. The place was blue with smoke. He made out no other details but went up into his saddle. And just then, as he was reining his horse sharply around, meaning to head along after Bud Briscoe, he for the second time glimpsed Alice. She was white-faced, her big eyes enormous with horror; she sat rigid in her saddle and stared at him.

He pulled his horse in and rode to her with the growing crowd milling around them.

"What are you doing here?" he demanded. "You and that precious uncle of yours?"

She spoke in a queerly hushed voice, and he thought that she was like some little girl walking in her sleep.

"Robert told me—that night you came for me, the night he died—that today at the bank—Oh, I wouldn't believe it! But I had to come. And

Uncle Dick—I think he followed you. And Charlie—"

"Bud is on his way out of town, where to, I don't know." He leaned out of the saddle and put his hand on hers, frozen to her saddle horn. "You go home, Alice."

She whipped her hand out from under his.

"Don't touch me—Don't ever touch me again! You killer! I just saw you kill Cass!"

He grew angry and jerked his shoulders up. Then again he whirled his horse on its two rear hooves, its forelegs flailing the air, used his spurs and shot away, out of town like Bud Briscoe, headed the same way.

Bud Briscoe had vanished. Jeff only knew that he had headed out of town in the general direction of Settlers' Gap, which was also in the general direction of Black Gulch, of Green Water Valley, of the wild mountains beyond. There was no trustworthy tale to be told by the tracks in the dusty road; several men had gone pounding out of town this way within a handful of minutes and there was still high dust hanging in the air. Bud Briscoe might have ridden steadily on in the road or he might have somewhere swung aside striking across its rocky rim, its dry yellow grass leaving a track you couldn't find unless you went back and hunted every foot of the way with a pair of eyes sharpened to the efficacy of a magnifying glass. That

216

way you'd lose time and you'd therefore lose your quarry—providing he kept on riding, providing he wasn't so dangerously wounded that he dropped out of his saddle.

"Here I've put Nate Briscoe in his place, and rightly I had no great quarrel with him," grumbled a disgruntled Jefferson Davis Morgan, "and here I've burned Cass Burdock down, leaving him holding the bag, and what the hell do I care about Cass Burdock? And here Bud Briscoe runs out on me again! Next time—"

He was riding as fast as his horse could slam hooves down, pick 'em up and slam 'em down again. He tautened his reins; he rode more slowly. He'd take his time. And the one thing he would do was find Bud Briscoe, dead or alive. He just yearned to find him alive—so that he could leave him dead.

He settled comfortably, loosely in the saddle, and rolled a slow cigarette.

CHAPTER XVII
A SIGNAL MEANT TO BE SECRET

WITH passing days, Jefferson Davis Morgan doggedly hunted down his quarry, just praying within his heart that Bud Briscoe hadn't died of his wounds. All that Jeff knew was that the man couldn't have gone very far, not clean out of the country; that he had ridden into Yellow Jacket from a certain general direction, that he had ridden out of town in a certain direction; that he must have holed-up somewhere over toward Settlers' Gap, over beyond Green Water Valley, somewhere in the dour, sharp-pinnacled mountains. And throughout those mountains Jeff Morgan sought him with the perseverance of a young lover seeking the star of his life.

"He won't die," said young Morgan. "He's too tough. Besides, he wasn't hurt bad enough for that. I'll find him all right. Hell's bells, that's what I am here for, or is it?"

Yes, that was what he wanted most on earth—or was it? He couldn't keep his thoughts from flocking like homing pigeons about Alice Briscoe's bright, proud head; and he couldn't very well forget how she had looked at him there in Yellow Jacket's dusty street, hateful of him, calling him "Killer!"

He came into a remote valley which a stranger entered all unexpectedly, a high green and fertile place reached through a crooked, narrow pass, and there was a bright stream cleaving it, and there were shady trees and a wall of rock down which a waterfall leaped into a great deep pool, and the place was not above a dozen miles from his own camp near Settlers' Gap. He said to himself, Ah! Here's the sort of place Bud Briscoe would hide in, secret and solitary, to lick his wounds. There'll be a cabin hid in the woods, or a cave shoving deep into the mountain, and there he'll be. Waiting for me!

He had his blanket roll with him, his rifle in its boot, a pack of food. He picked a spot in a young grove of firs, hidden, and bivouacked overnight. He communed with himself as solitary men always do; he said, flexing his muscles and filling his chest with the tangy air of these uplands, This is my valley, too. I have come home. Green Water Valley first, then this one, then all the running miles in between. And on a high place somewhere a house. I'll pick out a dozen likely spots; then I'll show them all to Alice and let her make her choice!

But he had to kill Bud Briscoe first. And you have to find your game before you can mark it down.

So he kept on hunting.

And he found Alice.

And he found Uncle Dick.

And he found something else!

He hunted throughout that secret place and back in the gorges behind it for three days. He named it, dealing right off the top, Waterfall Valley since that name would identify it; there were other waterfalls and they were bright and gay and full of life, singing eternally, making merry music echo somehow in a man's blood. Into the biggest pool, clear and cold and alive with trout, he dived and swam a brief moment only to gasp and laugh and crawl out with all speed. Drying himself the best he could, his restless eyes always roving afar, he said, Here's another place just made for a man to make his home on! I'll make it of those big flat granite rocks to start with, then great big logs, three feet thick and sixty feet long for walls! And a trail down to the bathing place. And he called that place, not looking at any time for fancy names, Bathtub Swimming Hole. And he wondered whether Alice could swim? It would be great, teaching her.

Then, only a few minutes later came the first of his three discoveries, if a discovery this one was. It was Alice. He found her—or she found him. She rode into his Waterfall Valley and they saw each other.

She was hauntingly pretty this golden young summer morning; he'd never be able to get her out of his head and he knew it. Also she looked somehow cool and distant—like, say, far off hill-tops with snow on them. She still remembered that day in Yellow Jacket, remembered him shooting down Cass Burdock.

"Well," he thought, "she's mighty darn young. She can't be much over sixteen, maybe seventeen." Himself, he felt very old, very mature. He thought, I guess for a nice girl like her it's not much fun watching men she knows, shooting at each other.

He knotted his bandana about his lean brown

throat and stepped along from where he had been sunning himself on a rock after his bath and swift dressing. He touched his hat brim; he tried to sound and appear quite casual, though she had set his heart leaping like those quick fish he had disturbed in their pool.

"I am looking for Charlie," she said.

He didn't speak. Her eyes drifted across his face, then away. She said:

"You have been looking for him, too."

He nodded. "Yes."

"Have you found him? Do you know where he is?"

He shook his head. He came closer and wreathed his hand in her horse's mane. She pulled the animal back, away from contact with him.

"No," he said. Then he added, "You're angry with me, Alice. You're hating me, anyhow you're trying to hate me. Why? You know I love you, that when you come right down to it you're the only thing in the world I do love."

She looked scornful; he wished she wouldn't look that way. She said bleakly, "Love? What is love, I wonder. You are looking for Charlie to kill him. You are hunting my brother down to kill him, and you say you love me!"

"I don't exactly want to kill him any longer," said Jeff, very deliberate. "I guess I used to; I don't now. But he's got to be killed, Alice; you know that."

"I don't know!" Her small, gauntleted hands were clenched; she even, though quite involuntarily, lifted her riding quirt. "You have no right!"

"I don't hanker for the job," he said, and it was the very first time she had ever heard that weary note in his voice. "Just the same, it's got to be done. He's got it coming. And, I tell you, you know it."

She sat there biting her lips; he saw her fighting back the tears; he understood how she had to struggle with herself before she could go on.

"Hank is dead," she said after a little while. "Robert is dead. Nate Briscoe is dead—"

"Nate? I didn't know that!"

"After the—after the bank robbery. They broke into the jail and dragged Nate out. He was begging with them, he was screaming—they didn't care. They took him out and threw a rope over the cottonwood limb—They were just like you are! Oh, they were hard, brutal, merciless men!"

"Nate Briscoe had it coming to him," said Jeff.

"Haven't you any pity in you? Any warm, human blood!"

"Yes, I have. I get sorry for folks too. But there's nothing you can do about it. They all get their chance; whatever a man does, he's got to take what comes. That's fair. Maybe kind of tough, times; but fair."

"And you! You've never done anything wrong in your precious life!"

"Yes, I have. I guess everybody slips up, times. I don't see how it's possible, but even you maybe sometimes slip. But I believe in keeping the law, Alice, and if not, then taking what comes."

"The law! You'd obey the law always, no matter what law!" She began to talk wildly; she knew it, just couldn't help it. She cried out, "If men made a law that you couldn't carry a gun—you'd obey that, wouldn't you!"

The first hint of a wintry smile touched his lips.

"Come now, Alice," he said gently, "I don't think they'd ever do a thing like that—no more than they would say it's against the law to breathe. You're just all worked up, that's all."

"Where is Uncle Dick?" she asked. She had curbed herself; her mood had changed; her voice sounded flat.

"I don't know. I haven't seen him since that day in Yellow Jacket. Maybe he is over at my place this side of Settlers' Gap."

"*Your* place?"

"Yes. I've come to stay, you know. I've picked up a little piece of ground there. Then there's this place." His arm swept out; his gesture had the effect of registering his personal claim to everything within sight. "I'm going to find out about it; I'm going to own it some day. I like it here. Then—The first time I ever saw Green Water Valley I sort of fell in love with it too."

"My!" she mocked him, anger still in her heart.

223

"What a big, loving heart you must have, Mr. Jefferson Davis Morgan! You can love all these things—and still have so much room for hate."

He rubbed his jaw. "I get kind of rattled, times," he said quite simply. "Yes, I can love. I can love like all hell, Alice. But I don't know so well about hate." He looked at her loveliness steadily and yearningly; he drew a deep breath and his eyes wandered away, taking in all the glory of the bright solitary valley of the waterfalls. "I can't right now," he finished, his eyes back on hers, his eyes not quite smiling but almost, yet grave, too, "I can't right now," he said, "seem to be able to do a right good, bang-up job of hating."

"Oh, Jeff!"

Then she saw in a flash that she had been led to misinterpret him; he just meant that he couldn't quite hate a man the way he would like to—but he could and would go on hunting him, shoot him down in cold blood.

"I hate *you!*" she flared out at him, and whirled her horse and fled away.

He had a dream that night, a funny sort of dream. In it he was squatting over a camp fire with Bob Lane, and Bob was just like he used to be, good-humored, chuckling, easy going; and Bob had said, "Aw, shucks, Jeff, you don't have to go kill this Briscoe hombre just because he killed me! I don't mind a-tall being dead, Jeff; it's kind of fun.

Yeah, it's different, but when you get used to it, it's the real stuff. I got a good rest for a change, and my feet sure rested up and the sore spots went away. I must have slept like a winter bear waiting for spring. Lately things have been bully; I don't have to do a lot of things that always was a damn nuisance anyhow, and I got the show to do all the things I always did want and never got around to. Hell, Jeff, let the critter go: You don't have to kill Bud Briscoe; you can just leave him be." And he dreamed that Bob stood up and grinned and stretched, and thwacked him on the back and said, "I got to be on my way, Jeff. Remember Molly I told you about once?" Bob's grin broadened. "She's dead, too; ain't that something? See that long, kind of bright cloud roosting on the hills where the sun's coming up? She's waiting there for me and I got to shake a leg. So long, Jeff."

That dream stuck in Jeff's head all day, as stubborn as a cockle burr in a horse's tail. He said to himself, "Well, it might be like that! Who knows, anyhow?" But as full day dissipated all shadows, all uncertainties seemed to take flight with them. "Hell, it was just a dream," said Jeff, and saddled and rode again.

He rode out of his valley of waterfalls, heading back toward the Settlers' Gap camp. He had hunted high and low, tirelessly, keen-eyed, and had found never a fresh horse track, never the print of a boot not his own. Well, it wouldn't be long. He felt in his bones that Bud Briscoe was no great distance away; that a meeting between the two was inevitable; as he quite simply put the matter to himself, it was in the cards.

His way wound through crooked ravines, across wooded flats, down steep rocky slopes, up over a ridge and into view of Settlers' Gap. He rode down through the pines, and as always he was alert, always watching for some track, some sign, listening for some sound foreign to the hushed breathing of the forests.

He caught a glimpse through the trees of a small upstanding blue smoke; he saw briefly the gray glint of the boulders about his own place, had a glimpse of the dark walls. But watchful as were his eyes there was something he did not see.

It lay across the top of a granite rock; it was as still and as deadly as a rattlesnake before it strikes. It was a rifle barrel, and behind it, crouching in the shelter of the bulwark of granite, was Bud Briscoe.

The crack of the rifle echoed snarlingly through the mountains. Jeff Morgan felt the shock of the bullet, and it shook him in the saddle. Beginning to pitch forward, he managed to pivot slightly; he caught belatedly the glint of sunlight on the rifle barrel and saw a man's hat. Just before he folded up with consciousness beginning to grow dim and fade out of him, he lifted his gun and blazed away. He fired the one shot, and after that he didn't know exactly what happened.

And the first thing he did know after that, he was looking in a puzzled fashion up into the shrewd, pinched-up face of Uncle Dick. He was lying on a bunk, and the bunk, he made out after scowling at everything in sight, was in his own stone house on the rim of the flats overlooking Settlers' Gap. And he remembered the rifle shot, and its blow as hard as a clenched fist in a man's face. Somebody, hiding in the brush, had shot him. Why, the dirty devil!

His first words were, "Who did this to me? Wait until I get him!"

Uncle Dick tucked in the corners of his tight mouth.

"Damn you, Jeff Morgan," he chirped cheerfully, "you're a hard man to kill. Here you be, with a Winchester thirty-thirty bullet through you—as close as I can figger it went square through your heart!—or have you got any heart, and where do you wear it?—and here you ought to be dead and you sort of look like you wanted a venison steak and a pot of beans!"

Jeff Morgan grinned; he grinned rather foolishly but that was all right because just then he felt foolish. He said:

"Dammit, Uncle Dick, I guess I'm going crazy!"

Uncle Dick snorted that noble snort of his. He remarked dryly:

"Most folks does. And most folks don't have to go very far! Now what, son?"

"I've got into a funny way of dreaming crazy dreams. I dreamed last night that my old pardner, Bob Lane—he's dead now—had a long talk with me, and so help me, Uncle Dick, it was just like the truth. And just now, dropping off in a sort of doze because of a bullet, I dreamed about Alice. I thought she was here! And that, just like dreaming about Bob, was so damn real!"

Again Uncle Dick snorted. This was probably the crowning snort of his entire career.

"So you dropped off into a doze, did you, Mr. Morgan." He wiped his brow with a grimy hand, gave a flip to his fingers. "Why damn you, Kid Morgan, you've been laying here flat on your back, 'ceptin' when I wrestled with you and flung you back onto the bunk, for four mortal days and nights! Crazy? We-ll, I reckon. I sure do agree."

Jeff tried to surge up on a treacherous elbow, fell back. He stared at the rafters.

"Then she was here," he said.

"Yep. She was. She ain't now. Mostly, I reckon it was her pulled you through. Then, seeing you was going to scrape through, she goes out and washes her hands and puts on her hat. 'I hope he dies!' she says, and goes away."

Jeff nodded weakly. Yes, that would be Alice. He said:

"Who shot me? Bud Briscoe, wasn't it?"

"Reckon," said Uncle Dick. "I heard the shooting, I drug you in here. I looked around. You shot him, too, I'd say. Behind a big rock where he had squatted there was a little splash of browny stuff that might be dried blood. There was likewise a couple empty Winchester shells. And there was about forty cigarette butts; them ends off'n his cigarettes tole me it was Charlie. Ever notice how he twists his cigarette end, pinching it out? Nobody else does that. He must have laid there a couple hours, waiting for you. You huntin' him, and he shoots you down!" He concluded with a very commendable snort.

"You say I shot Bud?" said Jeff. "You're pretty sure?" Then, when Uncle Dick nodded emphatically, Jeff asked, "You can't guess whether I hurt him pretty bad or just scratched him? Anyhow, he got away before you got there?"

"There was a good splash of blood," said Uncle Dick. "That's all I know. He got away and I don't know where he went. I guess he was pretty sure you was dead when he weaved up onto his horse and got going."

Jeff took his ease for a while. He even dropped off to sleep for a while and thereafter Uncle Dick fed him with a spoon.

Again slow days dribbled by. At first Jeff Morgan's returning strength came back to him very slowly; he had grown pallid and gaunt and haggard-eyed; he knew that he must have died save for Alice and Uncle Dick working over him and he knew that even now, though Alice did not come again, he was well nigh helpless without the shrewd-eyed Uncle Dick. Not used to illness of any sort, he found his condition vastly irksome, and grew short-tempered and irritable. But Uncle Dick, never raising any question about ceasing to take care of him, gave no sign of being affected by Jeff's sharpening tongue. And then one day, awaking to feel better and stronger, Jeff Morgan laughed.

"You've been a mighty good and long suffering friend, Uncle Dick," he said. "Some day when you need a keeper, yell for me and I'll come running. Now I've started to mend and you just watch me! I feel like poking around; I could go for a general clean up, shave and hair cut both." He rubbed his jaw and cheek, cloaked in a dark untidy growth. "I'll be forking a horse pretty pronto, too."

"I'll go shake up some coffee and flapjacks," said Uncle Dick. "Likewise some beans and bacon."

The cabin's interior during his incarceration had been made almost cozy and homelike; from Settlers' Gap Uncle Dick had hauled in an old second hand table, a couple of chairs, some odds and ends of kitchen things; there was even a piece of red oilcloth on the table. There was tobacco, a pipe, a hammer and a handful of nails and a short handled ax. Leaning against the wall was a pick; there was fresh dirt on it.

Uncle Dick took up a bucket, announced he'd

step along to the spring and get some water, and went out. Jeff lay quiet, a smile touching his bearded lips as he regarded the pick.

"The old cuss is on the trail to something," he told himself. "Bud Briscoe's cache, of course. Well, I hope he finds it!"

Something prompted him to slip out of his bunk and go to the door standing open. He saw Uncle Dick going on his way, blithe as a cricket, his bucket swinging and flashing in the newly risen sun. But he didn't go straight to the spring. Instead he veered into a clearing, crossed it to the bushes rimming it on the farther side, and drew forth a long, freshly-peeled pole. At the top of the pole a square white cloth was attached: Uncle Dick set the pole up in the heart of the clearing, shoving its butt into a hole already made and ringed about with rocks. This task done the old fellow stepped along to the spring.

Jeff shuffled back to his bunk. A white cloth atop a pole, huh? Something you could see from far off—say from the top of the ridge beyond Settlers' Gap. Yes, you could see it for miles—if you knew where to look for it—and if you happened to have a spy glass!

"Yep, it's time I was up and around," he said cheerfully when Uncle Dick, slopping water from his full bucket, returned. "I'm the same as on my feet right now. I've a hankering to make a couple of visits to a couple of folks."

"One of 'em might be Bud Briscoe, if you can find him?"

"Might."

"And one might be Allie, huh?"

"Might," grinned Jefferson Davis Morgan.

CHAPTER XVIII
THEY MET ON THE TRAIL

ON a lazy, sun-drenched afternoon—the summer was advancing and the world was a nice, warm and lazy place in which to abide—Jefferson Davis Morgan rode again down into Green Water Valley. As he drew near the long log cabin on the knoll there was a furious baying of dogs and, as once before, he thought of them as ravening, slavering wolves. He saw them, five or six of the great beasts, start toward him in a pack and involuntarily his hand dropped to his hip; the brutes, left to their own devices he was sure would like nothing better than to drag a stranger down out of the saddle and tear him to pieces. But instantly a heavy voice boomed out, commanding the dogs to shut up and lay down, and they withdrew, growling and grumbling and lapping their wet jaws with their red tongues, and returned to the yard in front of the cabin porch.

George Briscoe came out a few steps and looked to see who the newcomer might be.

"Howdy, stranger," he said gruffly.

"Howdy," said Jeff. "You're George Briscoe, I guess? Me, I'm Jefferson Davis Morgan."

George Briscoe regarded him soberly, nothing affable about him. Taking his time about it, at last he said,

"Thought you might be. I've heard about you. Well, what do you want?"

"Wonder if your dogs would eat me up if I got down to shake hands?"

"Might. And what do we want to shake hands for?"

Jeff swung down from the saddle, stepped forward and put out his hand.

"We're neighbors now," he said. "I've dug in for the time at Settlers' Gap. I am going to dig in deeper. Being neighbors, I thought I'd drop in. Likewise, maybe you want to sell and I might want to buy the Green Water. Likewise again, is Miss Alice at home? I'd like real well to see her."

The dogs came stealthily forward, growling and bristling. George Briscoe kicked one of them in the ribs, commanded, "Get back, damn you," and surrendered a big, thick hand into Jeff's.

"Come up on the porch and squat," he said. "We'll talk. Yes, Allie's in the house."

There were bench, rawhide-bottomed chair and crooked, home-made rocker on the small porch. They sat. The dogs drew off, a couple of them crawling under the porch, one lying in the yard a few feet away, muzzle between great paws and hard, suspicious eyes on the visitor, the two others betaking themselves out of sight to parts unknown.

"I've seen a good deal of your brother Dick," said Jeff by way of breaking the ice.

George Briscoe surprised him by saying in his heavy, blunt fashion,

"Dick ain't no brother of mine. You can tell him I said so. I don't know who the hell he is."

"Why, I thought—"

"So did I. So we all did. I know better now. I ain't seen my brother Dick since we was boys, forty years ago;. I wrote Dick a letter last year. After a while he answered. He said he was coming out here. This man comes and says he is Dick. He is a damn liar. Maybe he killed Dick and stole some of Dick's things, anyhow he had 'em. That's all I know. If ever he comes back here I'll shoot him on sight. I reckon somehow he knows that; anyhow he's keeping away."

"I'll be damned!" said Jeff.

"Me, too," said George Briscoe.

"What is he up to? What does the man want?"

George Briscoe's beefy shoulders rippled in a mild shrug.

"Like the feller says," he remarked dryly, "I don't know, don't care, ain't the least interested and don't give a damn—so long as he keeps out from under my feet. Now what about buying my place? Who told you I'd sell?"

"Uncle Dick did. How'd you figure out he wasn't your brother, after at first being fooled?"

234

"Something put it into my head, I don't rec'lec' just what it was at first. So I didn't say anything. After a while I asked him if he'd ever heard anything in late years about the Talbot boys that we used to swim with in the old swimming hole. Ben Talbot and Johnny, I said. And he took a minute to scratch his jaw, and then he said seems as though he'd heard how Ben got killed in the War and Johnny had moved west and took up with a squaw. Then I knowed for sure."

"But how—"

"There never was any Ben and Johnny Talbot that I ever heard of; I just made 'em up. And I never could swim, and there wasn't any swimming hole."

Jeff had to laugh. A slick old customer was Uncle Dick, but it would appear that he had measured his horns with one just as smooth.

Jeff said, "Well." And then they sat silent a while and after that prolonged silence, during which he was always listening, hoping for the sound of Alice's light quick footsteps, he was about to speak when George Briscoe forestalled him.

"So you think maybe you'd like to buy Green Water Valley?" he said.

"There's only one thing in the world I'd like better," said Jeff, still harkening for some sign of Alice's coming. Then he added, "Yes. Suppose we make a deal?"

"Got some money, have you?"

Jeff nodded. "Yes. I've got money."

"Maybe it's in your pocket, in a money belt," said George Briscoe. "Maybe you've got it in cash? Maybe in a bank?"

"Yes, in a bank. In my personal bank, one that belongs to me."

George Briscoe's heavy black brows went up. Uncle Dick had fooled him for a time, but he wasn't the man to be fooled by many or for long.

"So you've got a bank, too, all your own, huh? A thing like that comes in handy, times, don't it? This bank of yours, now; you didn't say where it was."

Jeff grinned at him and answered with a chuckle.

"A safe bank, mine. It's in a hole in the ground, under a rock. And the money is mostly in gold, the rest in a tin can inside another tin can. Under another rock."

George Briscoe evinced his approval. That was the kind of bank to have! Just look at what happened to the bank in Yellow Jacket only the other day. He considered.

"I'll take ten thousand," he said, and relighted his pipe.

"I'll give you five," said Jeff Morgan, for after all business was business.

Again George Briscoe, a fair man, considered.

"Five thousand is the hell of a lot of money," he conceded. "You get five thousand in your hands

all the same time, it's the hell of a lot of money."
He scratched his head. " 'Tain't enough though,
Morgan. You see I'm going home, back to
Virginia. When I get there I figure on buying back
the old place; it'll be dirt cheap now the way
things are back there, everybody broke flat and
damn little cash money in sight. But it'll cost me
something, and I'll have to fix up the old house
and the sheds and fences and things, and maybe
have to hire a man the first year to help me get
things in shape sort of like they used to be. And,
seeing as how I'm taking Allie with me, and a
young girl like her needs things that cost money,
and the two of us—"

"I can save you some money right at the jump,"
said Jeff coolly. "You don't have to take Alice
with you. You can leave her here; me, I'll take
care of her. You see, Mr. Briscoe, I intend to marry
her. Real soon, too."

Then for the first time he did hear a sound
within the house, and knew that Alice had been all
this while as still as a mouse listening to them, that
she had heard what he had just said, that she must
have started so that she knocked something off the
table against which she was standing. He cocked
his ears for some other sound from her, and
presently heard her quiet stealing away.

George Briscoe pulled for a while at his pipe. He
put up his big, heavy hand and wiped his brow.
The expression of his face did not change, but

then there hadn't been much of anything in the way of an expression upon his impassive features. At last,

"Allie promised herself to you?" he asked.

"No. But she knows I'm in love with her. And," and he lifted his voice so that Alice, he hoped, might hear, "and she loves me too. You know how it is."

Did George Briscoe know? His thoughts shot back across long dead years.

"I'll go get Allie," he said. "We'll talk this thing out."

He went into the cabin; he called, "Allie! Allie, come here." When there came no answer he passed through the string of rooms, calling, "Allie, Allie, where are you?"

He came back to the porch and sat down and re-lighted his pipe.

"She ain't here," he said. "She was here when you rode up, too; she must have got a glimpse of you or heard you talking to me. Now she's gone. That don't sound very much to me, Morgan, like my girl wanted anything to do with you. So suppose you get the hell out of here. And you don't have to come back."

"I'll be seeing you again pretty soon, Mr. Briscoe," said Jeff, and went to his horse and rode away.

But he rode slowly, and his eyes were in the back of his head. He did not strike straight north toward his own place in Settlers' Gap but instead until out of sight from the cabin rode south; one would have said that he was heading toward Black Gulch. In his favor were those several oak groves; he rode beyond one, beyond the next and, with a sharp glance over his shoulder, caught sight of the Briscoe barn. And he saw Alice, mounted already, as she seemed to hesitate a moment, to take note of him and his direction, and then she leaned forward in her saddle, using her spurs, as she shot north.

He used his spurs, too, then, still southbound. But in a crease in the floor of the valley he swung out at a right angle, sped down to the river with its fringe of bushes and vines and willows and aspens, splashed across at the first possible ford and, upon the other, hidden side, swung due north again. And once more he tickled his horse in the flanks with his spurs.

He overhauled her within two or three miles.

His way of overtaking her was after this fashion, because he felt happy to be well and in the saddle again, because it was a gay day in the sunbright world under the fragrant pines, because he anticipated the moment of her surprise; so he raced along, out of her sight with a timbered ridge between them, and got ahead of her and cut back into the trail he knew she was following—and when she rounded a sharp turn in the trail she came upon him, sitting his horse in a lazy sort of way and busying himself with the only thing that seemed to matter just then, that slow rolling of a cigarette with which he occupied himself at times like this one.

"Jeff!" she gasped.

"Alice! My, you look like something a man had dreamed, and then the dream had come true!"

"But—You were down at our place—I saw you riding south—"

"You been dreaming, too?" asked Jeff.

"Don't you dare laugh at me! If you think it's smart—"

"I had to thank you. You see, I got hurt the other day. Some man was out hunting, deer maybe or maybe only rabbits. Anyhow I stepped in front of his gun and got hurt. Hurt pretty bad, too, it seems as though. Then there was your uncle Dick, and he piled me back atop my horse and led me home. And then you happened in and that's what kept me from dying. Anyhow, that's what Uncle Dick says. So you see, I had to thank you. You don't mind much, do you? Any man has got to thank a girl for saving his bacon for him."

"Jeff—"

"You listen, Alice. And listen good. Things get tough, times, for folks; for everybody. But they always get better, give 'em time; they come right-side-up after a while. Now, take you and me—"

"No, Jeff. That's all over; it's something dead, that's all. I guess something is dead inside me, too. You and Charlie—you trying to kill him, him shooting you down, nearly killing you—No, Jeff. My father is going away, back to Virginia, and I am going with him."

She rode on again, still heading north; he rode along with her and for a while did not say anything. He saw a tragic sorrow in her eyes, he felt that life had beaten her down, yet he knew that hers was a valiant soul and would stand straight again—but that, too, hers was a steely determination and that he was on the ragged edge of losing her for all time.

"Alice—"

"Let's not talk, Jeff. . . . There's no use. And I'd rather be alone now."

"You can't be alone," he said, and his voice had a keen, brittle edge of anger. "And you can't run out on me like this. If you go away, I'll come and find you. If you go all the way back to Virginia, I'll come after you. You might as well get used to knowing that. I mean it, Alice."

She looked straight ahead and again they rode on in silence. Then Jeff said,

"You thought I was headed for Black Gulch, so you rode this way. Maybe you are planning on looking up Uncle Dick!"

She did flash her eyes at him then, and they were scornful, angry eyes.

"I heard my father tell you! You know as well as I do that he is not my uncle; he is just like all the rest of the men in the world, or nearly all of them anyway: He is just a cheat and a liar and a—a thief! Yes, I am going to see him; I suppose you and he are still living together! You would! Oh!" She bit her lip, then said hotly, "And I am going to make him give me back my ring and bracelet, the ones with the red stones. They are gone, and I know he stole them."

"Let him keep them," said Jeff gravely. "They are bad luck, Alice; there is blood on them and you know it. They are Big Belle's—"

"I don't care! I won't have that little thief of an Unc—of a Dick Somebody, if even Dick is his name and I bet it isn't—running off with them. I won't!"

Jeff sighed. "You know, it's a funny thing," he said. "Me, too, I've felt in my bones he was a crooked little devil, and just the same I sort of like him. And I guess he did save my life for me—anyhow," he concluded hastily, "he started saving it when he dragged me into the cabin and went to work doctoring me, and you two did pull me through. Yes, I sort of like the little cuss—and, same time I wouldn't trust him out of reach with a two-bit piece. Well, let's see: You want to drop in on Uncle Dick and grab him by the throat and make him come across with his thievings? All right, but I want to be along when you do it. The way I tell you, I don't trust the little geezer."

Alice, bereft of words, said "Hmf!" or something to that effect.

242

They rode on.

"I've told you I want to be alone!" Alice said when she could no longer just ride along like this, side by side with him, so close that they could have held hands, so far apart that the wide world rolled between them.

"You can't," said Jeff simply. "Not today."

So again they rode on.

They came to the place where Alice had tried to ford the stream, where her horse Apache Kid fell, where she ran calling to Jeff. They didn't say anything as they passed on but both remembered. She recalled how he had made the fire for her so that she could dry herself, how he had gone off and had kept whistling so that she would know he was giving her her privacy. That was fine of him; the memory warmed her. And though she was striving so desperately to use her brain as a driving power and to shut her ears to the whisperings of her insistent heart, she did remember how he had kissed her—and, after all, she was only nineteen.

"Jeff!"

"Yes, Alice?"

"Oh, it's no use! I was thinking—No, it's no good. Why don't you leave me, Jeff; you go your way and I'll go mine. Don't you see?"

"You bet I see!" he said emphatically. "Only I see things the way they are, the way they've got to be, and you don't. But you will. You will, Alice girl. If you didn't, why there wouldn't be any sense to anything. You will. And me, I'll wait. Take your time to get it all straight."

She turned her head away; he saw her brush an impatient hand across her eyes. He saw how vagrant strands of her hair brushed against her cheeks. He yearned with a terrible yearning to sweep her out of her saddle and into his arms, and to ride far and far with her, far from all the meshes of the web in which they were tangled. But that would be a violation just now; yes, he'd wait.

Without realizing it he began whistling "Her Bright Smile Haunts Me Still," very, very softly, for he too was thinking of that night when he had sheltered her in the ruin of a cabin, when he had held her so close to him, when she had given back his kiss. "I love her and she loves me and that's all there is to it," he was saying doggedly to himself. "Come hell and high water, she's mine."

Where the trail narrowed, snaking along the side of the gorge pressing in on the thin race of the river, he reined his horse back, letting her ride ahead. His eyes watched her as she swayed in the saddle, letting her body go as the horse under her went, a slim young embodiment of grace and loveliness, and the blue mountains and the tall pines and the great granite boulders splashed with sunshine were nothing. Just Alice Briscoe riding ahead.

When they rode abreast again, he said,

"You know what your precious uncle Dick is up

to, don't you? You know why he is sticking around my place up at Settlers' Gap?"

"He wants to keep out of our sight! I suppose he wants to be with you! Two of a kind!"

"And that's the whole of it?"

"Isn't it?"

"The way he strikes me, your uncle Dick is the kind of guy that likes to grab him off a few souvenirs wherever he goes. He grabbed the red ring and bracelet, you say? Well, what else along that same line might he be looking for?"

"I don't know what you mean!"

He spoke after his deliberate fashion, taking time out to think.

"There was a bank hold-up in Yellow Jacket the other day, wasn't there? Cass Burdock almost got away with a grab of gold, didn't he? Well, did some of the rest of the crowd get away with a few gold pieces? Maybe a few thousand dollars? It seems likely. They didn't eat the money, did they? They haven't had time to go out and spend it or gamble it away, have they? No, because folks were remembering about the thing and would notice if anyone showed up all of a sudden with a lot of spending money. So they took their money and salted it down some place, didn't they?"

"I tell you I don't know what you are talking about!"

"Of course you don't! But maybe Uncle Dick does? You see, I've got some money of my own,

Alice; I've got it hid under a rock. All right, these other men, they've hid their swag, hid it maybe for a long time. And is that what Uncle Dick is looking for?"

She didn't answer. And so, with Alice silent and thoughtful, they still rode on.

CHAPTER XIX
TREASURE TROVE

Now, there's nothing like riding together, two young people in a hushed wilderness, the sun warm upon them, the skies blue, the whisper of a little breeze through the pine tops. There is a rhythm, a quiet throbbing like the beating of steady hearts, and there is a bit of magic, wild woods magic, in the air.

A mile, another mile, still another mile, with the trail winding, a leisurely trail through pleasant places, with the high black cliffs throwing shadows down upon them yet with streaks of sunlight brightening the cliffs so that they were like grim faces contending with smiles, with the depths of silence about them yet with the silence threaded through by the purl of laughing water, with the liquid call of quail, with the whisper through the pines—and there is something very companionable in the creak of saddle leather, the muted jingle of bridle and spur chains, when two people ride together. The sun rays crashed silently into the boles of the pines, and exhilarating fragrances exploded in their softly bursting fashion, like flower petals opening.

There was that rhythm in their horses' hoof-beats; if you listened carefully you could fancy words rising up with the dust puffs, words in unison with whatever was in your heart. About the oldest words in the world are, there is no doubt of it, "I love you." Alice, like one in a dream, listened to the sounds about her, she heard messages in the drumming of their horses' shod hooves. But she kept her face averted from Jefferson Davis Morgan's, and she kept her thoughts locked in her tumultuous breast.

And she didn't speak a single word, and neither did Jeff, until they came into the narrow valley where Settlers' Gap squatted on one side of the winding stream and where Jeff's place was, beyond the other side. And then Alice said, with a quick lift of her voice:

"Why, it's that girl! It's Georgia Hill—she says she's Charlie's girl—with Uncle Dick! What in the world?"

"Sh," Jeff commanded. "We go slow here. Me, I'd like to look in on what the two of them are up to. I get a whiff of something on the wind."

She said scornfully, "You'd spy on them?"

Jeff said, and smiled at her tolerantly, "Ever use a spy glass yourself?"

"Oh! You—" but when he said "Sh!" again she fell silent with him.

Uncle Dick and Georgia had just darted into the stone house, Jeff Morgan's place; they seemed hurried and eager, and Uncle Dick was expostulating, though they failed to catch his words, and Georgia was hanging on to his sleeve.

"I tell you I kind of like that Uncle Dick of yours, uncle or no uncle," chuckled Jefferson Davis Morgan. "He's a great old coot, though maybe tricky."

"I love him," exclaimed the girl impulsively. "I can't help it, even when I know he's a wicked old rascal. And he's no more uncle of mine than he is of yours."

"Let's adopt the poor old devil. It would make it kind of tough and lonesome for him, don't you think, not being anybody's uncle?"

She almost smiled. Something had lifted her spirits up. What? Just riding along? But that would be silly! Still, maybe it's wise to be silly sometimes. How big the world was, how sometimes you felt like Atlas, carrying the whole thing on your shoulders, how much nicer it was to curl up in its embrace, let it mother you. She did smile, though she hurried to hide that shining fact.

"Listen," said Jeff, "and I'll tell you something. I've got what they call a hunch: Uncle Dick has been sticking around for quite a spell and he's been busy about his own business. He's got him a pick; I saw it in my shack. There was fresh dirt on it, and that means he's been digging. Digging for what? What would Uncle Dick be looking for up in this neck of the woods? You see!"

"Digging? Looking for something? Well, some folks say there is gold here, if you can only find it. And—" She pretended not to understand.

"Gold? Sure. Gold that has already been dug up once, that has gone to the mint, that's now in nice ten and twenty dollar gold pieces! The loot of many a bank robbery and stage hold-up, cached away somewhere not too far from Settlers' Gap. And it wouldn't surprise me very much if he has found it!"

She winced; he might as well have said, "Gold that your brother Charlie robbed men of, he and the rest, and hid until the time of a division of spoils." But she let that pass; she said:

"But that girl? Georgia Hill? Why is she here with him?"

"Maybe just looking for Bud? Or, maybe looking for the same thing Uncle Dick is after?"

"But what are they doing in your place?"

"Suppose we find out? What do you say?"

She didn't say anything, but they rode slowly on and slipped out of their saddles in the little grove before you reached the stone house; Jeff tethered their horses there among the young pines and they went forward on foot. Before they came to the door they heard voices, Georgia's first lifted almost into shrillness. She cried out:

"I tell you it's Bud Briscoe's! Bud's and mine! And you just keep your dirty paws off of it!"

Uncle Dick snapped back at her:

"And I tell you it's mine! It's on the public domain, that's what it is! It's what they call treasure trove, by thunder. It's mine, but seeing as how you horned in I'll let you have a share, say ten percent. That is if you've got any sense and will do like I say and keep your mouth shut."

"I won't! I tell you it's Bud's and mine. We're going to take it and go away from here, some-where else a long ways off, and start in living dif-ferent lives. Bud said so."

"So Bud says so, does he?" he mocked her. "And might I ask you where Bud is right now? And whether dead or alive, whether chasing off with some other female? Ain't you got any good sense, Georgia?"

"Bud's not dead! I know he's alive somewhere. Oh, he'll be back! And you can't make me believe anything different, like he's playing around with some other girl. I tell you—"

"Shucks," grumbled old Uncle Dick, "I thought you had some sense but you're just plain silly. Now you better run home—"

Jeff Morgan and Alice Briscoe stood in the doorway, looking into the stone house. Jeff said briefly:

"Hello; what's going on?"

The two whirled about as though his voice had

been a pistol shot; Uncle Dick's narrowed eyes flew wide open for once, giving him a comical look, the whites shining, and Georgia Hill gasped and clapped both hands to her mouth. While Alice Briscoe looked at them penetratingly, worried and half frowning, young Jefferson Davis Morgan began laughing.

"You two look like a couple of kids that have just got caught stealing the jam," he told them. "What's it all about? Not having a lovers' meeting, are you? Uncle Dick, shame on you if you are breaking this girl's heart, maybe eloping with her."

Uncle Dick's eyelids came down and Georgia dropped her hands to her sides, but her hands were tight clenched, and there was a high, hot color in her cheeks. Uncle Dick, a hard man to upset at any time, a man who knew the way back to his poise if for a moment he had lost it, treated them to a sort of dry cackle as though he saw the joke and it wasn't a bad one.

"You most scared me out'n my boots, Jeff Morgan," he said. "You popped up as sudden and as quiet as toadstools after a good warm rain. Hello, Allie—"

"So you found it, did you?" said Alice icily.

He looked the very part of bewildered innocence.

"Found it? Found what?" he asked.

"Where is it?" she demanded. "It doesn't belong to you, and you know it. And no part of it belongs to Miss Hill."

"Now, you look here, Allie! I don't know what you're talking about! But I do know that you never talked to your old uncle Dick like this before, and—"

"*Uncle Dick!*" she said scornfully, though even then with him getting ready to wheedle her she couldn't help feeling a glow of affection for the old rascal. "You are no uncle of mine and you know it and so do I. And so does my father! Who are you anyway?"

"Why, Allie! What's come over you? You—"

"Never mind all that. Just tell me this: Thinking 'way back to the time you were a boy, you remember the Talbot boys, don't you? Ben and Johnny Talbot? And the old swimming hole?"

"Why, of course I remember! Me and George was talking about them only last—"

"Only it happens," said Alice, cutting across his swift flow of words, "that there weren't any Talbot boys, either Ben or Johnny—and there wasn't even any swimming hole! You fraud!"

Uncle Dick blinked. He began scrubbing at his jaw, he ran his talons through his hair, thoroughly massaging his scalp. He studied her shrewdly, looked at Jeff and saw how Jeff, amused, was watching him flounder. Then Uncle Dick slapped his leg and giggled.

"Caught me, didn't you? Meaning George caught me. We-ll. Hm. So I got caught like a rat in a trap." He shook his finger at her. "Ain't you

252

shamed, Allie, doing a trick like that to me? Do you suppose, if ever I had caught you in a hole of some kind, I'd have tried to make it tough for you? You know better'n that, Allie! You know durned well, 'stead of getting cross with you, I'd have tried to help you out! Ain't you shamed, Allie Briscoe?"

She flushed. Actually, with him looking at her like that, she was almost ashamed. Certainly for a moment she was at a loss for words. Jeff spoke up again.

"Now, you look here, Uncle Dick," he said mildly. And he grinned and added, "Me, anyhow, I can call you Uncle Dick for a while yet, can't I? I haven't disowned you yet, you'll notice, and I'm doggoned if ever I do! You're an old he-dog that ought to be tin-canned and then hung, but you've been sort of like a mother to me while I was laid up with lead poisoning! Just the same you can't get away with murder like you're trying to do. You found Bud's cache, didn't you? You dug it up with that pick of yours, didn't you? And Georgia Hill crept up on you and figures it's fair to split it two ways—but to split it between her and Bud and leave you out in the cold. That's as clear as a big yellow punkin out in the middle of a bare field. You're a smart old devil, and I'm for you, but you're going to be out of luck this time. Where's the loot?"

Uncle Dick sighed, sighed as a horse sighs, his

chest heaving. Jeff Morgan remarked later that the old devil must have some horse blood in him, what with that windy sigh and his frequent equine snorts.

Jeff didn't need to ask the second time. There was a hurried interchange of glances between the old fellow and the girl Georgia; alarm was in the looks they shot at each other, and a caution too. And Jeff at that moment noted that the door leading from the main room into the dug-out at the rear was closed. And that door had stood half open, sagging crazily on its broken hinges like a drunk man on an unstable cane. And he remembered the pick with fresh dirt on it, and also the manner in which both these conspirators had dashed into the house, each seeming in haste to be ahead of the other.

His broad grin broadened still further.

"Why, it's the simplest thing in the world!" he chuckled. "Funny I didn't think of it quicker—the way you did, Uncle Dick! Why did Bu—why did somebody happen to be hanging around, and why pop me out of my saddle? Huh? We were getting too close to it, am I right? And you scratched that old head of yours—Yep, the way you're doing it right now!—and you said to yourself, 'Why, shucks! Of course!' And you and your pick got busy—and Georgia Hill, what with her poking into nooks and corners and old meeting places, poked out here and caught you."

254

"If I knowed what you was talking about, Jeff Morgan—"

"We'll take a look," said Jeff. "Come ahead, Alice; let's see what the neighbors brought in."

He shouldered the door open and Alice, daintily passing between a perturbed Uncle Dick and a hot-faced Georgia Hill without touching either of them, was close behind him. They looked into the dug-out, narrow and cool and damp and as dim as dusk. But, uncertain as the light was, they had no difficulty in seeing all they needed to see:

There was a place in the rear wall—and that wall was the side of the mountain into which the dug-out had been tunneled—a place of broken rock and earth, where Uncle Dick with his pick had excavated. He had been led luckily to the right spot by a gold piece on the floor, well trodden down, yet with a golden new moon of its rim winking back into his shrewd old eyes. He had picked and scooped and clawed, and in the end had come by his "treasure trove." Treasure trove with a vengeance! There on the floor where he had left it, interrupted in his labors, was a wooden cracker box; a side, half rotted away, was broken off, its contents were partly strewn on the ground. A big gold watch, as fat as a turnip, dangled by its heavy gold chain. There were a dozen other watches, a score, more likely, and there were small canvas bags; Jeff kicked one with a careless boot and it jingled softly. Gold, no silver, here;

gold in watches, in minted coins, in the contents of small, heavy tobacco cans where it was stowed away in honest gold dust or nuggets of all sizes.

Jeff whistled softly; Georgia, who had pressed close behind them, gasped; Alice went white and stared with incredulous eyes. And Uncle Dick, who had dropped back, caught up an old, rusty looking carbine from under a ragged blanket and drove its muzzle between Jefferson Davis Morgan's shoulders.

"Stick 'em up, kid," he said tartly, "and make it lively, else I have to kill you."

Jeff Morgan raised his hands as in duty bound. He turned slowly and regarded Uncle Dick for a time in a stony silence; he thought, "The old devil would kill at the drop of the hat." His eyes dropped to the carbine; he had never seen it until now, had never known that Uncle Dick carried any such weapon—and, also, he had never seen a weapon looking so old, so foul with grime and rust. Didn't look as though the darn thing would go off, but then you never could tell; might be just rusty on the outside yet with the bore as bright as a new silver dollar. No, you never could tell.

"That's a good boy, Jeff," said Uncle Dick approvingly. "I ain't looking for trouble with you any time, and you know that. And I'd rather chop both hands off than have trouble with Allie. And I can't even find it in my heart to hurt Georgie's feelings. But the fact is that this here treasure trove is mine and I'm piling it on my horse and moseying along with it right now. And you three folks has got to leave me be. What's right is right, Jeff; that's what I say. All of us respect other folk's feelings, and that way we all stay happy. *And* alive!"

Jeff had to laugh at him. Get mad at this old coot? You just couldn't do it.

"Suppose I get my hands down long enough to roll a smoke while I think?" he offered as a moderate suggestion.

A voice outside spoke with authority. All looked, startled, to the front door and saw, first of all, two rifle barrels trained upon them. Under his breath Uncle Dick muttered irritably, "Doggone the luck."

The voice spoke briefly and to the point.

And the voice belonged to Cass Burdock; there was no mistaking that, and naturally Jefferson Davis Morgan was somewhat taken aback, flabbergasted for the moment in fact, since he had indulged in the fancy that Cass Burdock was altogether out of the picture, safe in jail. But there were the two rifles, and the other man had to be taken into consideration, and more than ever was Jeff at a loss. For as sure as mud is mud, that other man was Rawlings. He had seen Whitey Rawlings dead, absolutely dead, on the floor of the shanty over by the covered bridge. Later he came to find out that he was both right and wrong in his certainty: It was Rawlings all right, but no Rawlings he had ever seen, just the dead man's twin brother. But they looked alike, like two peas in the same pod.

What Cass Burdock had to say, his meaning briefly couched, was:

"No trouble, unless you make it. What we want is what you're trying to steal. Watch your step and you get out of this alive. Step wrong and you're done for. You, Rawlings, step ahead and gather the stuff up. Me, I'm shooting the first one of them, man or woman, who moves a finger."

Rawlings put down his rifle at the side of the door and dragged out his six-gun and stepped forward. Jeff Morgan kept staring at Cass Burdock; he thought, I knocked hell out of him once with my fists, and I fooled him and shot him down the second time—and he hasn't forgot. And so, though Jeff obeyed orders, his hand was ready to leap to his side where his holster hung.

Rawlings, using his left hand, scraped up the fallen articles, watches mostly, and dropped them into the old broken cracker box, while his other hand kept its grip on his gun. He completed his task and stepped slowly backward, the box under his left arm.

Cass Burdock's eyes were everywhere at once; they rested only a second on Alice Briscoe's white face, and Burdock's mouth hardened; they flicked to Jeff Morgan and were hot with hate and the knuckles of the hand on his rifle shone white with tension.

Georgia Hill, watching fascinated as Rawlings stepped backward with the box under his arm, screamed out:

"No! No! You can't do it! That's Bud's and I won't let you steal it from him! You—you robbers!"

So Cass Burdock's eyes, murderous now, shifted instantly to her.

"Shut up, you little fool," he growled. "Do you want a bullet through you? And anyhow—Well, Bud's dead and—"

"It's a lie!" shrilled Georgia. "You lie, Cass!"

Cass Burdock ignored her as he grew watchful again of the two men. And Rawlings said to him out of the corner of a thin-lipped, twisting mouth:

"Hell with her, Cass. Hell with all of 'em. Let's get goin' while the goin's good. And don't you start any killin' less you have to—and if you kill one of 'em, for Gawd's sake kill 'em all so there won't be nobody talkin'. Dammit, Cass, let's get out of here."

Cass Burdock harkened to him and saw reason in his words and so for the present forgot his murderous intent, for there had been murder in his eyes as they burned into Jeff's. He answered curtly:

"Pile on your horse, Rawlings. Have mine ready. We're on our way."

Rawlings slipped out through the door.

"Tell me about Charlie, Cass," pleaded Alice. "Where is he? He isn't—he isn't—"

"I'm seeing you again, Alice," said Burdock. "Like I told you that other time, you set your trap for me and you caught me and, by God, you're going to keep me! I'll be back."

"But tell me about Charlie!"

Rawlings, hurriedly mounted, led Cass Burdock's horse to the door. Burdock, backing out, called back curtly:

"Shut the door, you Morgan, and don't open it in a hurry; I'll shoot the first one of you that looks out. Shut the door!"

He backed across the threshold, his rifle trained on young Morgan's chest. Jeff knew that, should he be of a mind to disobey orders, Cass Burdock could drop him in his tracks before he could get his hands down to a level with his belt. He kicked the door shut.

CHAPTER XX
A CAMP FIRE TO COOK BY

"Me, I feel the way a jackass feels," said Uncle Dick.

"How's that?" asked Jeff.

"Like a jackass."

They were sitting on a log out in front of Jeff's stone house. Uncle Dick was tinkering with his old rusty carbine and Jeff was staring off into vast distances. Uncle Dick said,

"I let Cass Burdock make a monkey out of me, and when a man has that happen to him what does he feel like? Like a jackass, the way I said."

"Like a start on a menagerie," said Jeff.

"No. Just what I said. No skunk and no weasel, and no lion and tiger cat neither. When a man makes a monkey out'n you, you're just a damn fool jackass."

He lifted his ancient blunderbuss and glared through the fouled sights.

"First time I ever saw a cannon like that," Jeff said.

"It's a doggone good one," Uncle Dick announced defensively. "I've had it purty near all my life and it's never let me down yet. See that cocky blue jay?"

A crested jay had just swept in a long clean line across the sky, had made a nice landing atop a pine a hundred yards away and had immediately screamed a challenge to all the world.

"I don't care much for jays anyhow," said Uncle Dick, and snuggled his head down against his left shoulder, puckering his eyes. "Watch me shoot his damn head off."

"Me, I kind of like these mountain blue jays," said Jeff, and he was grinning inwardly and a part of his grin got as far as the corners of his mouth. If Uncle Dick with that prehistoric carbine of his could hit that bird at that distance, he'd offer to eat Uncle Dick's boots and swallow his rusty old gun for dessert. "Don't hurt him, Uncle Dick."

"If you say so," said Uncle Dick with one of his long horse sighs. "We-ll, see that ripe pine cone just about two foot over the jay bird's head? Let's drop it on the pesky son-a-gun."

"Only be sure you don't hurt the bird too much," chuckled Jeff.

Uncle Dick got his sights lined up and said, "Here we go," and blazed away.

And the pine cone was cut away, very neatly, an incredible shot, and fell so close to the jay that the bird betook itself far away, screaming curses, and Jeff very simply, in full admiration, said,

"I'll be damned."

"It's a good gun," said Uncle Dick. "I trued up the sights last week. One time I got me two Injuns and one of the Injun's dogs the same shot." He blew down the barrel, puffing the smoke out. "Yep, she's sure a good gun."

"Seems as though there's a pretty good man behind the gun," grinned Jeff.

"I can shoot real good," admitted Uncle Dick modestly. "Not so doggone lightning quick like you, mebbe, but mebbe straighter."

"And you've got your gun all oiled up—inside, I mean!—to go out and get you some big game?"

Uncle Dick came pretty close to bristling. Actually the sparse hair on his head, certainly his eyebrows, bristled.

"What's mine, fair and square and honest,

belongs to me," said Uncle Dick. "And I never did like that feller Cass Burdock, nohow."

"Me, too, Pete," said Jeff in the parlance of the day. "Go ahead old boy, and here's wishing you luck."

"Thankee kindly," said Uncle Dick, and both stood up. "Might be I'll be needing it. So long, Jeff boy."

"Ride lucky, Uncle Dick," said Jeff, and meant it.

He watched the old fellow go down for his horse, saddle and ride away. Then he went into his stone house and made his own preparations: He, too, saw to his rifle; it was as right as rain. He whirled the cylinder of his Colt belt gun; it ran oilily, as smooth as silk. The chambers were charged and there were shells aplenty in his cartridge belt. He made his small pack: Blankets, frying pan, handful of food. He went whistling down into the meadow for his horse.

He rode again for the dozenth time to the spot where Bud Briscoe had lain behind his boulder to shoot him down. He said to himself, as he had said before, "Sure, Bud figured I was sticking here looking for his cache. So he knocked me over and went on his way—but not laughing his head off, because I gave him back pretty near as much lead as he gave me." And, as he had done before, he tarried here a while and looked east, west, north and south; and he said, "I'm right; he headed back toward my other place, up beyond my Waterfall Valley."

So he rode to Waterfall Valley.

He thought to put one across on Uncle Dick, and the thought amused him. It was his idea that he was going to come upon Bud Briscoe holing-up somewhere on the rim of Waterfall Valley, and that when he found Bud he would find also Cass Burdock and Rawlings. It was likely, he estimated, that Bud was still walking gingerly from the bullet in him, and had grown uneasy with Jeff Morgan and Uncle Dick making their headquarters fairly on top of his hidden loot, and so had sent them to do his errand. And Uncle Dick with his ancient carbine had slanted off at an angle, off to the southwest on a trail that should miss the Waterfall Valley country by ten miles.

Jeff had already figured out his trail. He had asked himself time and time again which way a man would ride from Bud's rock if that man was pretty badly hurt and wanted to get under cover the shortest way, wanted to keep out of sight of folks who might shoot him down on account of the bounty on his side because of his nefarious doings, wanted to come with no great delay to his own secret lair, that lair being presumably somewhere near the Waterfall Valley country. So, having, so to speak, put his money down on his chosen card, Jeff struck out along a little used trail, one that could have been only a deer runway.

• • •

He found Bud Briscoe. But not in Waterfall Valley, and not that day. He found him three days later and a good thirty miles beyond the high, sweet valley; found him in a long abandoned prospector's cabin at the base of Smoky Mountain. It was there that Bud Briscoe had betaken him like a stricken animal about to die, to suck his paw in loneliness and to die without molestation. A fine thing, to die all alone with no one bothering you—When you come to think of it, this dying business is a man's job; it's tough and goes against the grain; a man likes to be left alone when he goes about it.

Jeff found him because he had used his head, he had figured out for himself the kind of man Bud Briscoe was, the sort of trail Bud Briscoe would follow. And he was pretty certain that Bud Briscoe instead of just Cass Burdock and Rawlings alone would have showed up at the stone house, if Bud weren't pretty badly hurt. Well, at any rate young Jefferson Davis Morgan found Charles "Bud" Briscoe in the old prospector's hut when Bud was about ready to cash in his last chips and call it a game. One more lost game, the last of all games in this world.

"I'm double damned," muttered Jefferson Davis Morgan. He began to lose patience; here he had hunted this man down over half the world, it seemed to him, and every time he came up with him he found him laid by the heels. How could you shoot a man already dying? What good would it do, and what fun to be had from the doing of it? None. So he lost his temper.

There lay Bud Briscoe, his eyes roving-wild, his beard and uncut hair unkempt, hot spots of fever somehow shining through his tangle of beard, his hands as loose and lax as a man's newly dead. On the floor, where it had fallen from his nerveless hand, was a six-gun.

Bud Briscoe rolled his eyes at the newcomer. His tongue ran along his blistered lips; he tried to rear up and couldn't. He said in a thin, reedy whisper—it was the best he could do—and his eyelids dropped down before the last of the few words was spoken.

"Here you come again, do you, Morgan? Well, hell take you. I'll kill you yet if you just leave me time enough to get up and drag my boots on. Where the hell's my gun? Stole it, you—"

Bud Briscoe's head flopped down loosely on his tumbled blanket. Jeff Morgan glared at him a moment, then went out and slammed the door and climbed into his saddle and rode away.

But he didn't ride far. A few hundred yards only. Returning, he found the spring close behind the cabin and he found a rusty tin can that would do for a cup. He brought the fever-ridden bandit a brimming drink of clear, cold water.

And so it went.

Bud Briscoe had had a bullet through him, Jeff's bullet no doubt, just grazing his lung, and his wound was festering. Jeff cleaned the wound, gritting his teeth while he did so, and made the best rough-and-ready bandage he could. It sickened him to touch the man's white body. He straightened up the bunk, getting the worst of the hills and valleys out of the untidy blanket. He looked around for some sort of nourishment, so obviously needed, and found no scrap. He took his rifle and went out to bring back something better at a time like this than bacon and flapjacks. He nailed a fat young buck within twenty minutes and set to work to make a kind of soup. "It'll taste like hell," he said, and jammed some aromatic leaves down into the bubbling broth, "but he won't know the difference, the half-dead fool. I hope he chokes on it."

Bud didn't choke and he didn't die just then. He was as tough as saddle leather or he would never have weathered out as many harum-scarum days, threaded with gunfire, as he had. Jeff nursed him like a mother and cursed him like the devil. Day after day it went on, with Bud's strength returning, with the fever gone out of his blood; with the old hard, bright look coming back into his eyes.

"There's an old ax standing over there by the fireplace," he jeered. "Why didn't you bash my brains out?"

Jeff, being altogether a human young animal, started to say, "You haven't got any brains to bash out," but thought better of it and kept his mouth shut.

He waited on Bud Briscoe hand and foot, as they used to say. He attended upon him not only like a damned fool mother but like a nurse in a hospital; he took care of his every need though it sickened him. And Bud Briscoe, getting his strength back in a heady stream, always jeered at him.

"You got funny ideas, Morgan," he jibed. "You're a damn fool. Well, anyhow, I'm glad. It won't be long now."

"No, it won't be long," said Jeff.

But it was long. One day Bud got up out of bed and with Jeff's help got dressed. They got his boots on—and he went a sick white and toppled over in a dead faint. Jeff had to put him back to bed.

They got to talking about things. "There's mountain quail up beyond the spring where there's a sort of flat place with squirrel grass and with live oak trees shutting it in," said Bud. "They make good eating. And if you go about two-three miles up, there's a creek where the trout come out and bite you. They go pretty good too, if you put 'em in a pan and brown 'em."

At night, all the light they had came from the fireplace. There was a rickety bench; Jeff sat on it and rolled his cigarette and smoked while Bud either slept or, propped up in his bunk, smoked with him.

They talked.

Bud Briscoe, convalescing, was a genial sort of chap. Hard as it was to take, Jeff came grudgingly to see how it was that Alice Briscoe loved this big blond brother of hers.

"It's like fattening a hog to kill for Christmas time, ain't it, Jeff?" Bud Briscoe said, and his white teeth flashed through the tangle of his yellow beard. "Getting me on my pegs so you can knock me over."

"That's what I aim to do," said Jeff.

They ate together, no escaping that. They slept in the same room. Sometimes one would say, "Listen to that damn old timber wolf; he keeps a man awake." Or, "Say, I'd give a lot for a can of tomatoes. How'd it be to have a real steak off of a cow instead of this damn deer meat? You know there's a place in Yellow Jacket where you can get a big box of dog candy for four dollars?" Or, "Looks like a thunder storm boiling up."

There was no getting away from the fact that Bud Briscoe was a pleasant companion. He had a ready laugh, there was a deep stratum of gen-erosity in him, he was downright likeable and he was a simple, friendly and warmly human sort of individual. He had the makings of a fine man in him, had Bud Briscoe, only the devil had got him in one his loose-riding, thoughtless days and had greased the skids down to hell for him. A killer now, an outlaw, a man who ought to be hanged from the first handy tree. Or shot between his candid, smiling eyes.

"I could fight it out with you right now, Jeff," he said, "only the hell of it is that here's another time I've got plugged through the right side, putting my gun arm out of commission."

Jeff said thoughtfully, "Well, at that, I could use my left hand, too. But I guess it wouldn't be fair for two reasons: You haven't got your strength yet, being sort of shaky, and I'm pretty good at left handed shooting."

Bud grinned. So Jeff was pretty good at left handed shooting, was he? Well, he'd better be! Bud Briscoe had never shot with anything but his left hand in all his life. And Bud was not the last man to take advantage of a situation. He didn't care to budge from this altogether comfortable camp until he was entirely himself again, for he had some hard riding to do. What he did was regain his strength rapidly, his a superb vitality, yet also he did all that he could to conceal how swiftly that strength flowed back into him.

Jeff Davis Morgan, not exactly any man's fool, grew into the way of looking Bud shrewdly in the eye.

"I'm thinking it won't be long now," he said one morning.

"If this damn shoulder of mine wasn't so stiff and numb-like—" Bud muttered.

That morning Jeff, growing impatient, gave Bud Briscoe's gun back to him.

"I'll be watching you," he said, very grim and hard about the mouth. "Maybe you are stronger than you let on. Anyhow, you are welcome to your hardware and any time you want to start anything, blaze away. It's up to me not to give you a chance to shoot me in the back."

He stood with his thumb hooked into his belt. Bud Briscoe took his gun back, hefted it, fondled it, shoved it into its holster and laughed.

"You know damned well, Jeff, after all you've done for me—"

"Oh, go to hell," snapped Jeff.

And that same morning Alice Briscoe found them.

She had seen in the distance the morning column of smoke from their chimney, then had seen a man come out and go with a bucket that flashed the sun, to the spring. Even from afar she knew him by his carriage. She watched him return to the cabin, and for a time she hesitated; he had not glimpsed her where she sat her horse at the rim of a shadowed grove; she could turn aside. For it was not Jeff Morgan she was seeking—or so at least she had been telling herself a hundred times a day, every time she heard a sound in the forest or glimpsed something stirring, though sound and glimpse might easily have been afforded by bear or deer. It was Charlie that she sought, knowing

271

him wounded and deserted, knowing him—or believing that she knew him—robbed by his robber companions, Cass Burdock and the man Rawlings. And she knew, too, something of Uncle Dick's vanishing, of his subsequent activities— and that he was no friend of Charlie Briscoe's. So here was the excellent opportunity to demonstrate to herself that she had been honest with herself and had no wish to find Jeff Morgan—

She rode slowly into the open and straight to the cabin. Nearing the open door, about to call, she heard voices. And one of the voices was Bud Briscoe's!

"Charlie!" she called, between an eager joyousness and a great fear. It was so good to find him, to know that he was alive and could talk in that great strong voice of his—but what did it mean, finding Jeff Morgan with him? She leaped to the one sinister yet logical conclusion that Jeff Morgan held her brother here a prisoner.

Jeff Morgan, every whit as eager as she, hurried out long-stridedly to meet her. He pulled off his hat and stared looking up at her, the sun in his hair, her loveliness bright in his eyes. She flashed down out of the saddle and brushed by him. Her heart was beating wildly but she clung to her self-assurance that it was Charlie and not Jeff Morgan whom she had sought, whom she wanted and had found.

"Charlie!" she said again as she saw him propped up on his bunk.

He grinned at her and stuck out his paw of a hand.

"Hello, Allie," he said in his affectionate and vastly good-humored way. "Say, you look sweeter than a bee-tree full of honey! How in the world did you happen—"

Her brow gathered into puckers of puzzlement.

"What are you doing here, Charlie? You were hurt, I know—but you don't look ill now. Are you here because you can't travel—or is Jeff Morgan—Oh, Charlie, I don't understand!"

He chuckled at her, looked from her to Jeff standing watching them from the door, turned his eyes back on her.

"Shucks, I'm doing fine," he said. "I've been laid up; not quite ready to travel yet but it won't be long now. And—Well, this Morgan man, he found me like this, only worse. And he's been playing doctor to me. We're great friends now, ain't we, Jeff?"

Alice whirled about, her face brightening.

"Oh, I'm glad! *I'm glad!* Oh, Jeff—"

But all the bright glow faded swiftly and even her eyes darkened. Just the look at Jeff's face before he said a word was enough.

"Bud Briscoe's a liar now the way he always was," he said. And Bud's grin only broadened. But when Jeff turned abruptly from him to look at Alice, Bud's grin grew warped and twisted and his eyes narrowed—then suddenly he realized that

Alice's eyes hadn't immediately run to a meeting with Jeff's but were still bent searchingly upon him—and again he laughed easily.

"Don't mind Jeff," he bantered. "He talks tough but he's got a heart soft as a baby's."

Alice stayed that day, and that night, too. Toward nightfall Jeff moved out, giving her his bunk, doing what he could with fresh-cut pine and fir tips to make it pleasant, and established himself outside, far enough away to give brother and sister their chance for talk, were they of a mood for it, close enough for him to keep guard over the one door lest Bud Briscoe tried to make his getaway. And the girl and the bandit did have a long talk, and next morning after breakfast Alice and Jeff sat on a log at the edge of the brook spilling downward from the spring, and were silent a good deal; words for a time came hard for them. Suddenly Jeff began laughing when he discovered that he and she both were constantly reaching down, taking up a twig, snapping it carefully, tossing the ends away, reaching for another—

But no responsive smile came from the girl.

"How can life be so hard, so all without mercy? When I always thought it was meant to be so fine and splendid, so gay and good! You see, I am not asking you any more, Jeff, to let Charlie go. I saw both your faces. One of you is going to kill the other and very soon. And now that I am here, now that I can't tear myself away—Dear God in Heaven! Do I have to see it happen!"

Jeff broke some more twigs but didn't laugh again. He stood up and pushed his hat back and mopped his brow that had gone suddenly wet. He was remembering that dream he had had of Bob Lane, Bob being dead and happy, doing now the things he had always wanted to do, hurrying off to a gay meeting with Molly—"Remember Molly I told you about once? She's dead too; ain't that something?"—Bob grinning and slapping him on the back; Bob saying, "Hell, Jeff, let the critter go; you don't have to kill Bud Briscoe; just leave him be." Bob heading for that long bright cloud roosting on the hills where the sun was coming up, where Molly was waiting—

"Just a fool dream—just to make things easy for myself in my sleep—"

"What are you saying, Jeff?" Alice demanded. "Why do you look like that?"

Jeff tucked in the corners of his mouth.

"What about Uncle Dick?" he asked. "Seen or heard anything of him?"

Uncle Dick, Alice declared, was an unmitigated old rascal—maybe you had better call him a scoundrel and be done with it—and yet she found it hard to be as sweeping in her denunciation as she felt she should; she didn't quite make excuses for him but the tone of her voice at times did: Uncle Dick, it would appear had left the country for good, but had not gone empty handed. She had seen him just once; he hadn't come down to the house in Green Water Valley, having, as he was frank to admit with that sly smirk of his, no intention of upsetting Alice's father; but he had hung around for a chance to meet her on one of her rides. And, she was perfectly confident, he had lied to her like the horse thief he probably was.

Nope, he hadn't seen hide nor hair of Cass Burdock and Rawlings. Nope, didn't know where they was. Yep, he had heard folks say that they had headed down Mexico way, maybe meaning to go clean to South America; he had a hunch anyway that they'd never be seen up around this way any more. And Uncle Dick told her good-bye and she could swear that there were tears in his eyes. And he had given her a ragged piece of paper with pencil scribblings on it and had said, "This here is a letter to you, Allie, to you and that young feller Jeff Morgan. And you ain't to read it, nuther of you, until you both read it together." And then he had looked at her for a long time in a queer way, looked at her as though his mind were taking a picture of her, one he meant to keep—and then he ducked into the brush where his horse was hidden, and that was the last of Uncle Dick.

"What did his letter say?" Jeff asked.

"I tell you that he said neither of us was to read it alone. Do you suppose—"

Again he smiled, though a bit crookedly this time, as he said,

"Of course you did! What was it about?"

"I could slap your ugly face!"

"You did though, didn't you?"

Out of the pocket of the boy's shirt she was wearing she snatched the torn scrap of paper and flung it at him. He got it unfolded, smoothed out most of the creases and read aloud, having trouble with the scarcely decipherable scrawl:

"Good luck Allie and Jeff and goodbye from your cussed old Unkle Dick and here is what I done I went looking for them varmints that stold all my gold but they got away and went off somewheres well good riddance like the feller sez and I can promise you theyre gone for good and wont never come back and bother you and then I went to the sheriff over to Black Gulch and I give him the red ring and braselet because they was bad luck and anyhow Big Belle had a kid she was a girl kid that got hurt and got one leg cut off and maybe the money will buy her a new one and anyhow I knowed Big Belle and she was real good and I am giving you Allie and Jeff a going away present and I hid it by the big pond over to Jeff's waterfall valley and its under a rock there and it was mine come by honest so dont worry and you remember that kind of pretty girl Gorgie Hill well she sez goodby to because shes coming along of me because she sez as how I aint nobodys unkle now and so she will take care of me and I will tell you Allie about your real unkle Dick he was awful sick and he died on the Panama boat and he told me where he was headed and all, and I knowed you folks would be terrible sad with him dying like that so I was sorry for you and made out I was him to make you folks happy and I will close now your respectful unkle Dick."

Jeff whistled softly. Looking up from his reading he saw Alice hurrying away, back to Bud in the cabin.

"And so Uncle Dick has dug out of the country already, and without finding Burdock and Rawlings, huh?" said Jeff incredulously to the scrap of paper. "After oiling up his old cannon and truing up his sights! Hm. But somehow he's dead sure those two are never coming back? I'll bet a man!"

He tore the paper into tiny fragments and watched them drift down the creek—

And there was Georgia Hill, too, Bud's girl! Going along with Uncle Dick! Just why? For the sake of his beautiful eyes? Jefferson Davis Morgan emitted a mild snort, reminiscent of Uncle Dick's. Whether Uncle Dick in his scrawl had told some part of the truth about the real Uncle Dick, George Briscoe's brother, or trimmed the entire fabric of that tale with a lace-work of lies, there was slight chance of ever knowing.

Alice, having returned to the cabin, found Bud up and about, stirring restlessly. She knew him well in certain ways, she knew the look in his eye now, and she was swift to sense trouble. For one thing, he didn't look ill enough to be shut up indoors. For another, she noted for the first time that he was wearing a gun, the one that Jeff had returned to him.

"Charlie," she said gently, "Jeff Morgan saved your life, didn't he?"

"Who says so? Morgan say so? Maybe he told you he shot me in the first place!"

"I know that you shot him first. We both know that he found you here helpless, and that he has taken care of you—"

"To get me up on my feet so that he can shoot me down again!"

"Charlie! Oh, Charlie! Can't you see how foolish this is, how crazy! Why can't you two leave each other alone? Why can't one of you go away; the world is big enough; you'd never need see or hear of each other again as long as you lived."

He patted her shoulder, his big hand become gentle.

"Now don't you go to worrying, Allie! If it comes to trouble I can take care of myself—"

"One of you will be killed; I know it! If not you, then—*Charlie!*"

His hand on her shoulder rested very still as he stared steadily at her.

"So you're in love with him, are you?" he demanded.

She started shaking her head; then her eyes dropped before his steady gaze, and next the warm color ran up into her cheeks—and then she lifted her chin high and brought her eyes back to his, as steady as his own, and said,

"Yes! I love him with all my heart."

"Oh, hell!" said Bud Briscoe disgustedly.

She pleaded with him; she all but got down on her knees to him. He stood stony-faced and she could not tell whether he even listened. It seemed to her that everything here spelled tragic death, the gun so loose in his holster, Jeff's rifle leaning so convenient against a wall, the very remoteness of this mountain place, the iron wills of these two men.

"Charlie, don't you see—"

He was standing in the center of the room; the door stood open; he was first to see Jeff Morgan moving toward the cabin. Of an instant as Bud whipped back and to one side she saw his purpose leap up into his eyes. The next instant he had jerked his belt gun out and held it leveled toward the open door; transfixed with horror she saw Jeff Morgan's long shadow before she saw Jeff himself—

She knew then that Bud Briscoe meant to shoot him down without warning, and she knew that since she was with her brother there was a chance that Jeff might not look for such an act and so might be taken off his guard. She started to scream a warning—

That would mean that in all likelihood they would kill each other—

Galvanized into lightning-swift action she whirled and snatched up Jeff Morgan's rifle. Behind Bud Briscoe, she jammed the rifle barrel hard against his spine.

"Drop that gun, Charlie," she gasped, "or so help me God I am going to kill you! *Drop it!*"

Bud Briscoe stood perfectly rigid, not even breathing for a moment. Slowly the tense fingers of his hand opened and the heavy weapon slipped from them and fell to the floor. And that was just when Jeff came fully into sight, not a score of paces away.

"Jeff," she cried out wildly. "Stay where you are! *You stay where you are!*"

"So I am to stay where I am?" said Jeff. He took in the scene within the cabin; he took stock of the attitudes of the two, even of their expressions; of the rifle and of the fallen weapon. He even noted that it had fallen from Bud Briscoe's left hand. "So you're left handed after all, are you, Briscoe?" he said thoughtfully. "Lying to me all the time about your gun arm, huh? Waiting your chance—"

And now it was with Jefferson Davis Morgan that Alice Briscoe half pleaded while almost she

281

commanded, the muzzle of the rifle still against Bud's great body.

"Jeff, please! Give me just a minute—two or three minutes! I tell you, stay where you are! No; back off a little way. Let me alone with Charlie a few seconds—Oh, Jeff, if you love me!"

"I'll wait," said Jeff. "I'll back up and wait. Take your time."

He withdrew another score of paces. Then Alice, white and shaken yet never so determined in all her life, said,

"You walk over into that corner, Charlie! Quick!"

Bud Briscoe pretended to laugh at her and half turned. He heard her say scarcely above a whisper. "Oh, dear God, help me—forgive me—"

And Bud Briscoe gave over laughing and obeyed, stepping into the cabin's corner.

Then Alice stooped quickly and caught up his gun; as fast as finger and trigger could work together she fired the six shots into the floor; that done she threw the weapon far under the bunk.

"And now, Charlie Briscoe, you are going away from here," she said, and the color rushed back into her face and her eyes were flaming. "You are going straight out through that door and to your horse and you are going to ride and keep on riding. Do you hear me?"

"You're crazy, Allie! The minute I step out there without a gun on me that damn Morgan is going to shoot to kill!"

"That's just what he won't do! If you had a gun on you, yes! But you walk out with both hands in the air and he'll let you go! He will have to let you go! He is not coward enough to shoot you unarmed; he isn't bully enough to beat you with his fists because you've been hurt. Now—*Go!*"

Bud Briscoe went. But first he shouted, "I'm coming out, Morgan, but I'm coming out without a gun, and my hands up!"

As for young Jefferson Davis Morgan, beyond looking at Alice and marveling and falling in love with her all over again, there seemed at the moment nothing much he could do about matters. So Bud Briscoe went on his way—

And Jeff went to Alice.

She stood looking queerly, as though in a daze and not understanding, at the rifle in her hands. Suddenly she threw it from her and a shudder shook her slight body from head to foot, and she put her face in her hands and began to cry.

Jeff had to take her into his arms. "There, there, Alice girl," he said. And, feeling her body sobbing against him, added for full measure, "There, there—"

At first Alice couldn't say anything; she just snuggled closer and trembled in his arms and nothing had ever felt so good, so comforting, so homelike as his embrace. But at last, clutching him tight, she managed,

"He is gone for good, Jeff; I know. He won't

come back; he'll be safe some place far off—Hold me tight, Jeff. I'm just waking from a bad dream."

. . . And Bud Briscoe did go fast and far that day, but not as Alice meant. He headed straight back toward Jeff's Waterfall Valley and still on toward Settlers' Gap, and he reached Settlers' Gap on a horse ready to drop dead under him in the late afternoon. He dismounted at the rear of the unkempt old saloon where Jeff had first seen Georgia Hill, and entered through a back door. Alone, brooding at the far end of the all but deserted bar, he drank his two or three great gulps of whisky; he beckoned a man over to him and the man went out to return presently with a six shooter which Bud shoved into his empty holster. Bud asked a few questions: Where were Cass Burdock and Rawlings? Where was Georgia Hill?

He got no satisfactory answer.

He had another couple of drinks and, in as morose a mood as any man had ever seen him, started out. The man who had staked him to the revolver caught him by the sleeve and whispered a warning: Better look out; the sheriff from Black Gulch was in town, a deputy with him.

Bud went out meaning to get a fresh horse. It would soon be dark and he wanted to be away. At the far end of the street he saw two men sitting their horses; they were talking with a man on foot. Bud knew them for Sheriff Jameson and a man named Dave Wilson. In front of the saloon was a tethered saddle horse; Bud climbed into the saddle, dug his heels in and in a rush headed out of town, southbound. A shout rose from behind him; Jameson had seen him. When Bud did not stop, Jameson fired and missed; Bud whirled in the saddle and fired back and fired again and a third time. He saw Dave Wilson claw at the air, then begin sliding out of the saddle. He fired the fourth shot and saw Jameson's horse rear high in air. He dug his spurs in then and rode. The dark couldn't come any too soon now to suit him.

He rode hard with the sheriff hard after him, with other men calling back and forth, finding what it was all about, some of them taking to horse and pounding along after Jameson. Somewhere along the road Bud Briscoe might have turned aside; still it was most shadowy in the hollow where the main trail ran and he would have taken chances on a ridge anywhere. Also he had a good fresh horse and may have thought to outrun all pursuit. Also he was in a rage and his quick hard drinking on an empty stomach did not conduce to clear thinking. Maybe he just forgot. Anyhow he returned to Green Water Valley—and his dogs got him.

Jameson saw it happen where the starlight shone down softly on a clearing.

Jeff Morgan did not get the whole story for some days; he made sure that Alice never did get the details.

Later Long Jameson told Jeff, and made a wry face in the telling:

"He had lamed his horse; I had almost caught up with him. Then those damn dogs of his must have scented him on the down wind. They rushed him like a herd of wolves. I heard him yell at them; he started shooting. He knocked one over and the rest went at him all the savager. He shot another. Then he stopped shooting. When I looked at his gun I saw he had only the two shots left."

The sheriff mopped his brow.

"I shot the other three dogs," he said.

Jefferson Davis Morgan and Alice tarried ten days in the Waterfall Valley country, lost to all the world. The summer was expanding, the lengthening days were but swift moments of golden glory under the bluest of blue skies. They might have been Adam and Eve in the first instead of this second paradise. A camp fire to cook by, trout and game to be had for the taking, even a handful of flour and coffee from Jeff's pack; a shelter created over them by the interlocking branches of the forest; chairs on log or stone or mossy bank; beds of balsamy fir tips; orchestral music in the running water of Waterfall Creek and the murmurous